The Misadventures of
SALEM HYDE

1

Spelling Trouble
Frank Cammuso

AMULET BOOKS
NEW YORK

Hardcover ISBN: 978-1-4197-0803-9
Paperback ISBN: 978-1-4197-0804-6

Text and illustrations copyright © 2013 Frank Cammuso
Book design by Frank Cammuso and Sara Corbett

Printed and bound in China
10 9 8 7 6 5 4 3 2 1

Amulet Books are available at special discounts when purchased in quantity for premiums and promotions as well as fundraising or educational use. Special editions can also be created to specification. For details, contact specialsales@abramsbooks.com or the address below.

ABRAMS
THE ART OF BOOKS SINCE 1949

115 West 18th Street
New York, NY 10011
www.abramsbooks.com

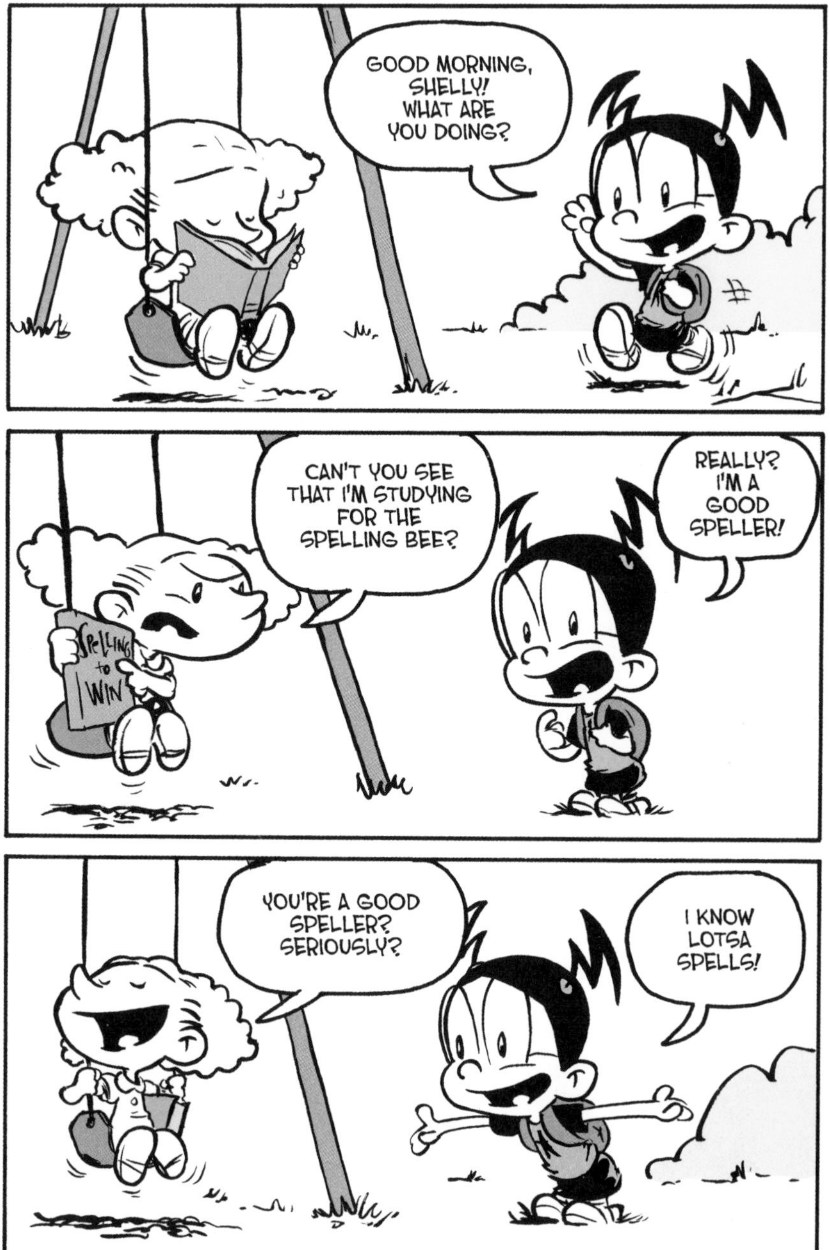
GOOD MORNING, SHELLY! WHAT ARE YOU DOING?
CAN'T YOU SEE THAT I'M STUDYING FOR THE SPELLING BEE?
SPELLING to WIN
REALLY? I'M A GOOD SPELLER!
YOU'RE A GOOD SPELLER? SERIOUSLY?
I KNOW LOTSA SPELLS!

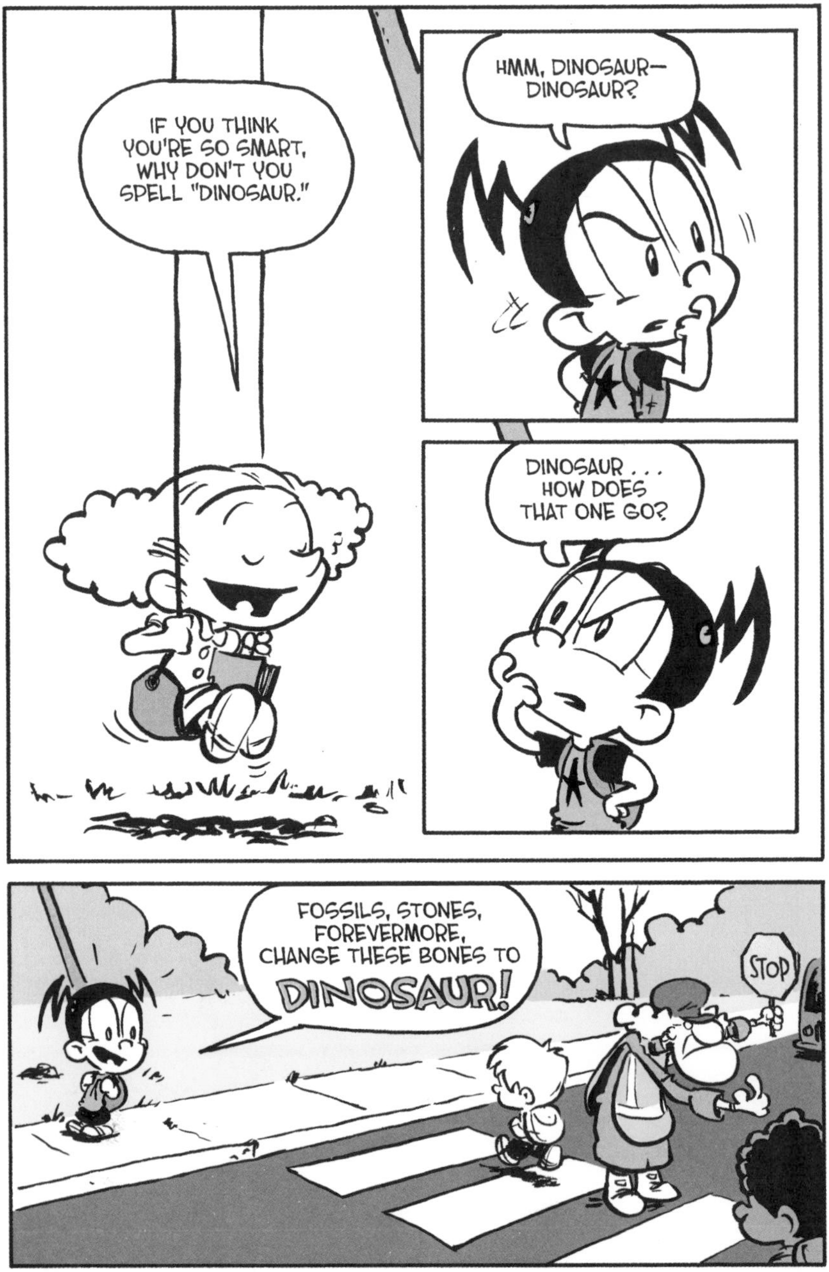
IF YOU THINK YOU'RE SO SMART, WHY DON'T YOU SPELL "DINOSAUR."
HMM, DINOSAUR-DINOSAUR?
DINOSAUR . . . HOW DOES THAT ONE GO?
FOSSILS, STONES, FOREVERMORE, CHANGE THESE BONES TO DINOSAUR!
STOP

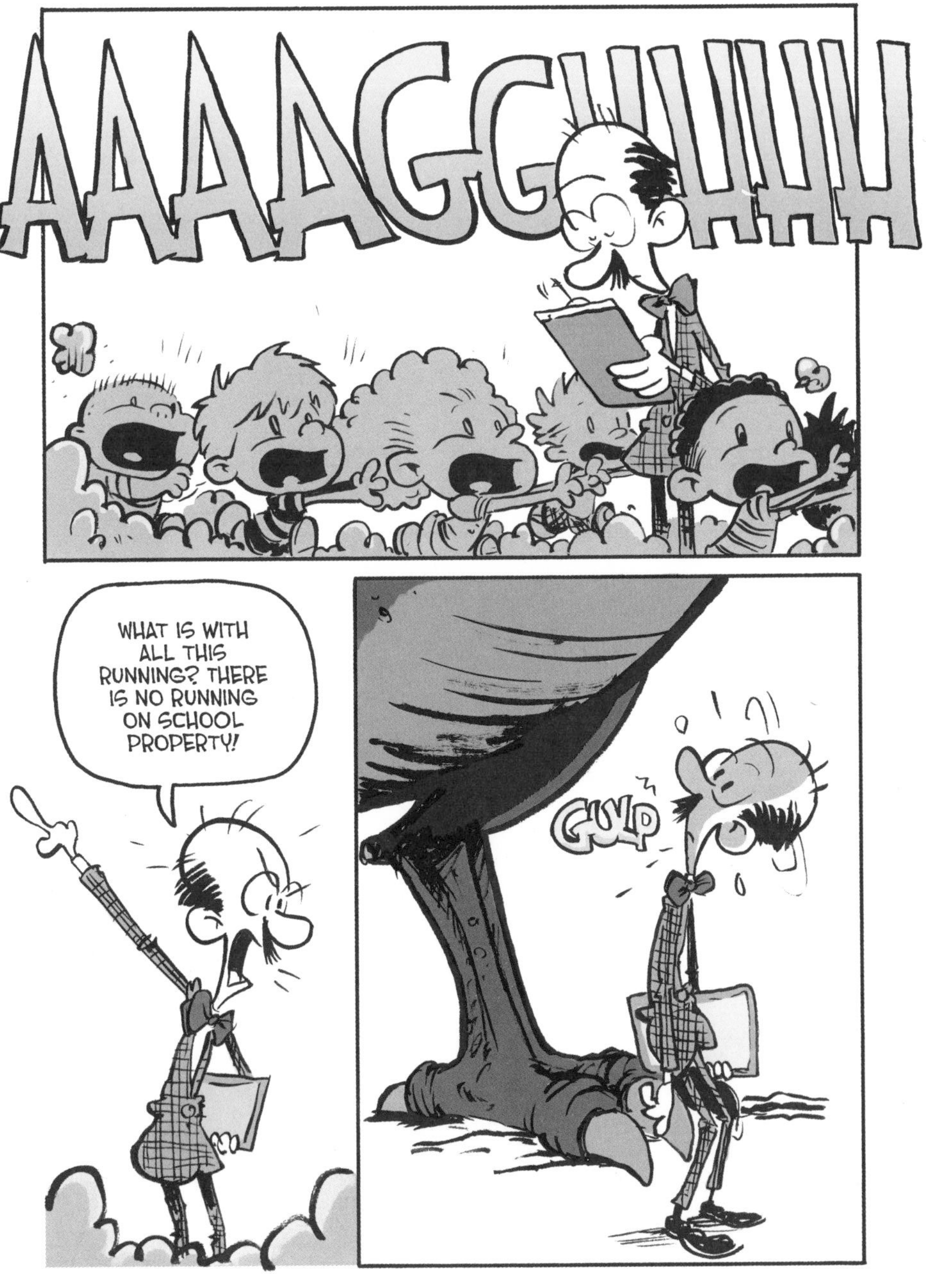
AAAAGGHHHHH
WHAT IS WITH ALL THIS RUNNING? THERE IS NO RUNNING ON SCHOOL PROPERTY!
GULP

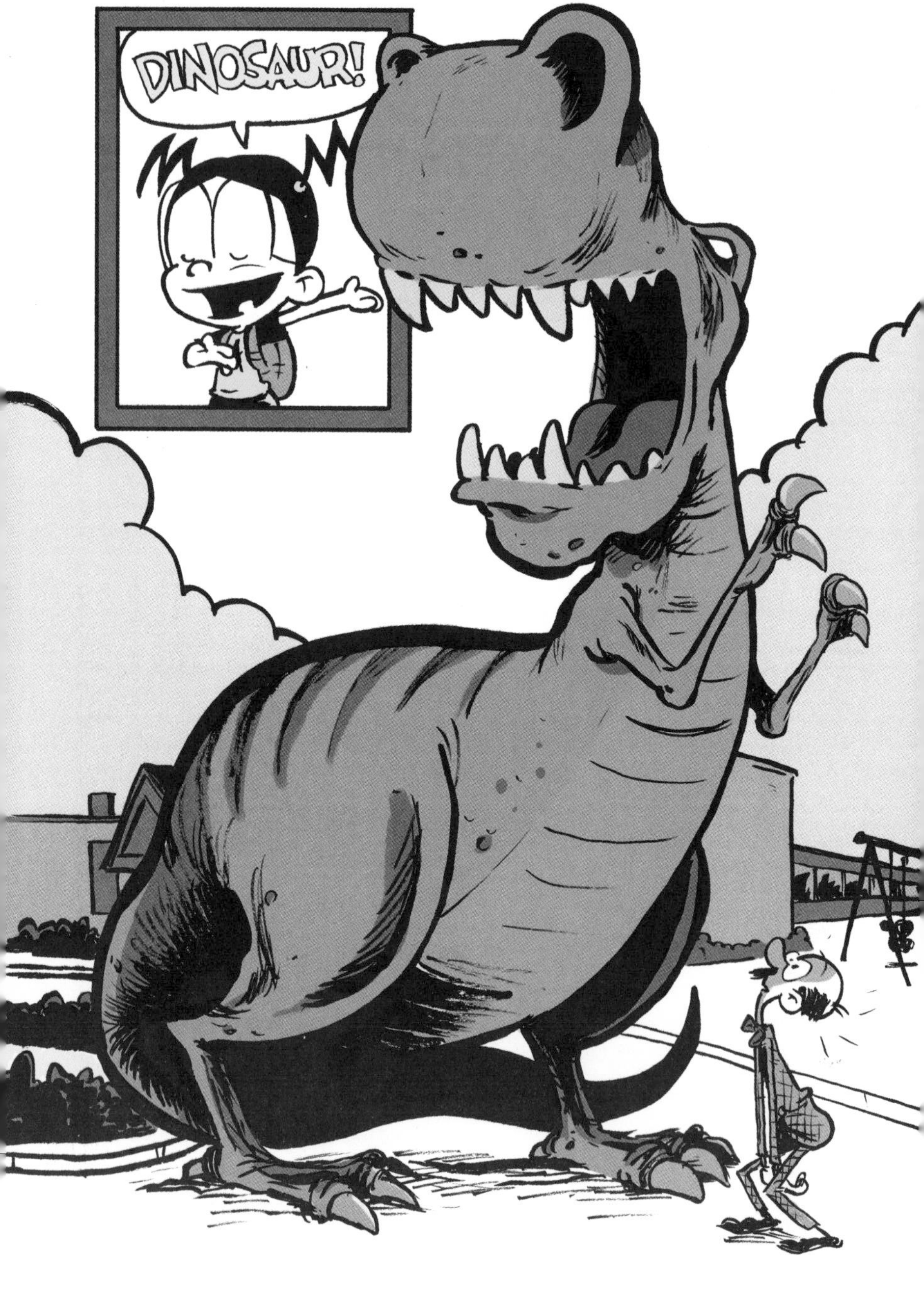
DINOSAUR!

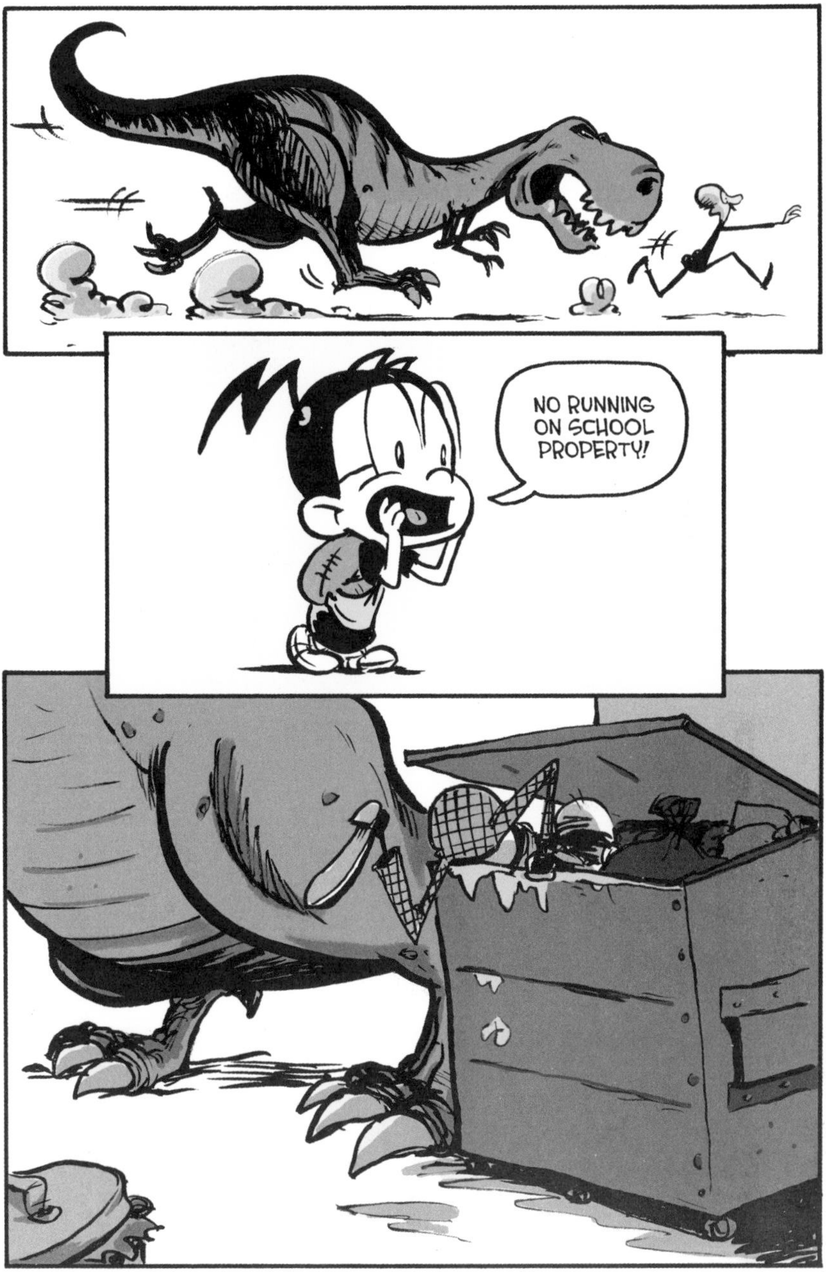
NO RUNNING ON SCHOOL PROPERTY!

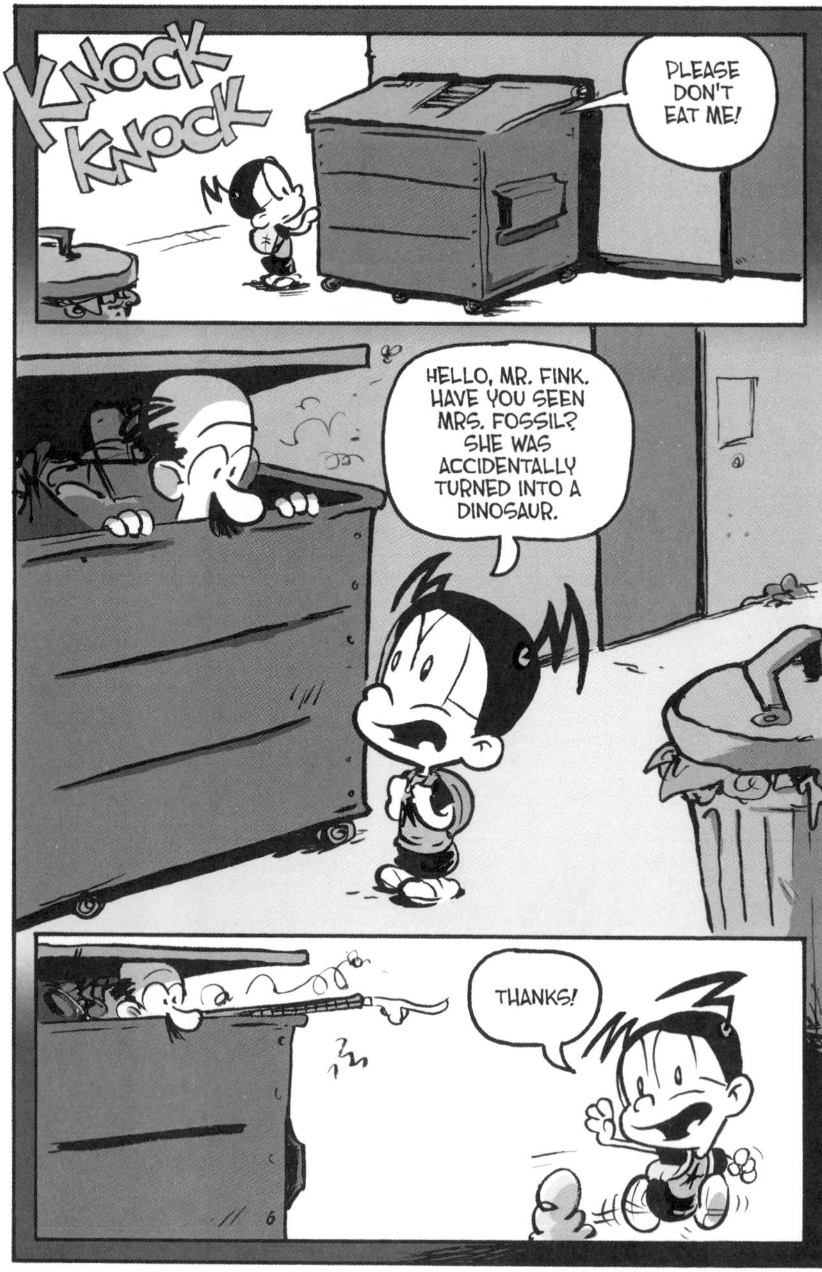
KNOCK KNOCK
PLEASE DON'T EAT ME!
HELLO, MR. FINK. HAVE YOU SEEN MRS. FOSSIL? SHE WAS ACCIDENTALLY TURNED INTO A DINOSAUR.
THANKS!

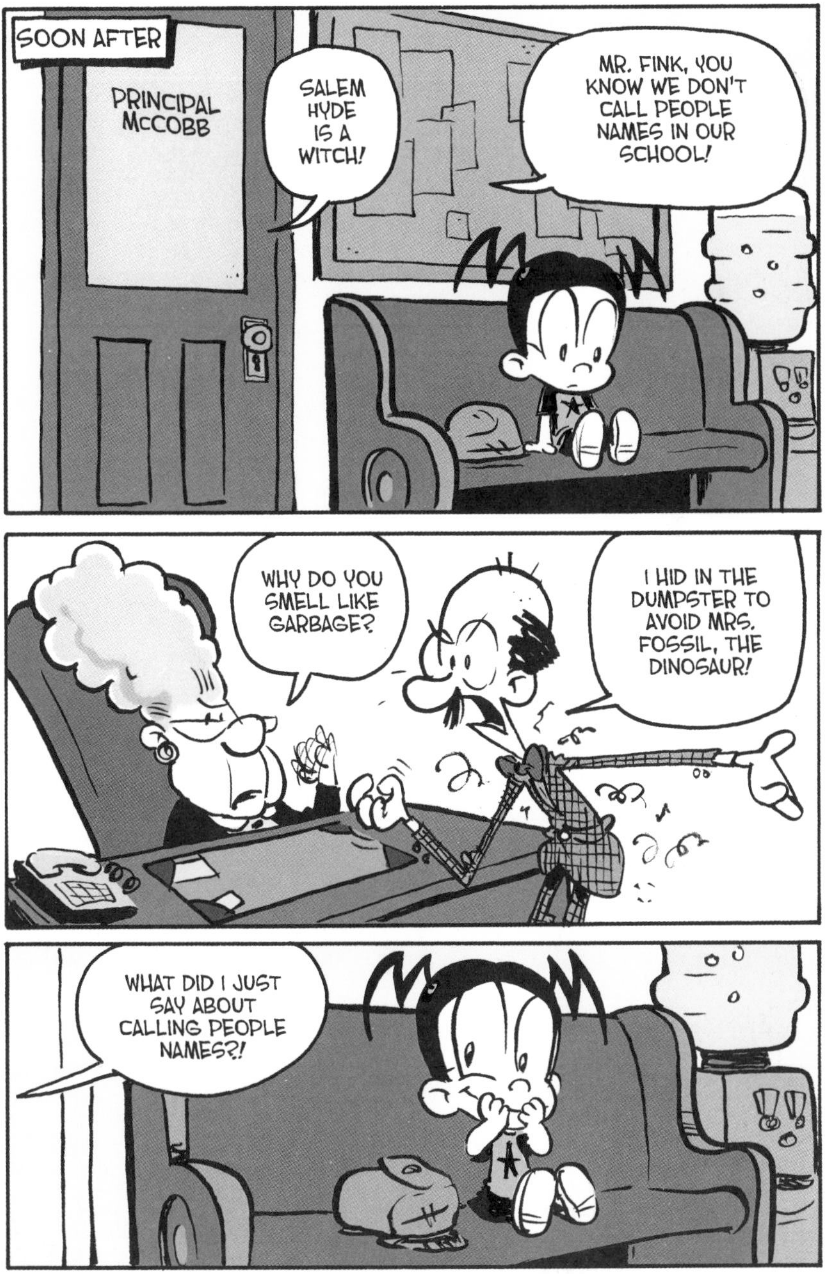
SOON AFTER
PRINCIPAL McCOBB
SALEM HYDE IS A WITCH!
MR. FINK, YOU KNOW WE DON'T CALL PEOPLE NAMES IN OUR SCHOOL!
WHY DO YOU SMELL LIKE GARBAGE?
I HID IN THE DUMPSTER TO AVOID MRS. FOSSIL, THE DINOSAUR!
WHAT DID I JUST SAY ABOUT CALLING PEOPLE NAMES?!

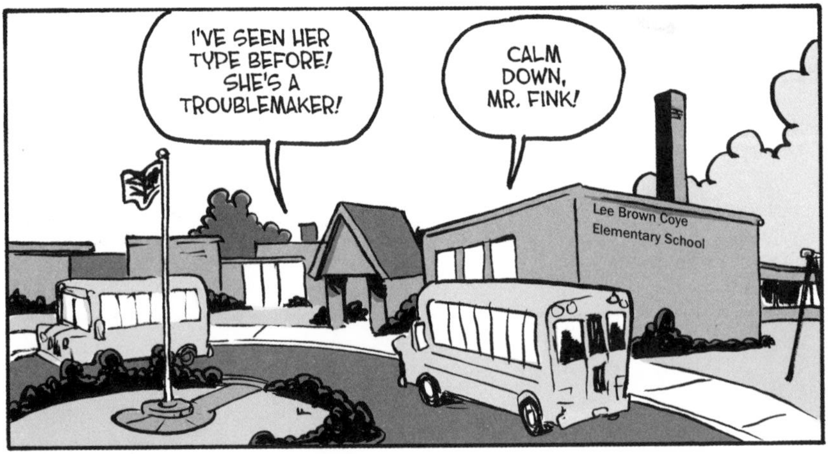
I'VE SEEN HER TYPE BEFORE! SHE'S A TROUBLEMAKER!
CALM DOWN, MR. FINK!
Lee Brown Coye Elementary School

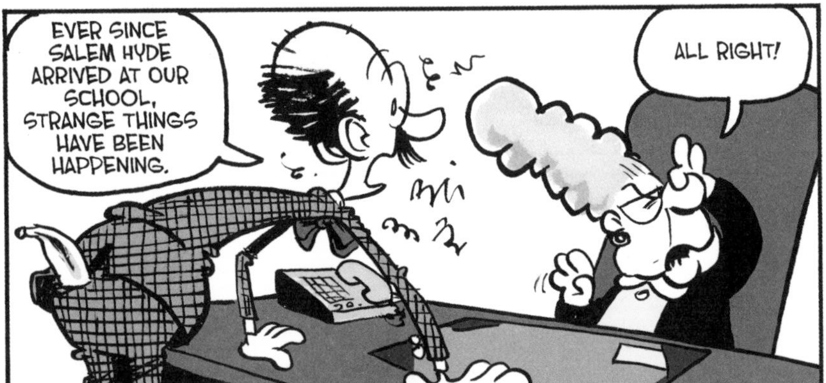
EVER SINCE SALEM HYDE ARRIVED AT OUR SCHOOL, STRANGE THINGS HAVE BEEN HAPPENING.
ALL RIGHT!

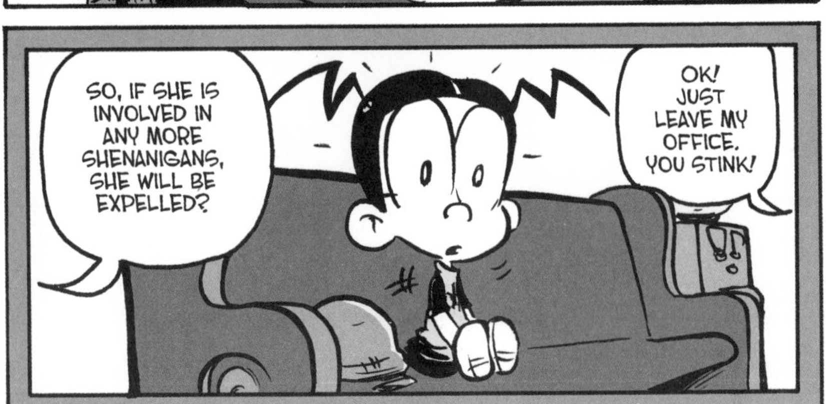
SO, IF SHE IS INVOLVED IN ANY MORE SHENANIGANS, SHE WILL BE EXPELLED?
OK! JUST LEAVE MY OFFICE. YOU STINK!

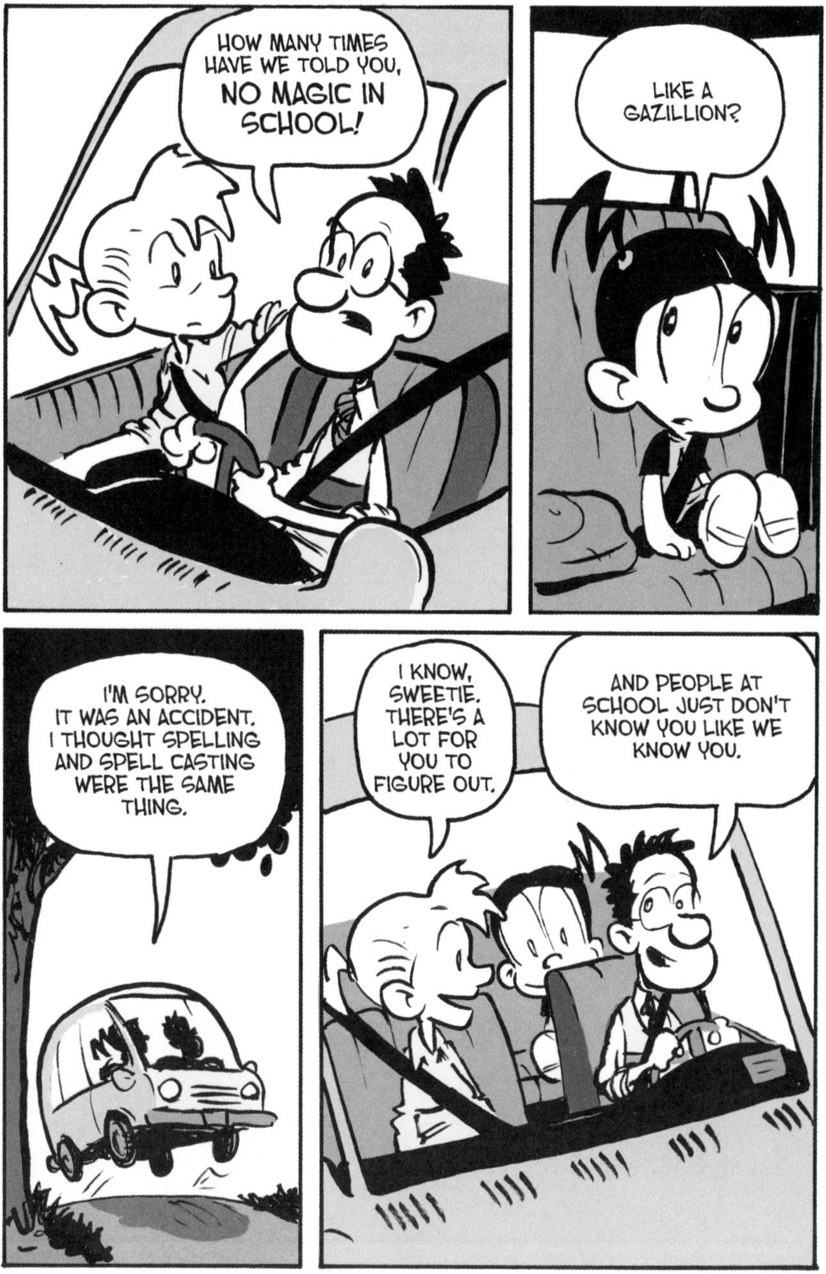
HOW MANY TIMES HAVE WE TOLD YOU, NO MAGIC IN SCHOOL!
LIKE A GAZILLION?
I'M SORRY. IT WAS AN ACCIDENT. I THOUGHT SPELLING AND SPELL CASTING WERE THE SAME THING.
I KNOW, SWEETIE. THERE'S A LOT FOR YOU TO FIGURE OUT.
AND PEOPLE AT SCHOOL JUST DON'T KNOW YOU LIKE WE KNOW YOU.

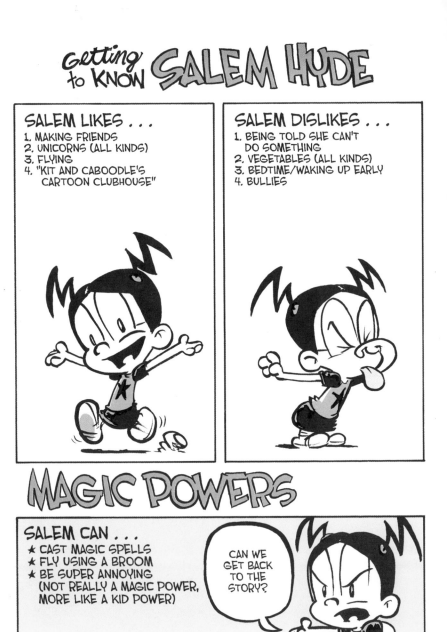

Getting to Know SALEM HYDE

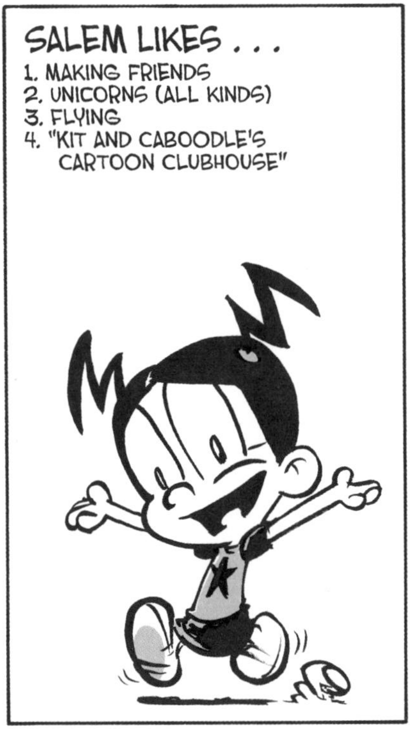
SALEM LIKES . . .
1. MAKING FRIENDS
2. UNICORNS (ALL KINDS)
3. FLYING
4. "KIT AND CABOODLE'S CARTOON CLUBHOUSE"

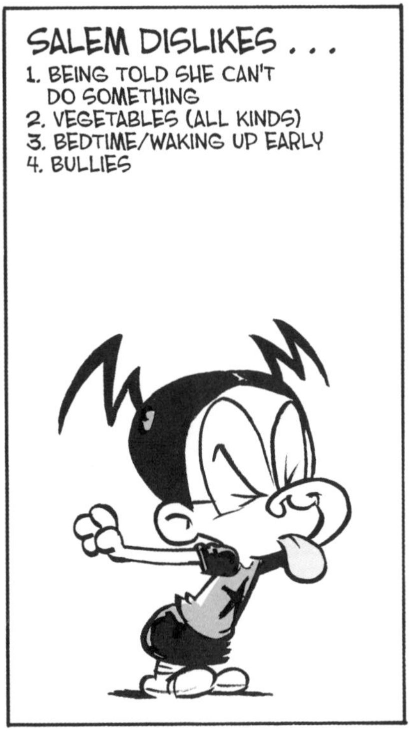
SALEM DISLIKES . . .
1. BEING TOLD SHE CAN'T DO SOMETHING
2. VEGETABLES (ALL KINDS)
3. BEDTIME/WAKING UP EARLY
4. BULLIES

MAGIC POWERS

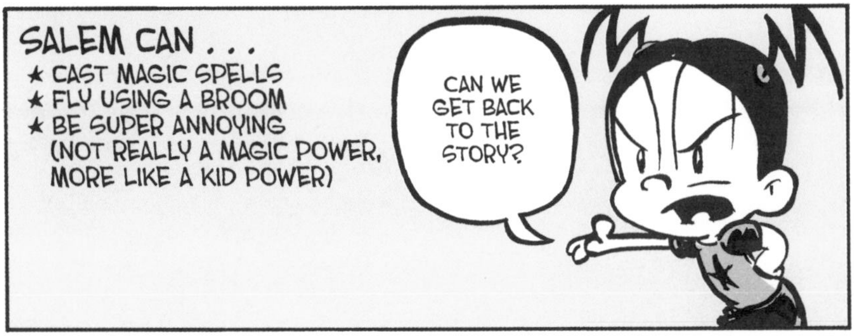
SALEM CAN . . .
★ CAST MAGIC SPELLS
★ FLY USING A BROOM
★ BE SUPER ANNOYING (NOT REALLY A MAGIC POWER, MORE LIKE A KID POWER)
CAN WE GET BACK TO THE STORY?

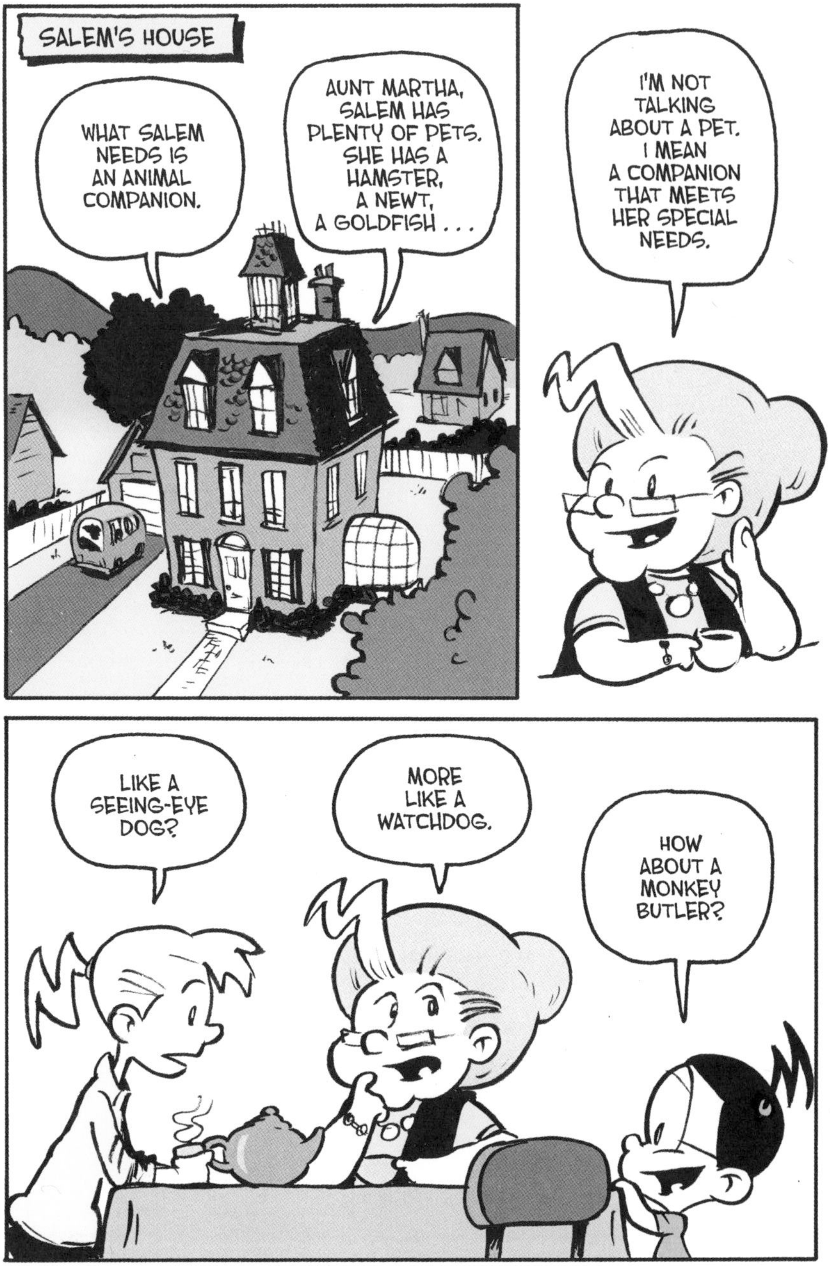
SALEM'S HOUSE
WHAT SALEM NEEDS IS AN ANIMAL COMPANION.
AUNT MARTHA, SALEM HAS PLENTY OF PETS. SHE HAS A HAMSTER, A NEWT, A GOLDFISH . . .
I'M NOT TALKING ABOUT A PET. I MEAN A COMPANION THAT MEETS HER SPECIAL NEEDS.
LIKE A SEEING-EYE DOG?
MORE LIKE A WATCHDOG.
HOW ABOUT A MONKEY BUTLER?

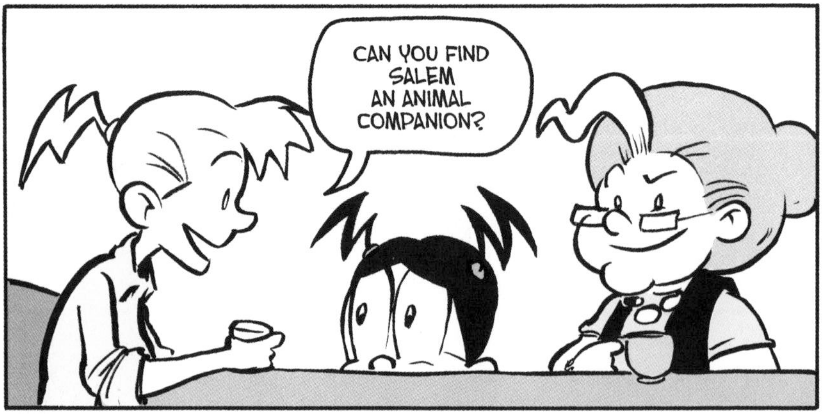
CAN YOU FIND SALEM AN ANIMAL COMPANION?

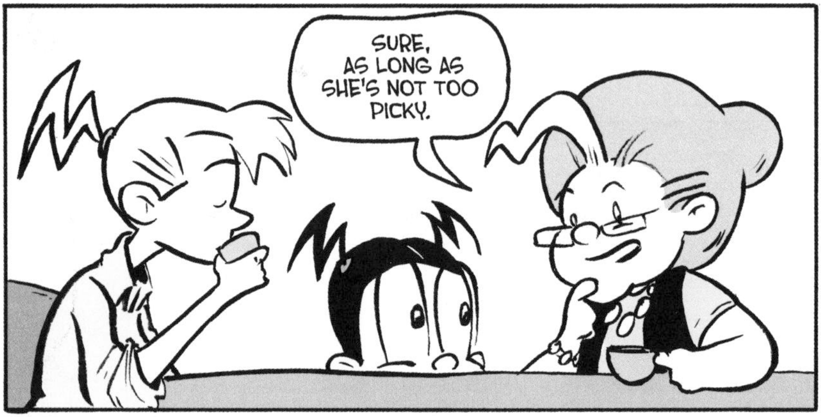
SURE, AS LONG AS SHE'S NOT TOO PICKY.

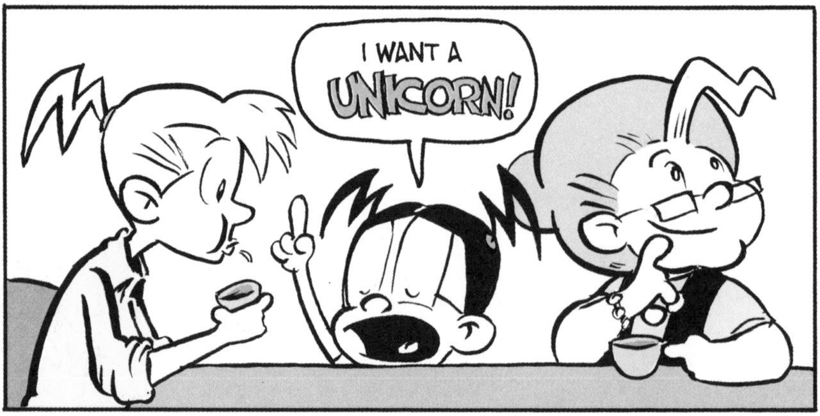
I WANT A UNICORN!

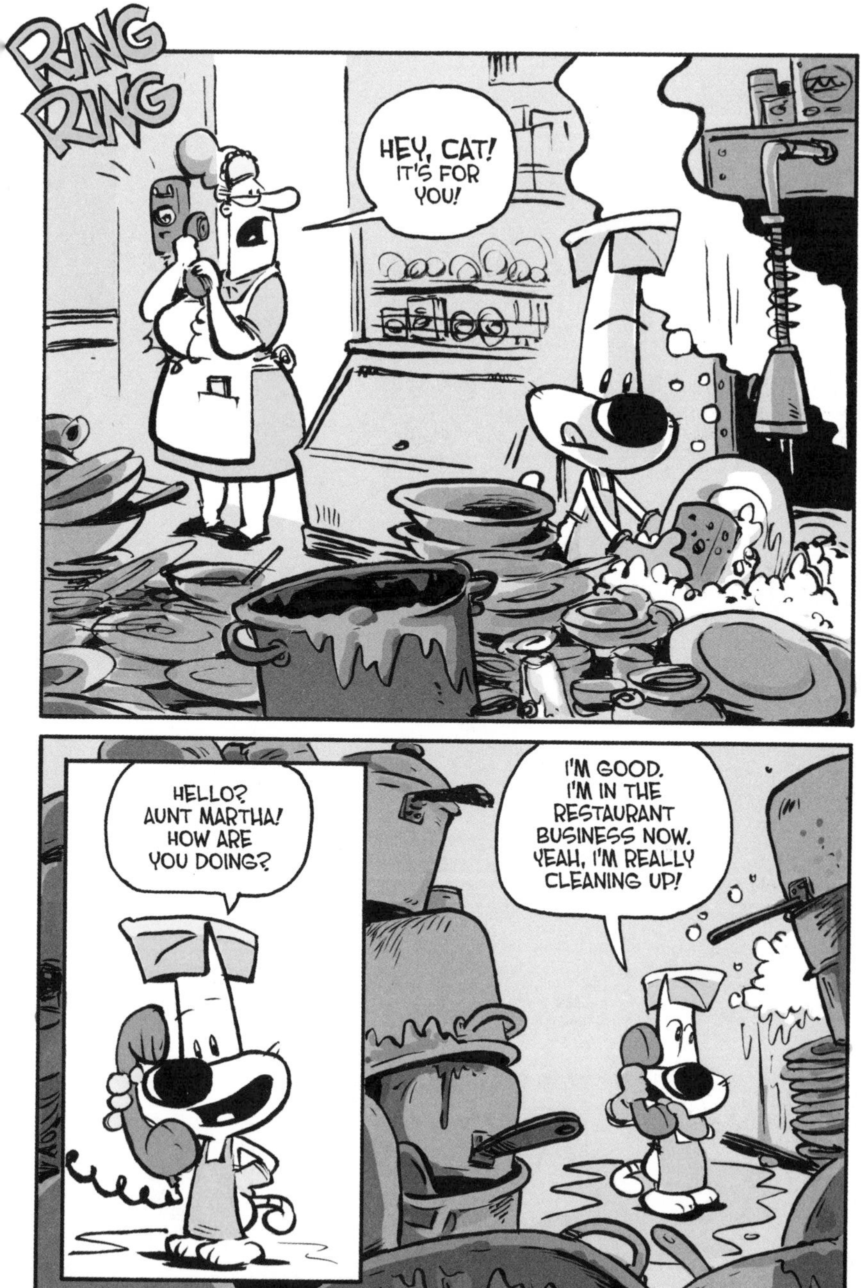
RING RING
HEY, CAT! IT'S FOR YOU!
HELLO? AUNT MARTHA! HOW ARE YOU DOING?
I'M GOOD. I'M IN THE RESTAURANT BUSINESS NOW. YEAH, I'M REALLY CLEANING UP!

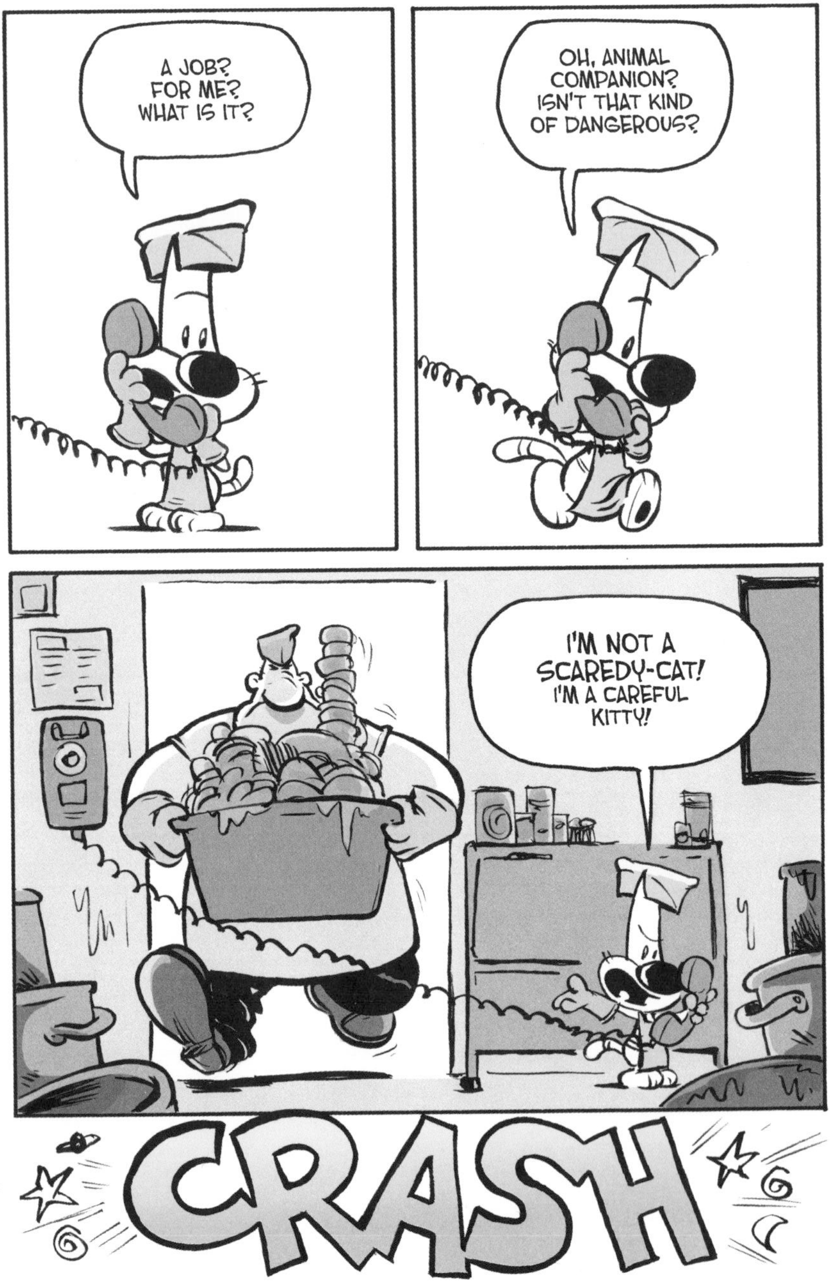
A JOB?
FOR ME?
WHAT IS IT?
OH, ANIMAL COMPANION?
ISN'T THAT KIND OF DANGEROUS?
I'M NOT A SCAREDY-CAT!
I'M A CAREFUL KITTY!
CRASH

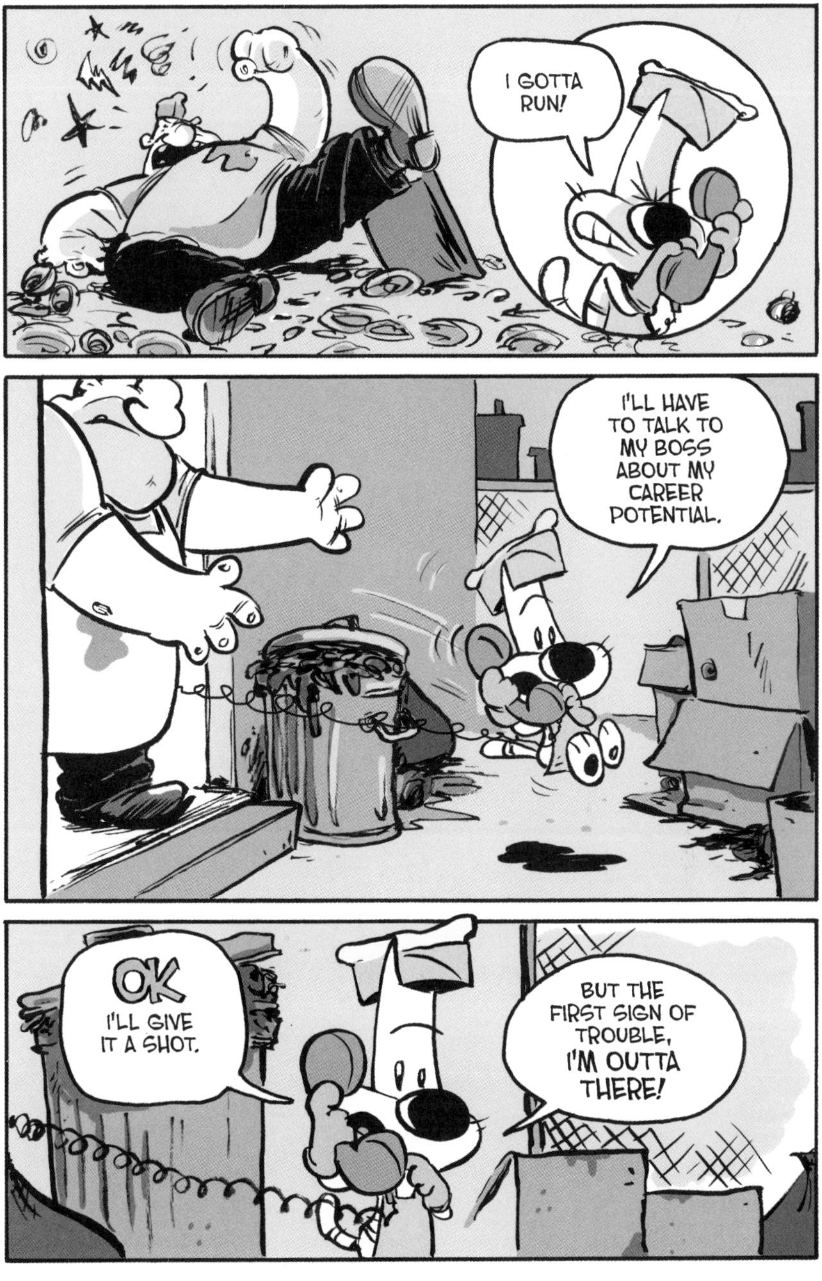
I GOTTA RUN!
I'LL HAVE TO TALK TO MY BOSS ABOUT MY CAREER POTENTIAL.
OK I'LL GIVE IT A SHOT.
BUT THE FIRST SIGN OF TROUBLE, I'M OUTTA THERE!

Getting to KNOW WHAMMY

WHAMMY LIKES...

1. TELLING STORIES
2. PIZZA (ALL KINDS)
3. TUMMY RUBS
4. PIÑATAS

WHAMMY DISLIKES...

1. FLYING
2. TROUBLE (ALL KINDS)
3. BEING CALLED A SCAREDY-CAT
4. FLYING

MAGIC POWERS

SURPRISINGLY, WHAMMY DOESN'T HAVE ANY MAGIC POWERS, BUT HE DOES HAVE...

★ SUPER-SENSITIVITY (EASILY OFFENDED)
★ OVER 800 YEARS OF EXPERIENCE
★ 5 OF HIS 9 LIVES LEFT

DID I MENTION I HATE FLYING?

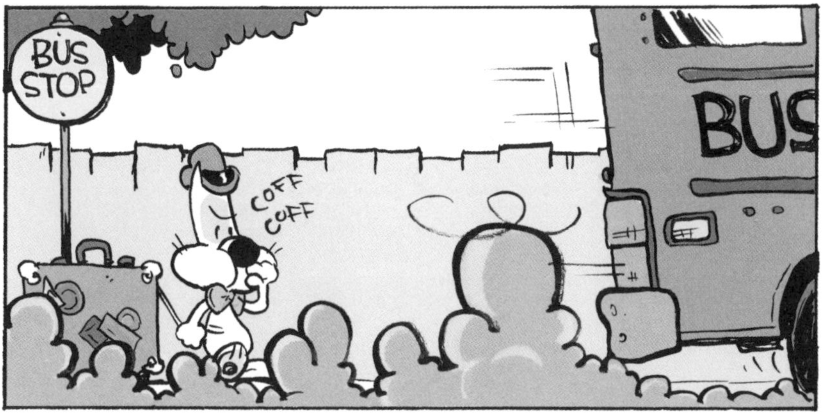
BUS STOP
COFF COFF
BUS

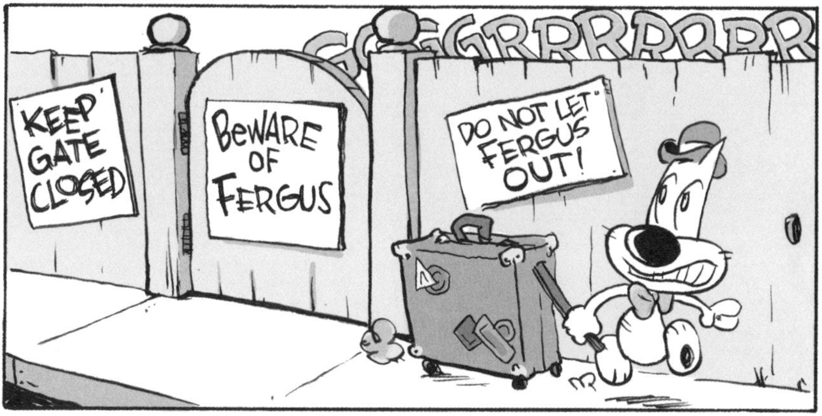
GGGRRRRRRRR
KEEP GATE CLOSED
BeWARE OF FERGUS
DO NOT LET FERGUS OUT!

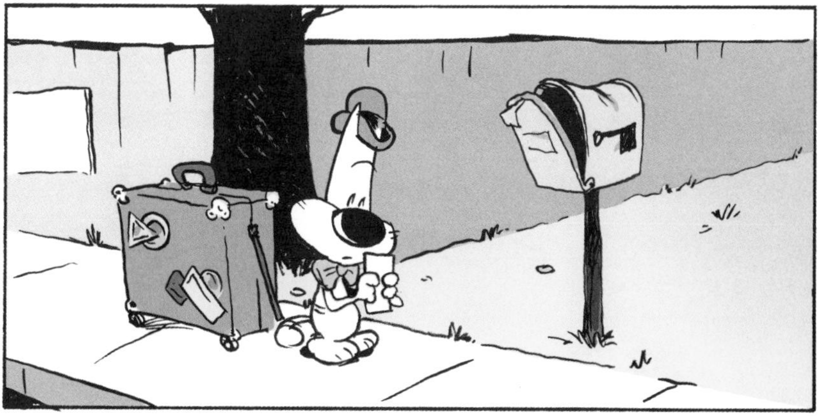

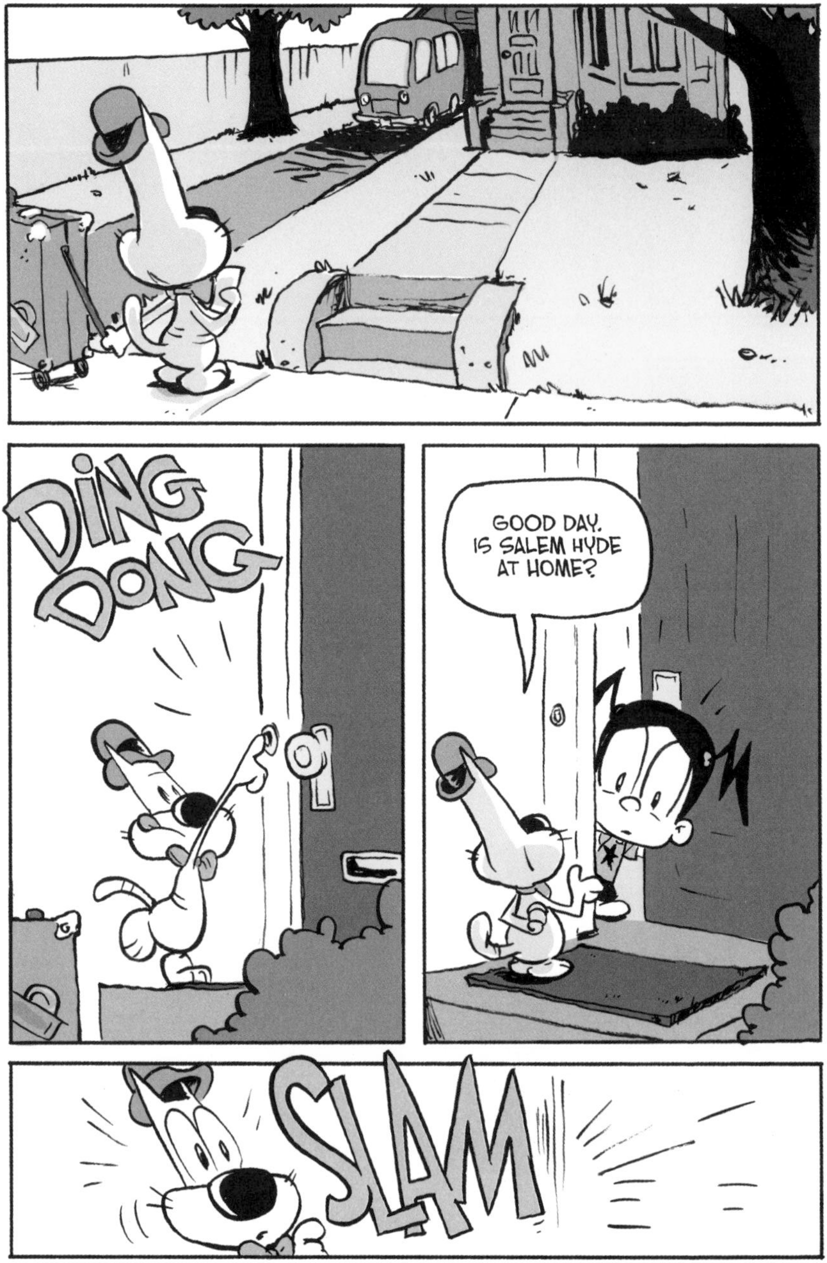
DING DONG
GOOD DAY. IS SALEM HYDE AT HOME?
SLAM

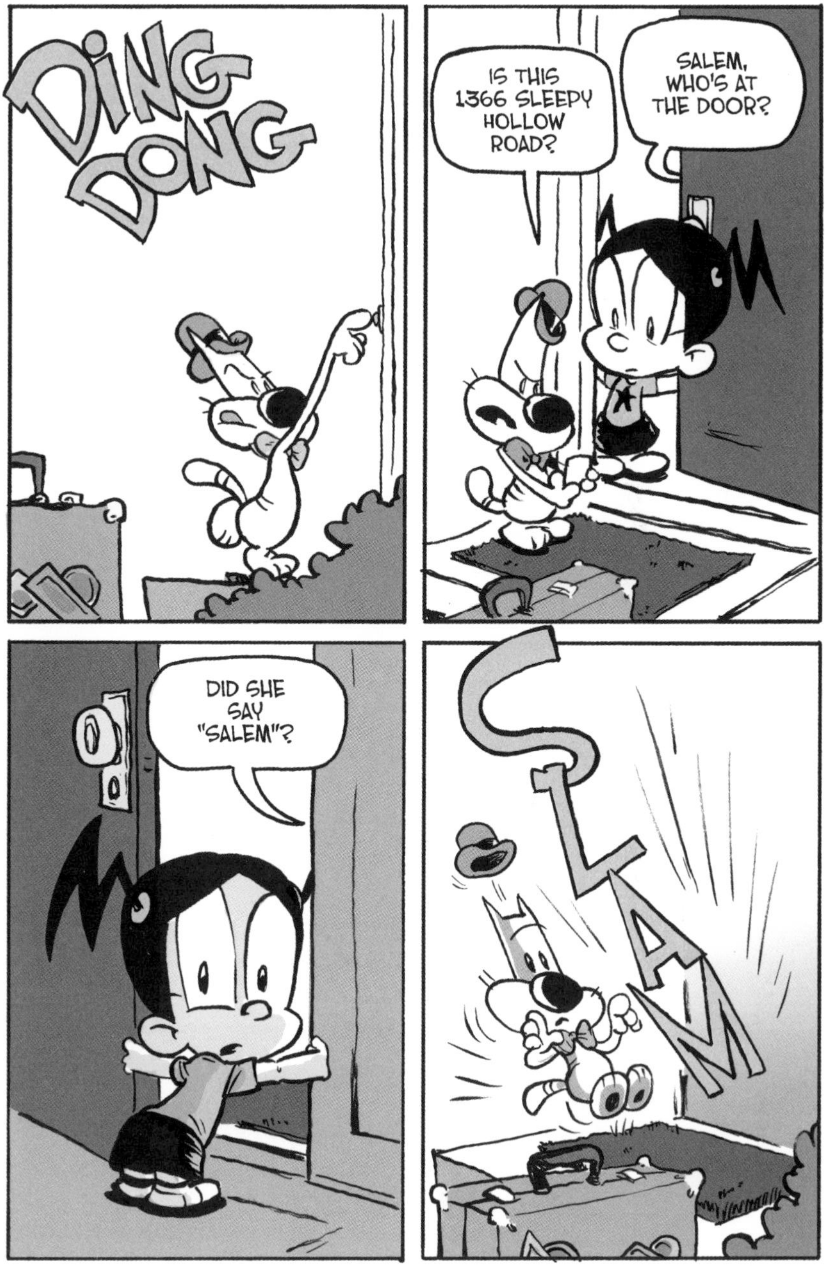
DING DONG
IS THIS 1366 SLEEPY HOLLOW ROAD?
SALEM, WHO'S AT THE DOOR?
DID SHE SAY "SALEM"?
SLAM

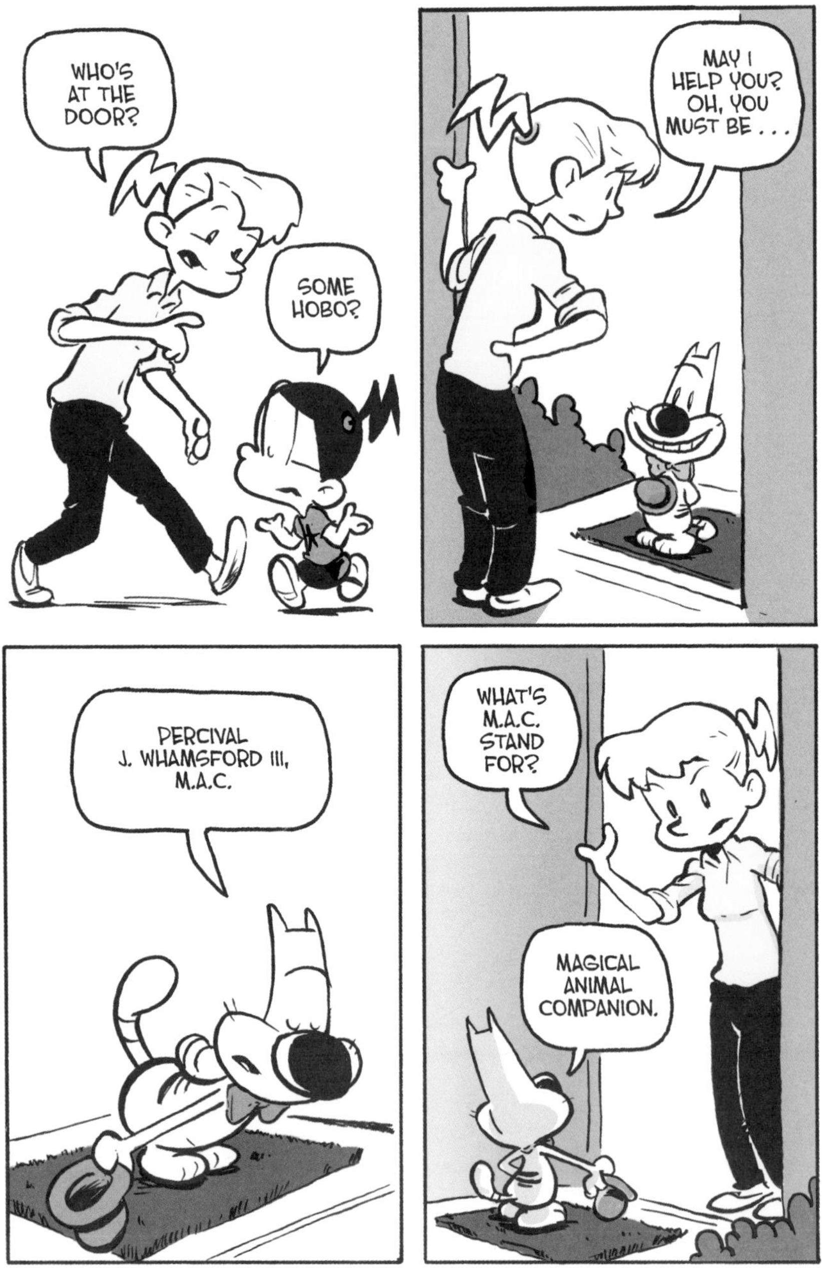
WHO'S AT THE DOOR?
SOME HOBO?
MAY I HELP YOU? OH, YOU MUST BE . . .
PERCIVAL J. WHAMSFORD III, M.A.C.
WHAT'S M.A.C. STAND FOR?
MAGICAL ANIMAL COMPANION.

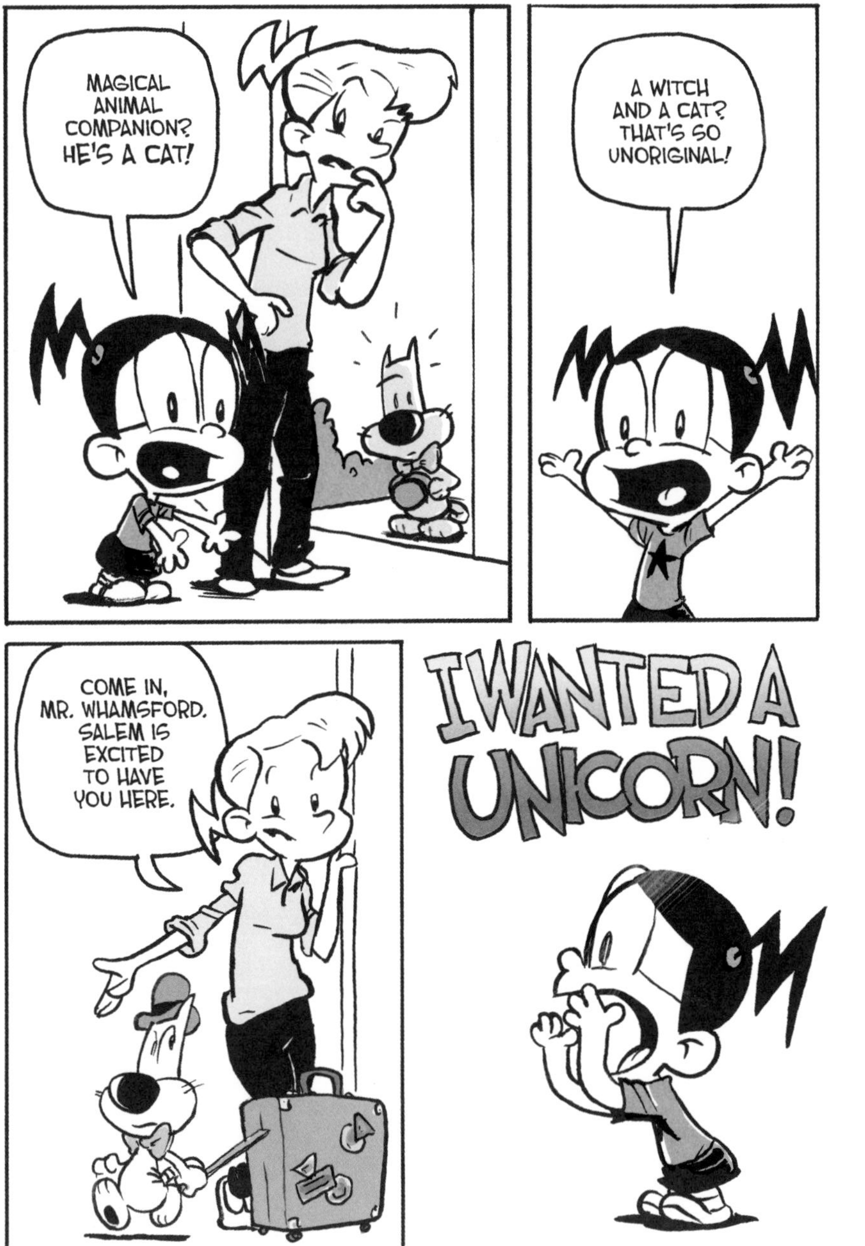
MAGICAL ANIMAL COMPANION? HE'S A CAT!
A WITCH AND A CAT? THAT'S SO UNORIGINAL!
COME IN, MR. WHAMSFORD. SALEM IS EXCITED TO HAVE YOU HERE.
I WANTED A UNICORN!

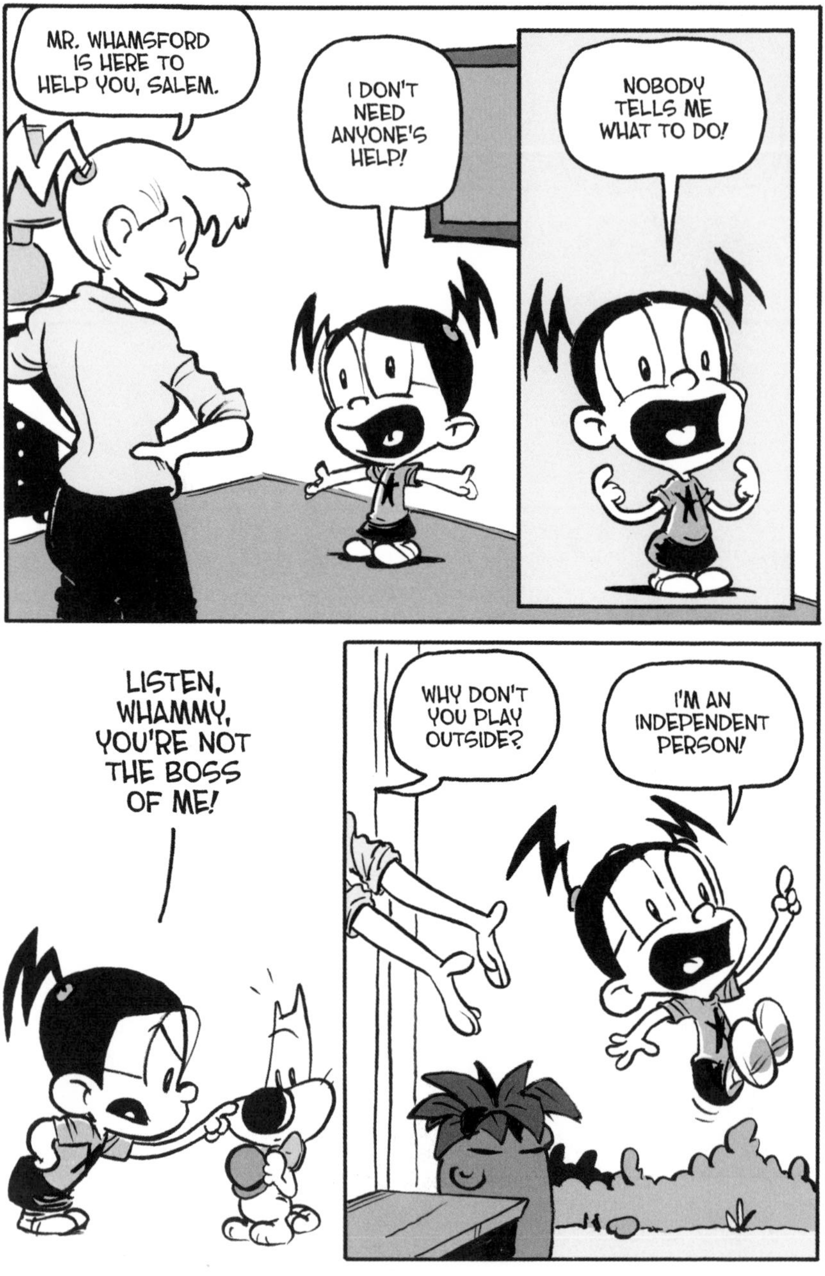
MR. WHAMSFORD IS HERE TO HELP YOU, SALEM.
I DON'T NEED ANYONE'S HELP!
NOBODY TELLS ME WHAT TO DO!
LISTEN, WHAMMY, YOU'RE NOT THE BOSS OF ME!
WHY DON'T YOU PLAY OUTSIDE?
I'M AN INDEPENDENT PERSON!

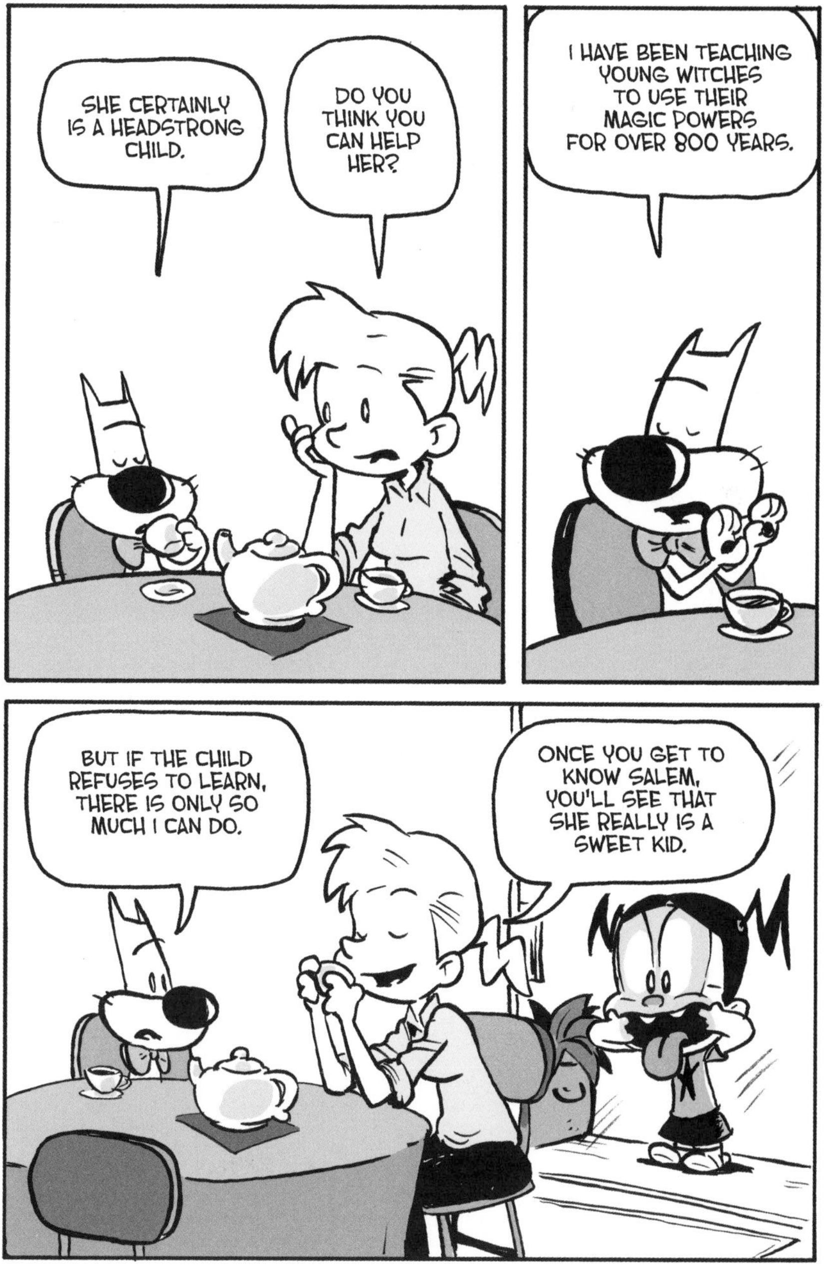
SHE CERTAINLY IS A HEADSTRONG CHILD.
DO YOU THINK YOU CAN HELP HER?
I HAVE BEEN TEACHING YOUNG WITCHES TO USE THEIR MAGIC POWERS FOR OVER 800 YEARS.
BUT IF THE CHILD REFUSES TO LEARN, THERE IS ONLY SO MUCH I CAN DO.
ONCE YOU GET TO KNOW SALEM, YOU'LL SEE THAT SHE REALLY IS A SWEET KID.

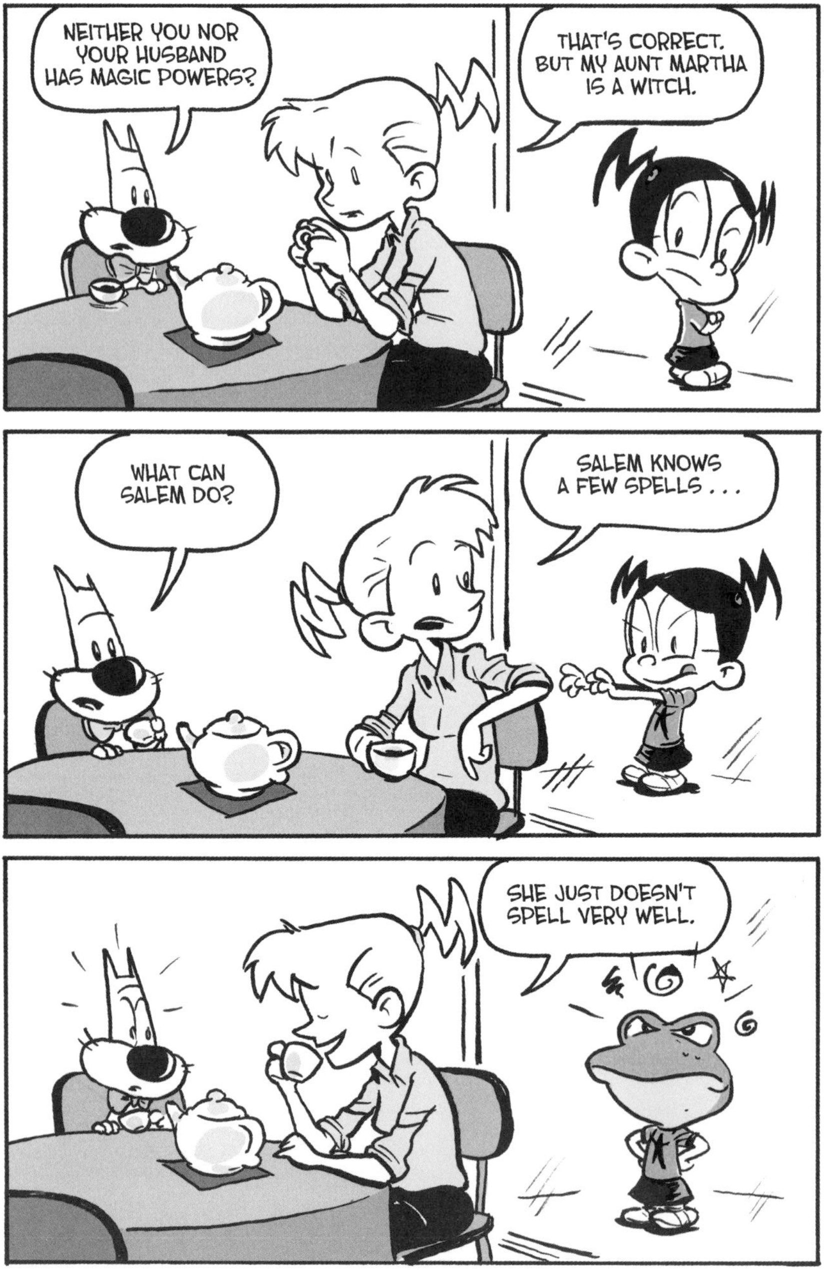
NEITHER YOU NOR YOUR HUSBAND HAS MAGIC POWERS?
THAT'S CORRECT. BUT MY AUNT MARTHA IS A WITCH.
WHAT CAN SALEM DO?
SALEM KNOWS A FEW SPELLS . . .
SHE JUST DOESN'T SPELL VERY WELL.

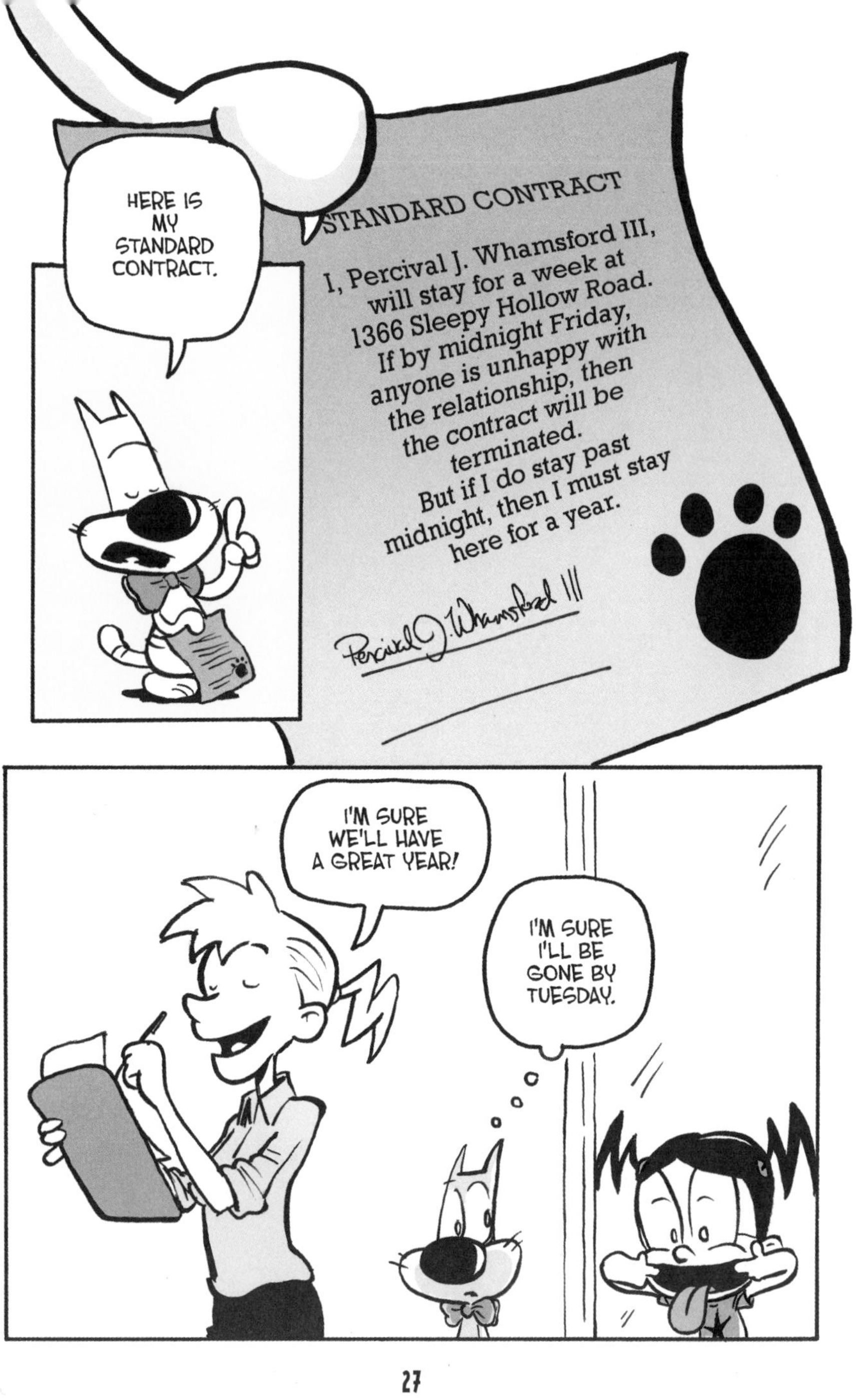
HERE IS MY STANDARD CONTRACT.
STANDARD CONTRACT
I, Percival J. Whamsford III, will stay for a week at 1366 Sleepy Hollow Road. If by midnight Friday, anyone is unhappy with the relationship, then the contract will be terminated. But if I do stay past midnight, then I must stay here for a year.
Percival J. Whamsford III
I'M SURE WE'LL HAVE A GREAT YEAR!
I'M SURE I'LL BE GONE BY TUESDAY.

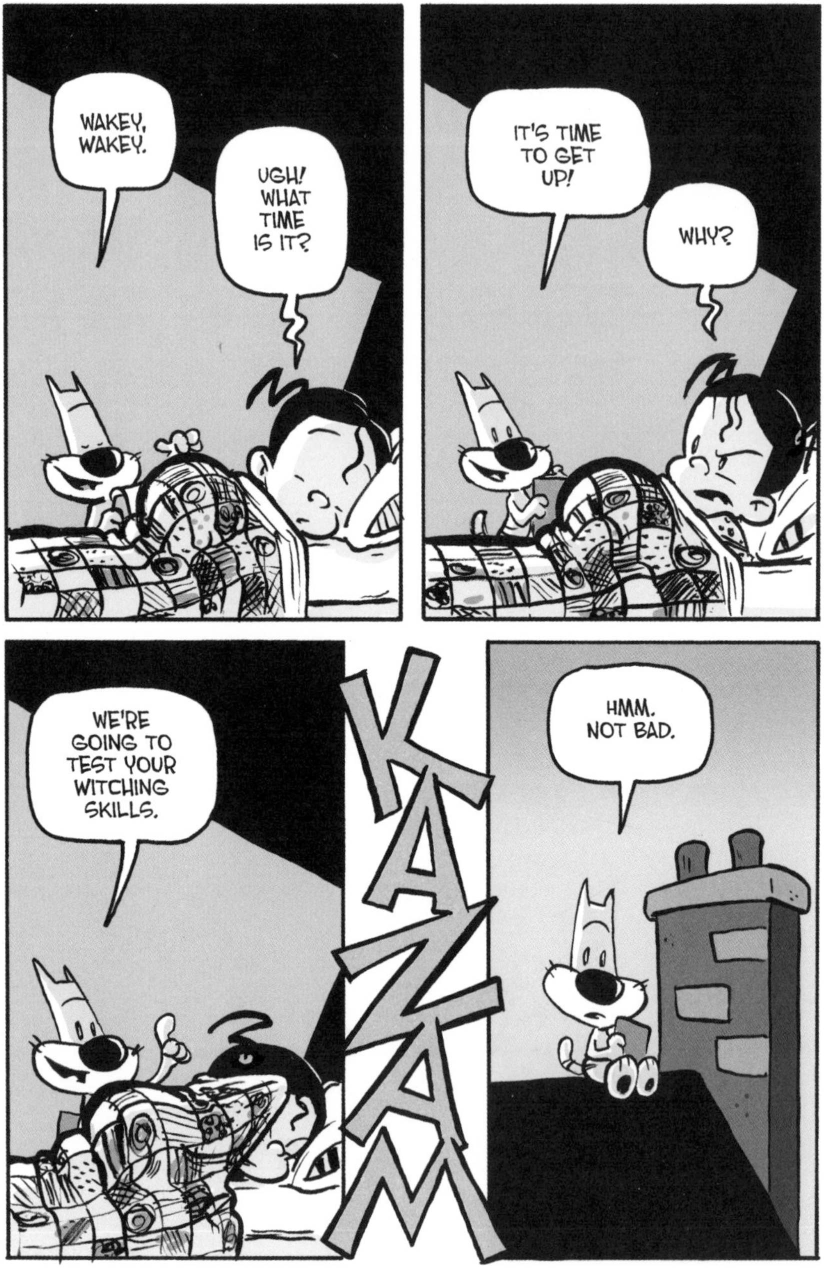
WAKEY, WAKEY.
UGH! WHAT TIME IS IT?
IT'S TIME TO GET UP!
WHY?
WE'RE GOING TO TEST YOUR WITCHING SKILLS.
KAZAM
HMM. NOT BAD.

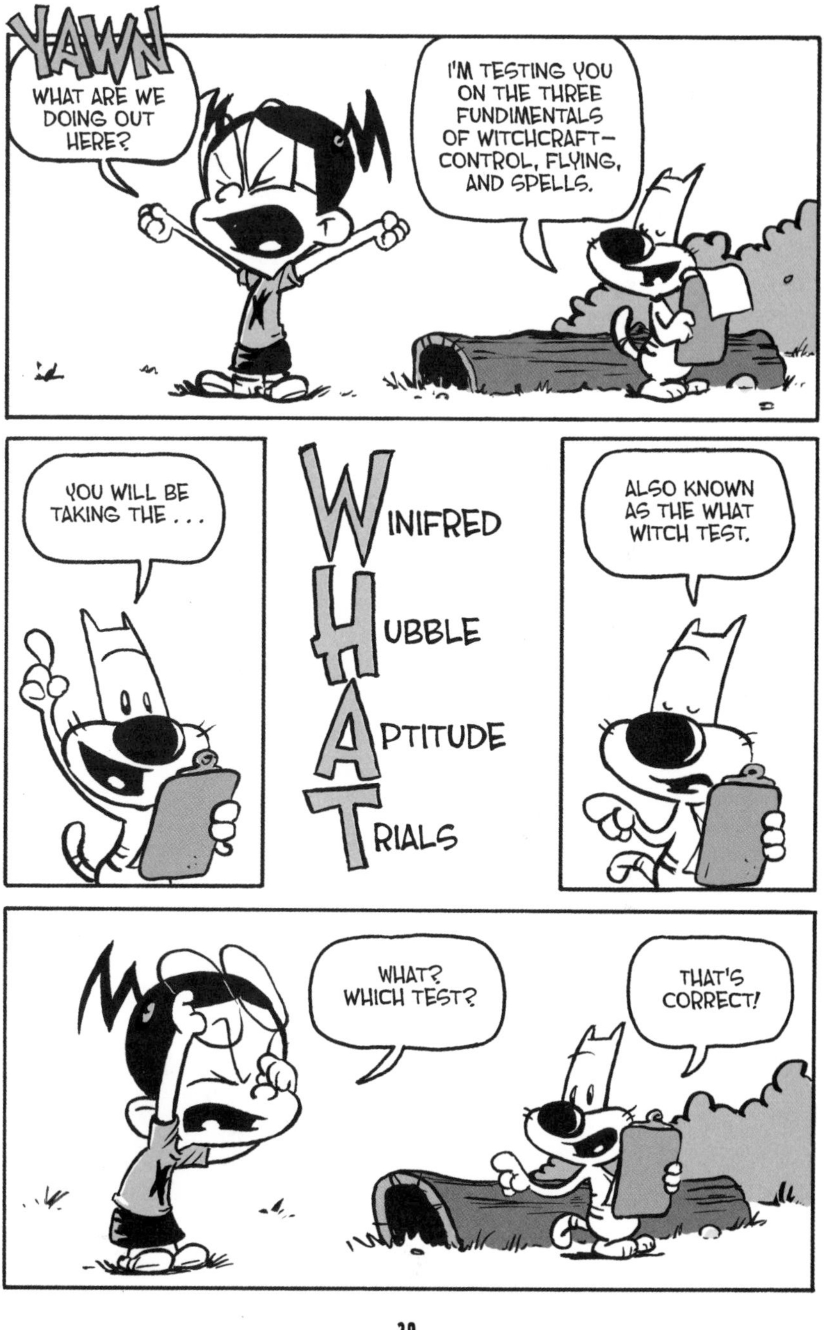
YAWN
WHAT ARE WE DOING OUT HERE?
I'M TESTING YOU ON THE THREE FUNDIMENTALS OF WITCHCRAFT– CONTROL, FLYING, AND SPELLS.
YOU WILL BE TAKING THE . . .
WINIFRED
HUBBLE
APTITUDE
TRIALS
ALSO KNOWN AS THE WHAT WITCH TEST.
WHAT? WHICH TEST?
THAT'S CORRECT!

PART 1: CONTROL

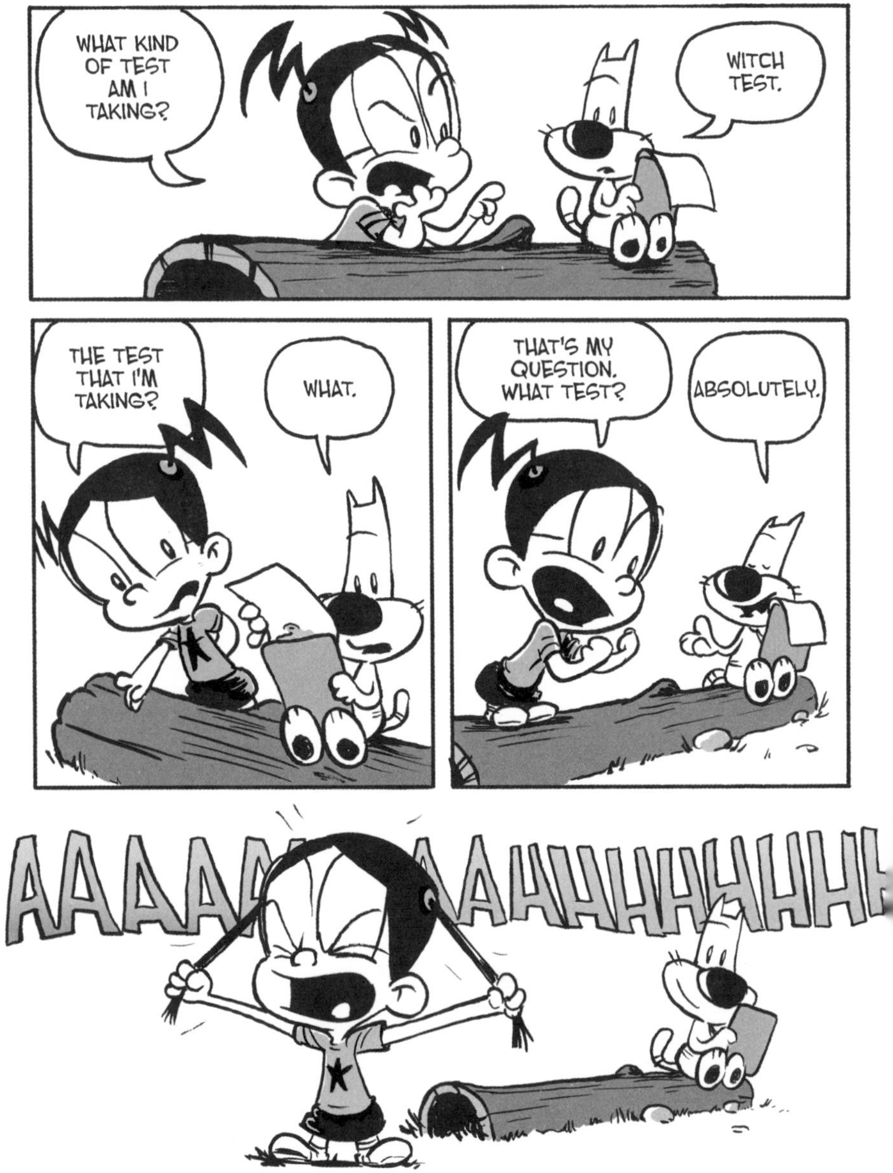
WHAT KIND OF TEST AM I TAKING?
WITCH TEST.
THE TEST THAT I'M TAKING?
WHAT.
THAT'S MY QUESTION. WHAT TEST?
ABSOLUTELY.
AAAAAAAAHHHHHHHH

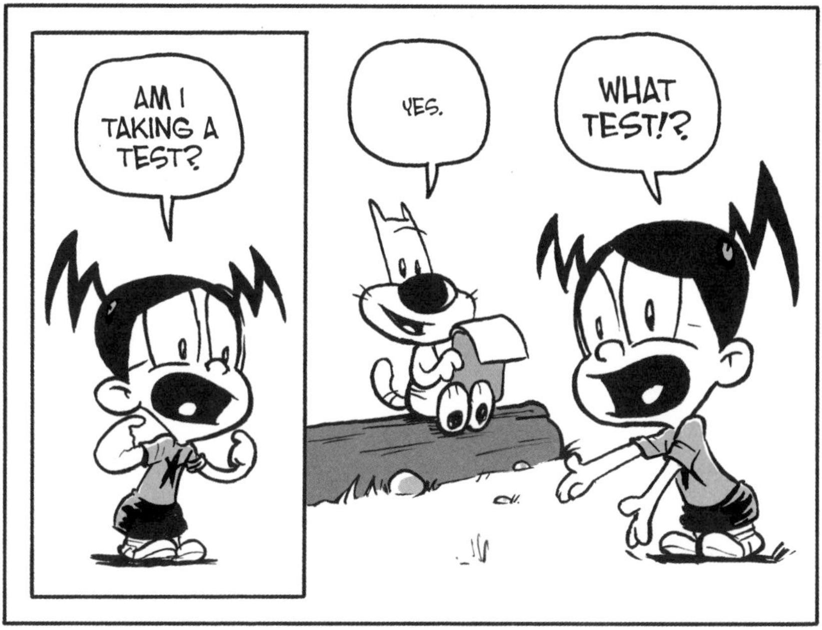
AM I TAKING A TEST?
YES.
WHAT TEST!?

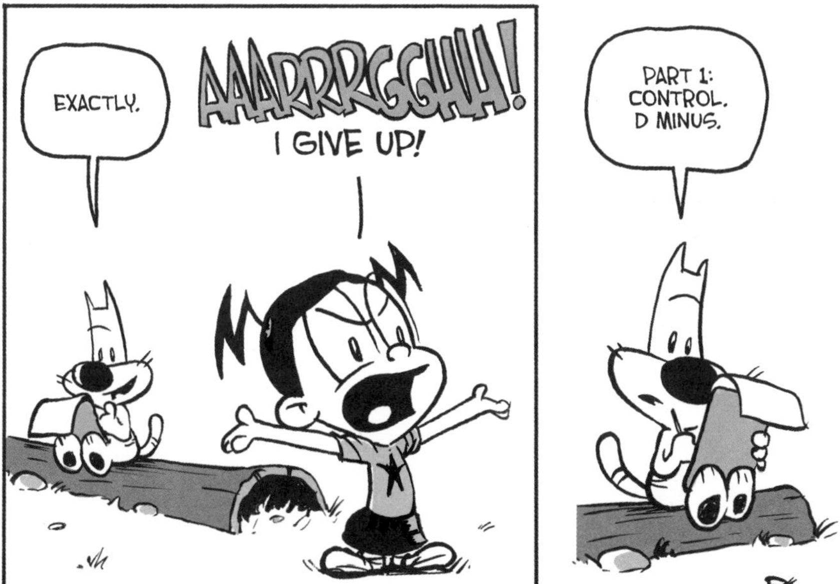
EXACTLY.
AAARRRGGHH!
I GIVE UP!
PART 1: CONTROL. D MINUS.

PART 2: FLYING

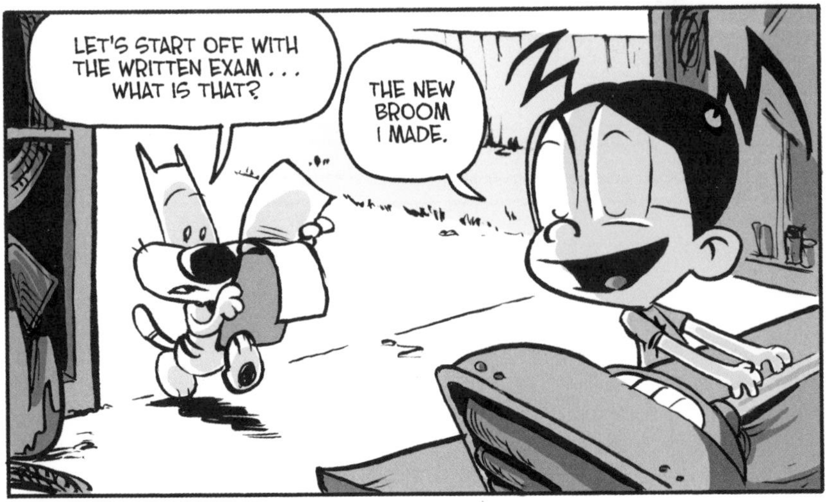

LET'S START OFF WITH THE WRITTEN EXAM . . . WHAT IS THAT?
THE NEW BROOM I MADE.

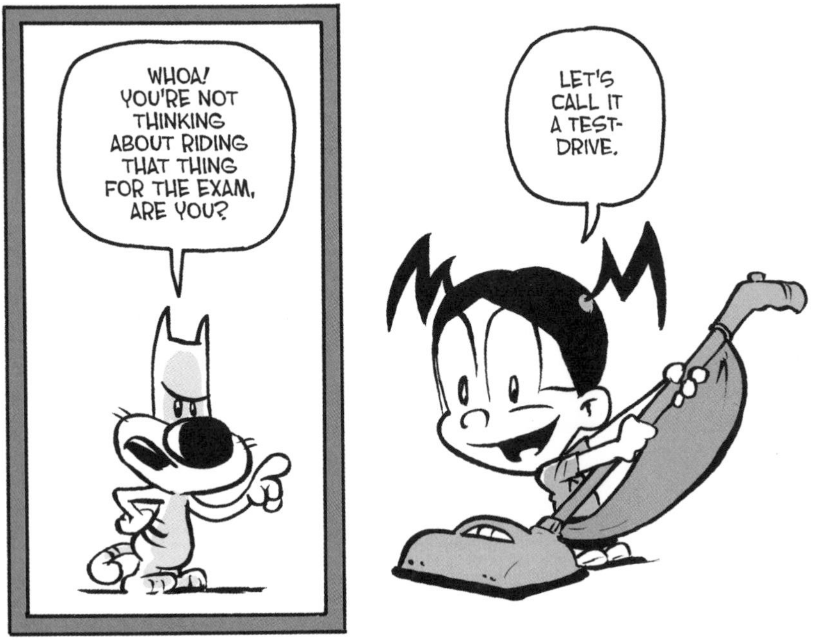

WHOA! YOU'RE NOT THINKING ABOUT RIDING THAT THING FOR THE EXAM, ARE YOU?
LET'S CALL IT A TEST-DRIVE.

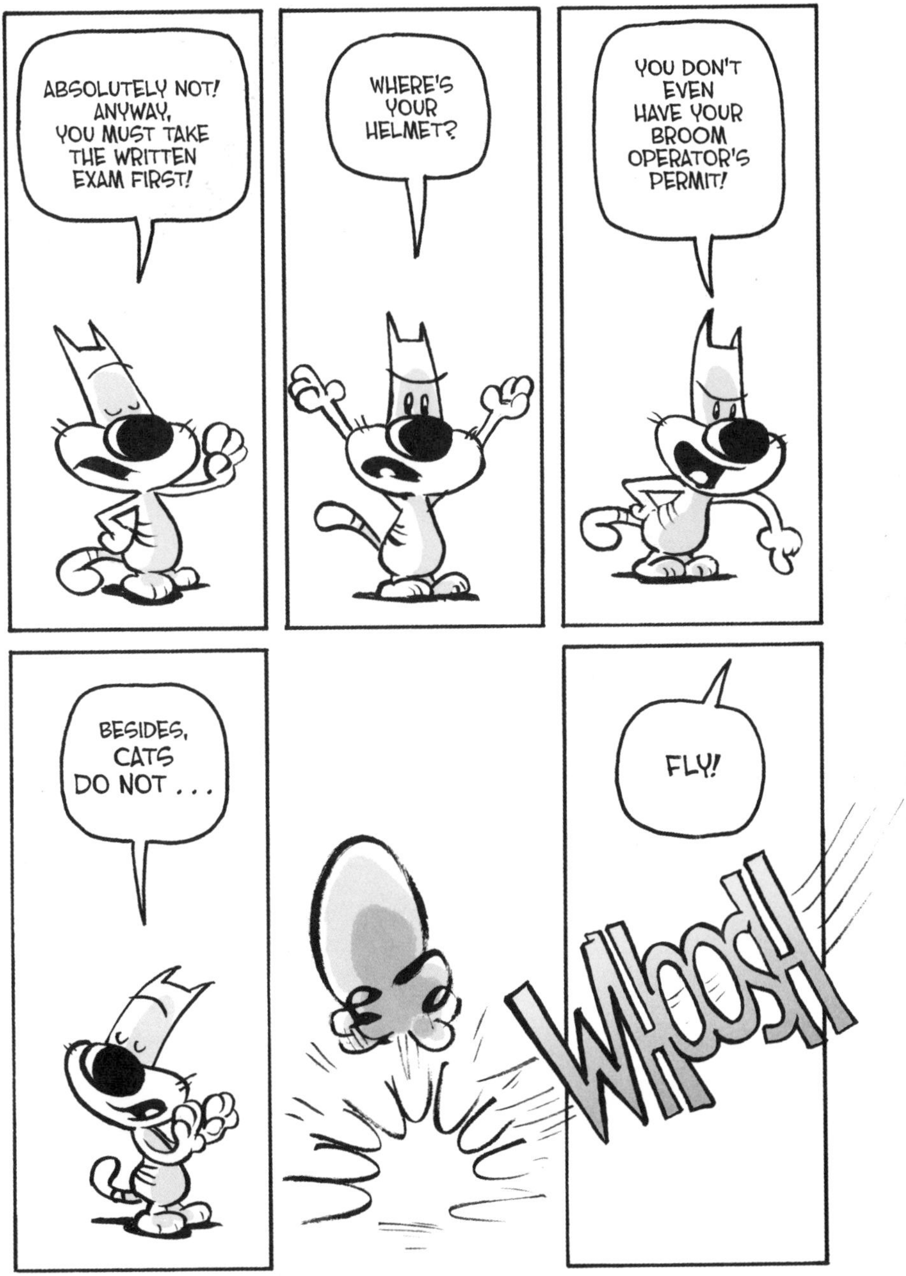
ABSOLUTELY NOT! ANYWAY, YOU MUST TAKE THE WRITTEN EXAM FIRST!
WHERE'S YOUR HELMET?
YOU DON'T EVEN HAVE YOUR BROOM OPERATOR'S PERMIT!
BESIDES, CATS DO NOT . . .
FLY!
WHOOSH

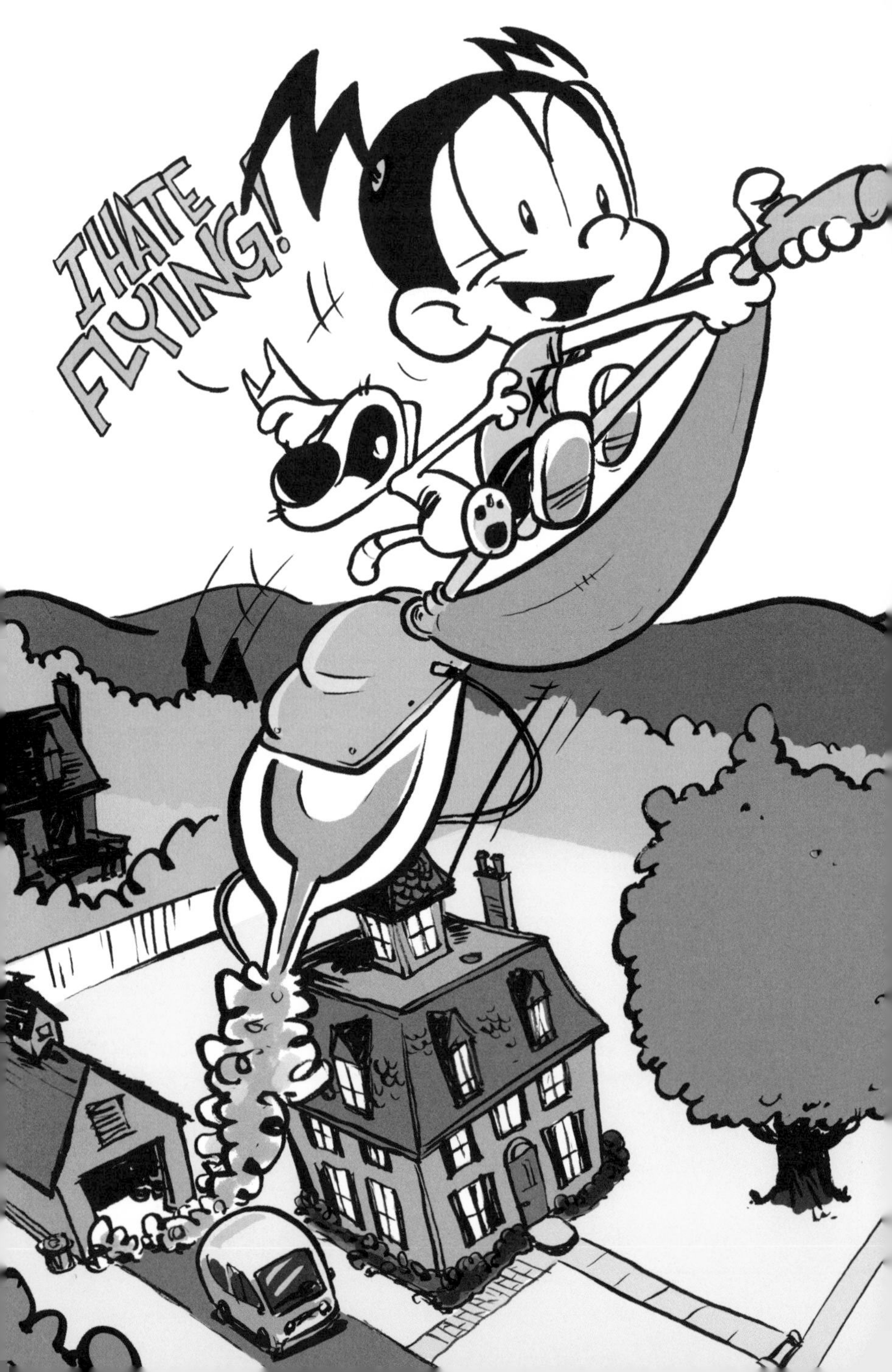
I HATE FLYING!

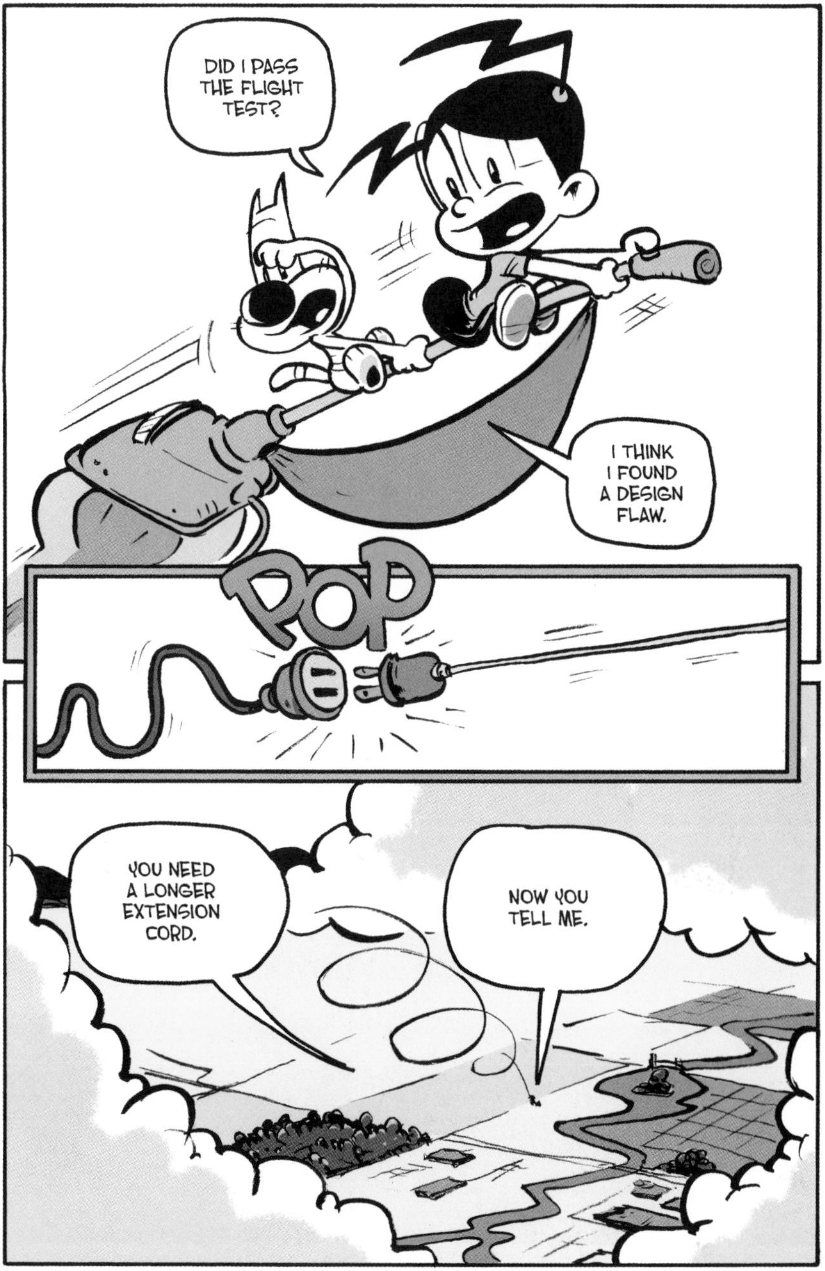
DID I PASS THE FLIGHT TEST?
I THINK I FOUND A DESIGN FLAW.
POP
YOU NEED A LONGER EXTENSION CORD.
NOW YOU TELL ME.

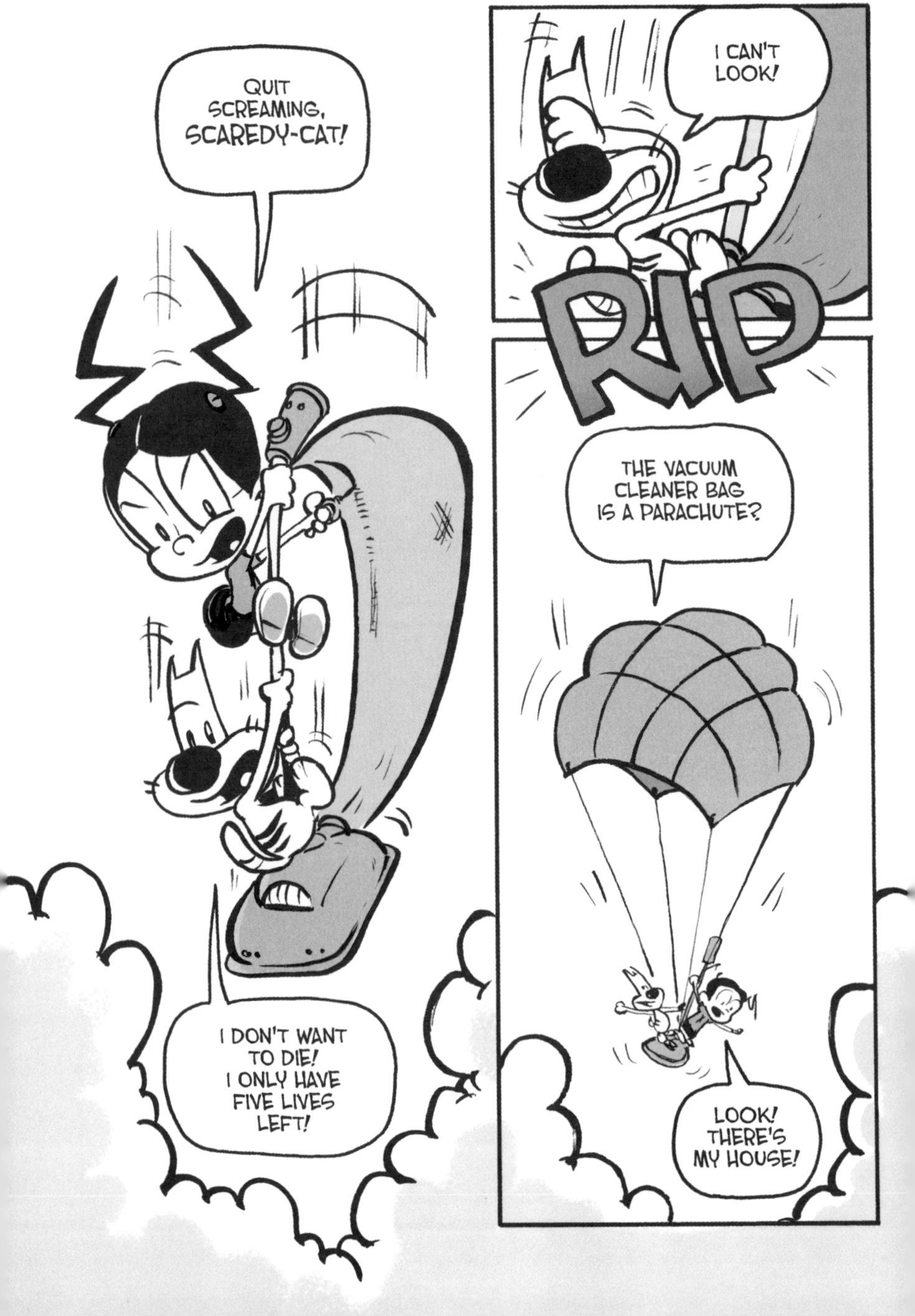
QUIT SCREAMING, SCAREDY-CAT!
I DON'T WANT TO DIE! I ONLY HAVE FIVE LIVES LEFT!
I CAN'T LOOK!
RIP
THE VACUUM CLEANER BAG IS A PARACHUTE?
LOOK! THERE'S MY HOUSE!

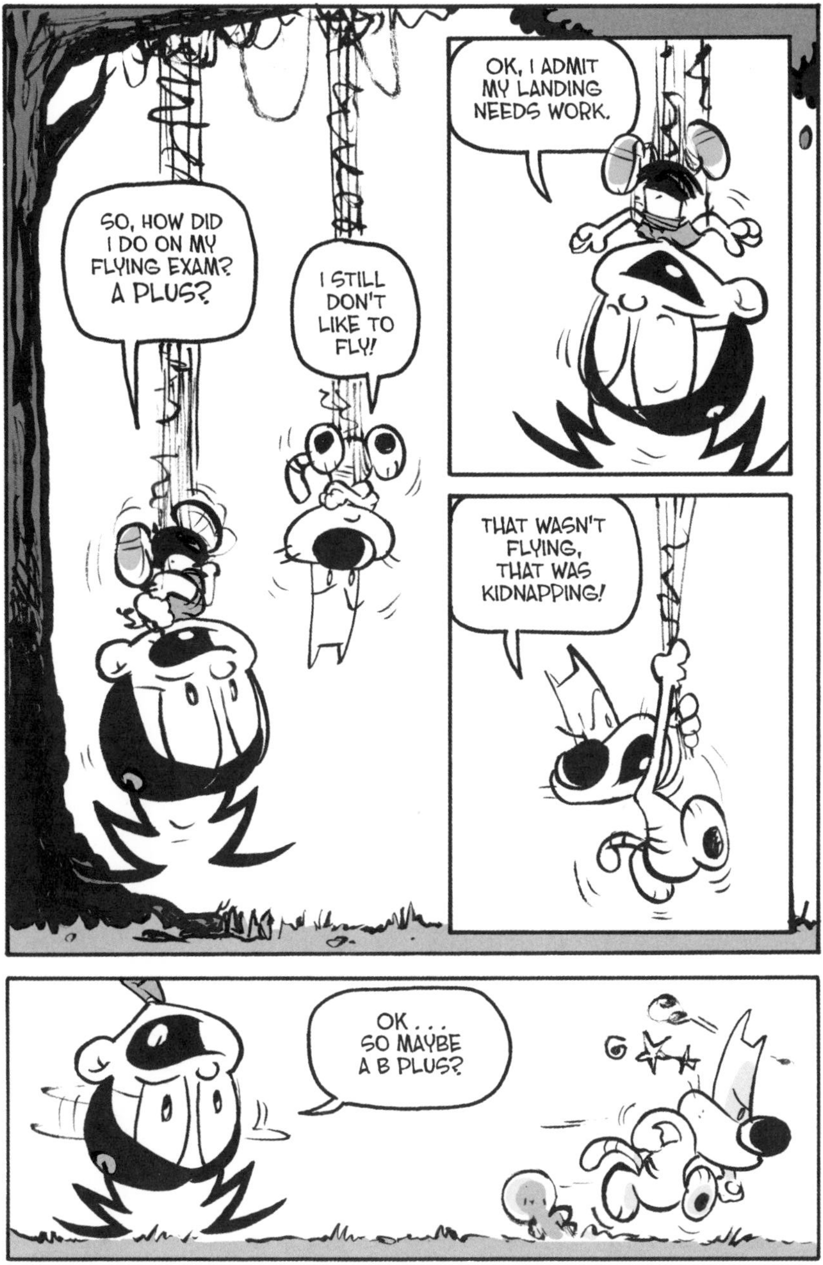
SO, HOW DID I DO ON MY FLYING EXAM? A PLUS?
I STILL DON'T LIKE TO FLY!
OK, I ADMIT MY LANDING NEEDS WORK.
THAT WASN'T FLYING, THAT WAS KIDNAPPING!
OK . . . SO MAYBE A B PLUS?

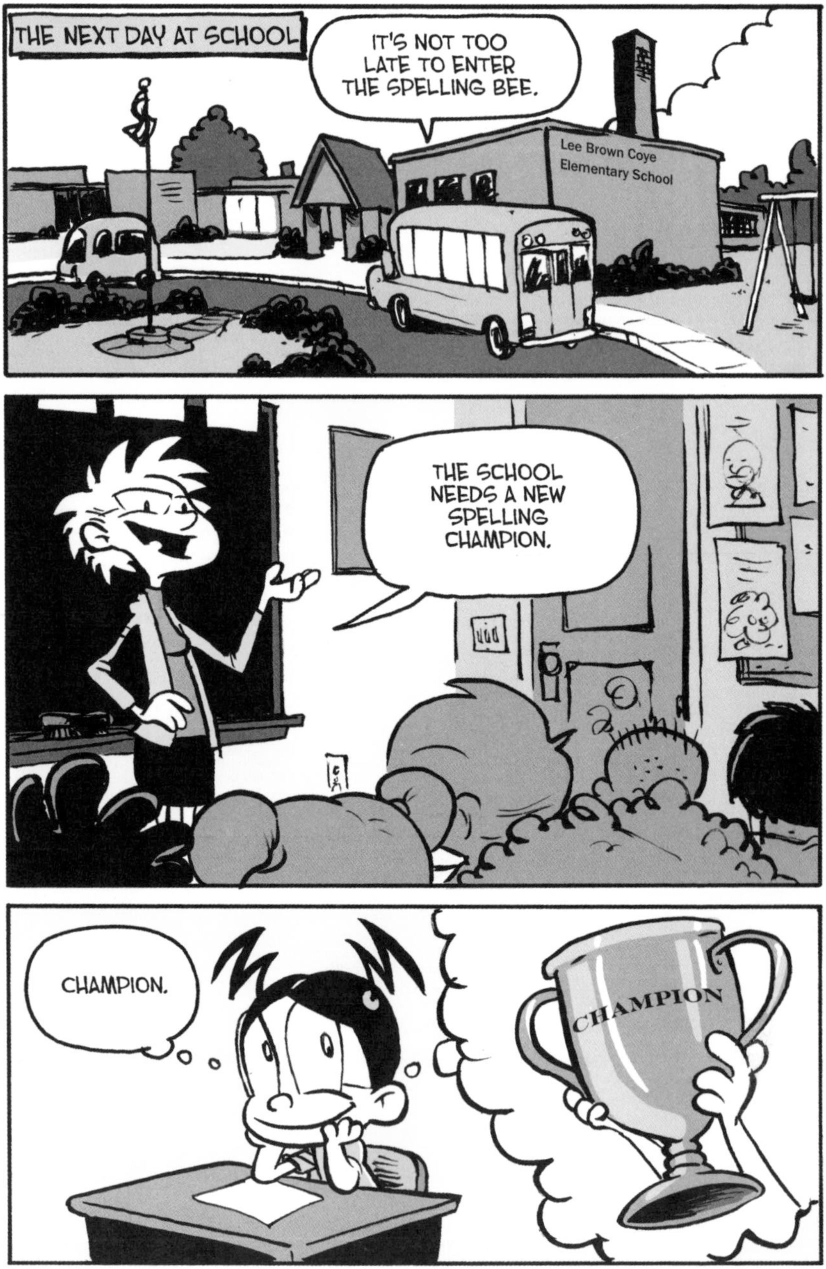
THE NEXT DAY AT SCHOOL
IT'S NOT TOO LATE TO ENTER THE SPELLING BEE.
Lee Brown Coye Elementary School
THE SCHOOL NEEDS A NEW SPELLING CHAMPION.
CHAMPION.
CHAMPION

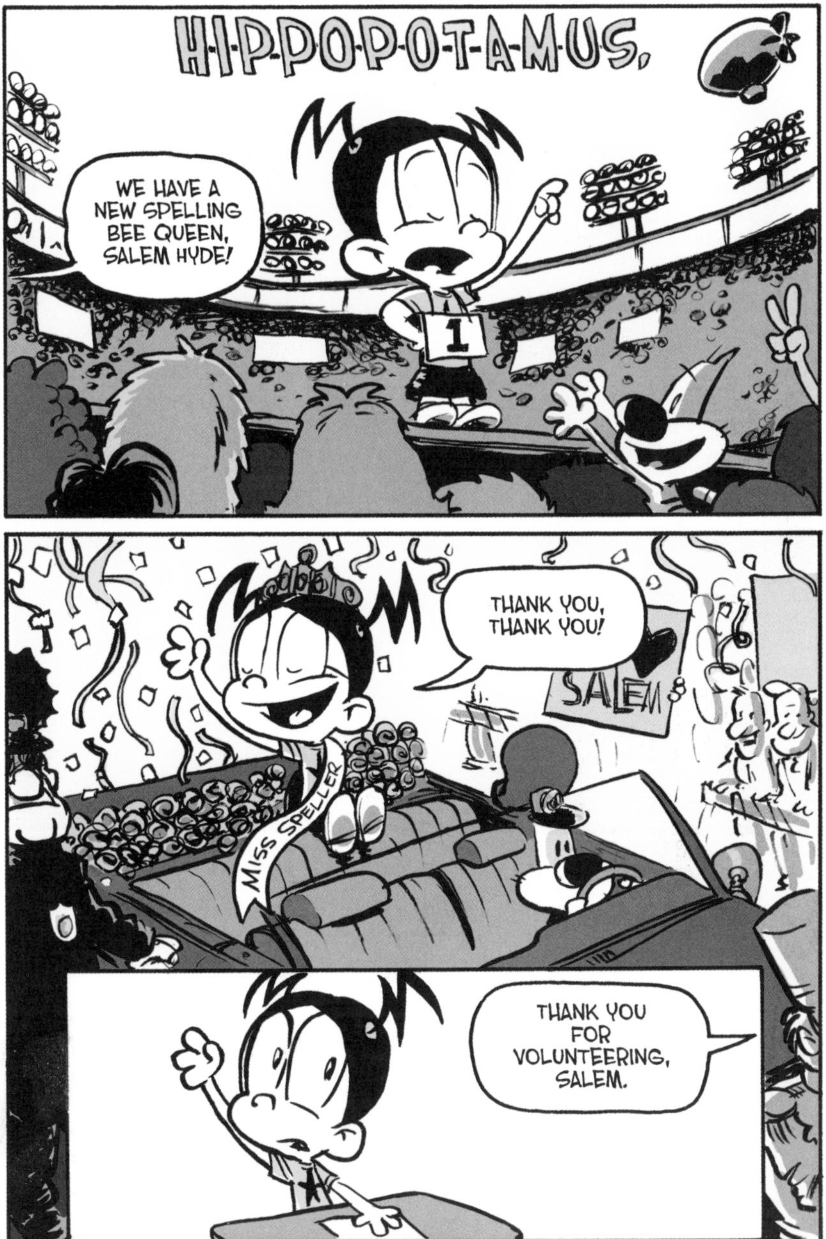
H-I-P-P-O-P-O-T-A-M-U-S,
WE HAVE A NEW SPELLING BEE QUEEN, SALEM HYDE!
1
THANK YOU, THANK YOU!
SALEM
MISS SPELLER
THANK YOU FOR VOLUNTEERING, SALEM.

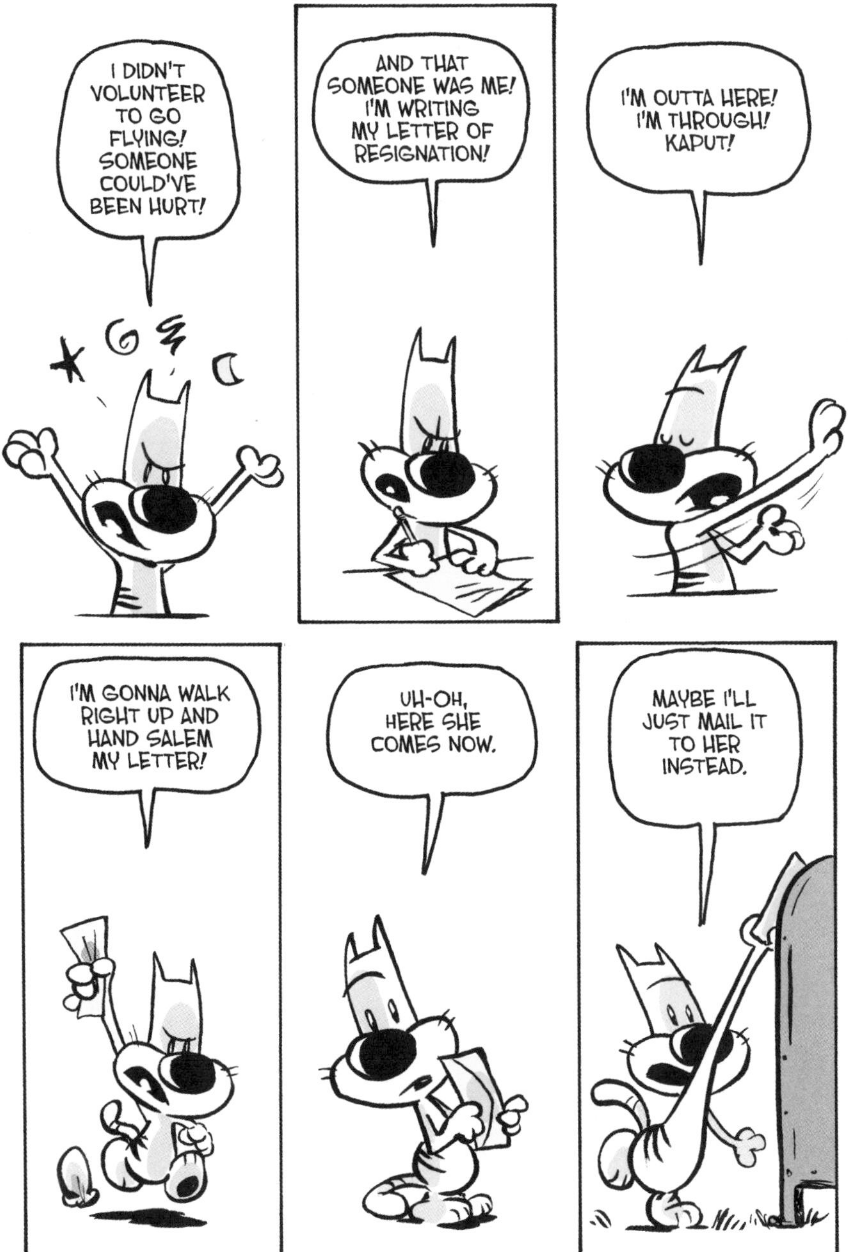
I DIDN'T VOLUNTEER TO GO FLYING! SOMEONE COULD'VE BEEN HURT!
AND THAT SOMEONE WAS ME! I'M WRITING MY LETTER OF RESIGNATION!
I'M OUTTA HERE! I'M THROUGH! KAPUT!
I'M GONNA WALK RIGHT UP AND HAND SALEM MY LETTER!
UH-OH, HERE SHE COMES NOW.
MAYBE I'LL JUST MAIL IT TO HER INSTEAD.

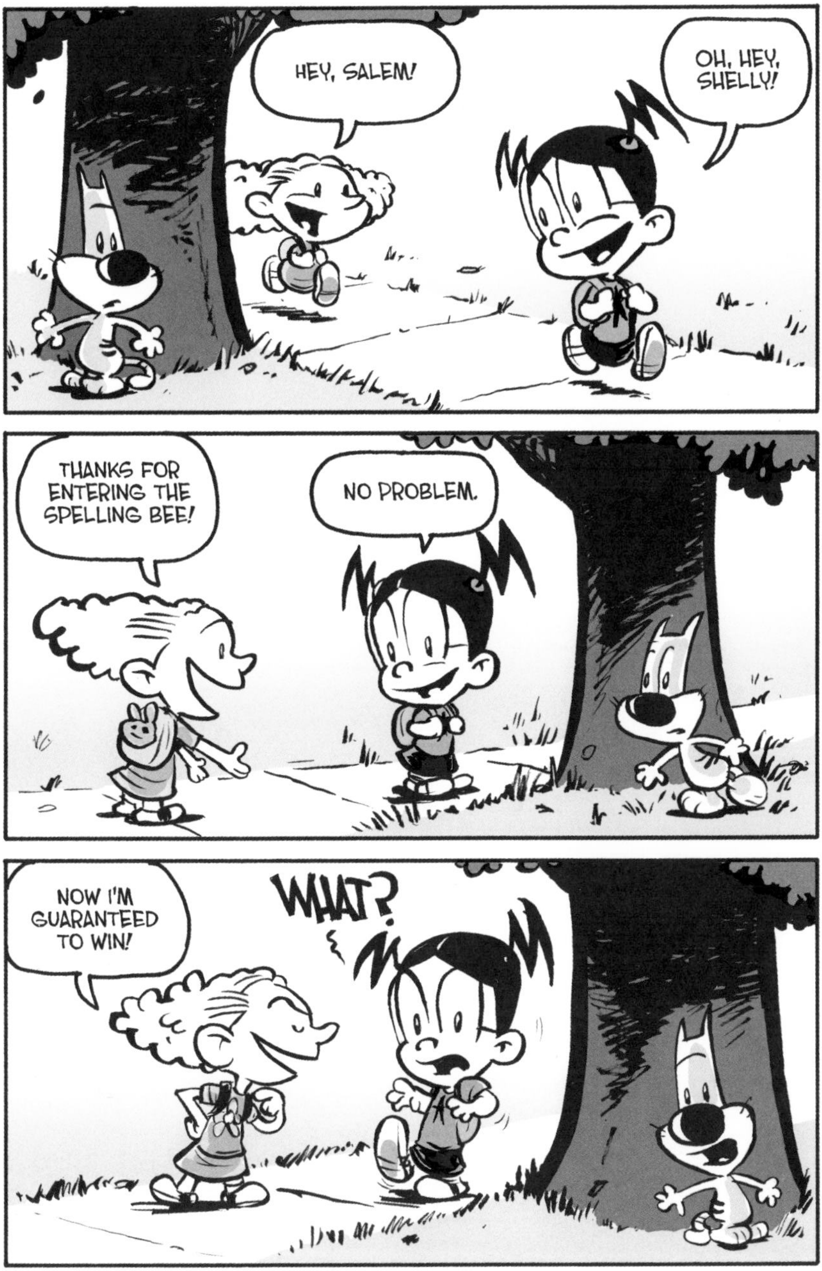
HEY, SALEM!
OH, HEY, SHELLY!
THANKS FOR ENTERING THE SPELLING BEE!
NO PROBLEM.
NOW I'M GUARANTEED TO WIN!
WHAT?

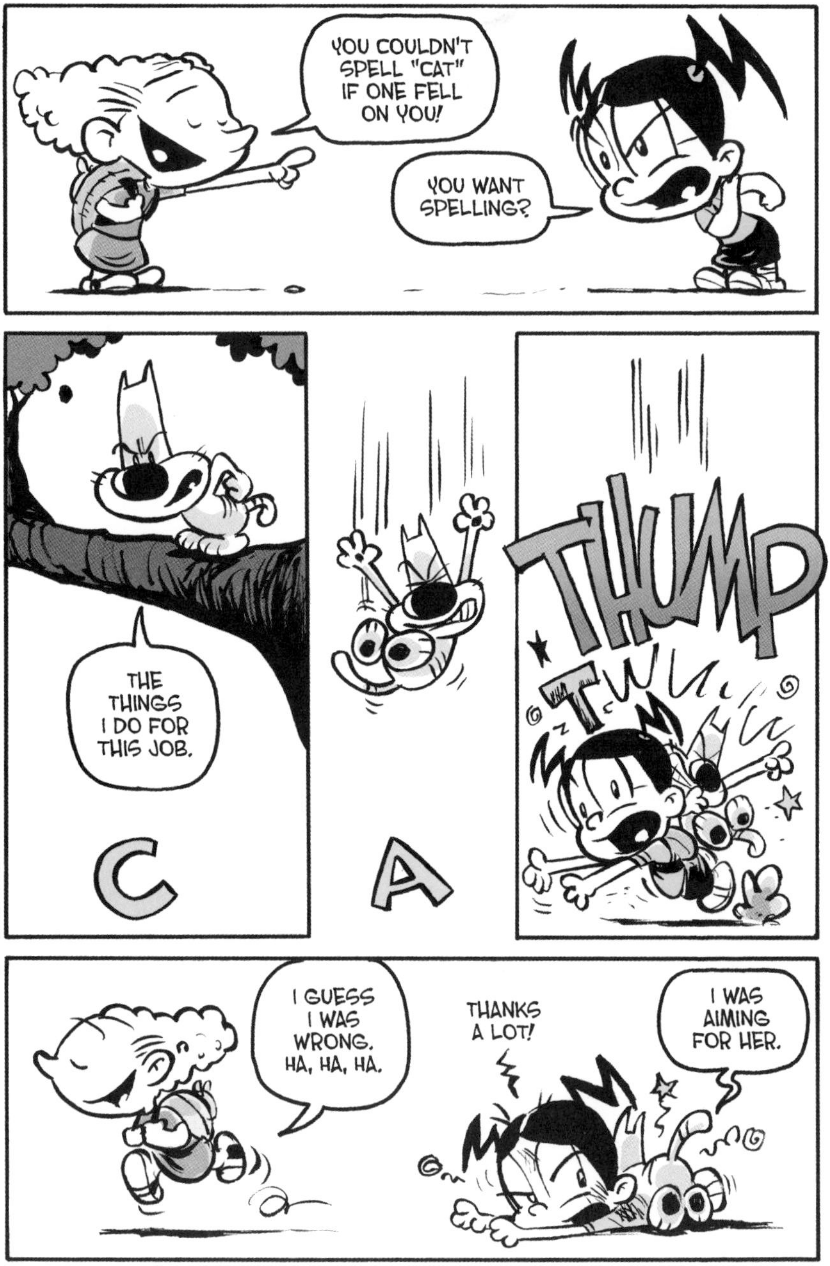
YOU COULDN'T SPELL "CAT" IF ONE FELL ON YOU!
YOU WANT SPELLING?
THE THINGS I DO FOR THIS JOB.
C
A
THUMP
T
I GUESS I WAS WRONG. HA, HA, HA.
THANKS A LOT!
I WAS AIMING FOR HER.

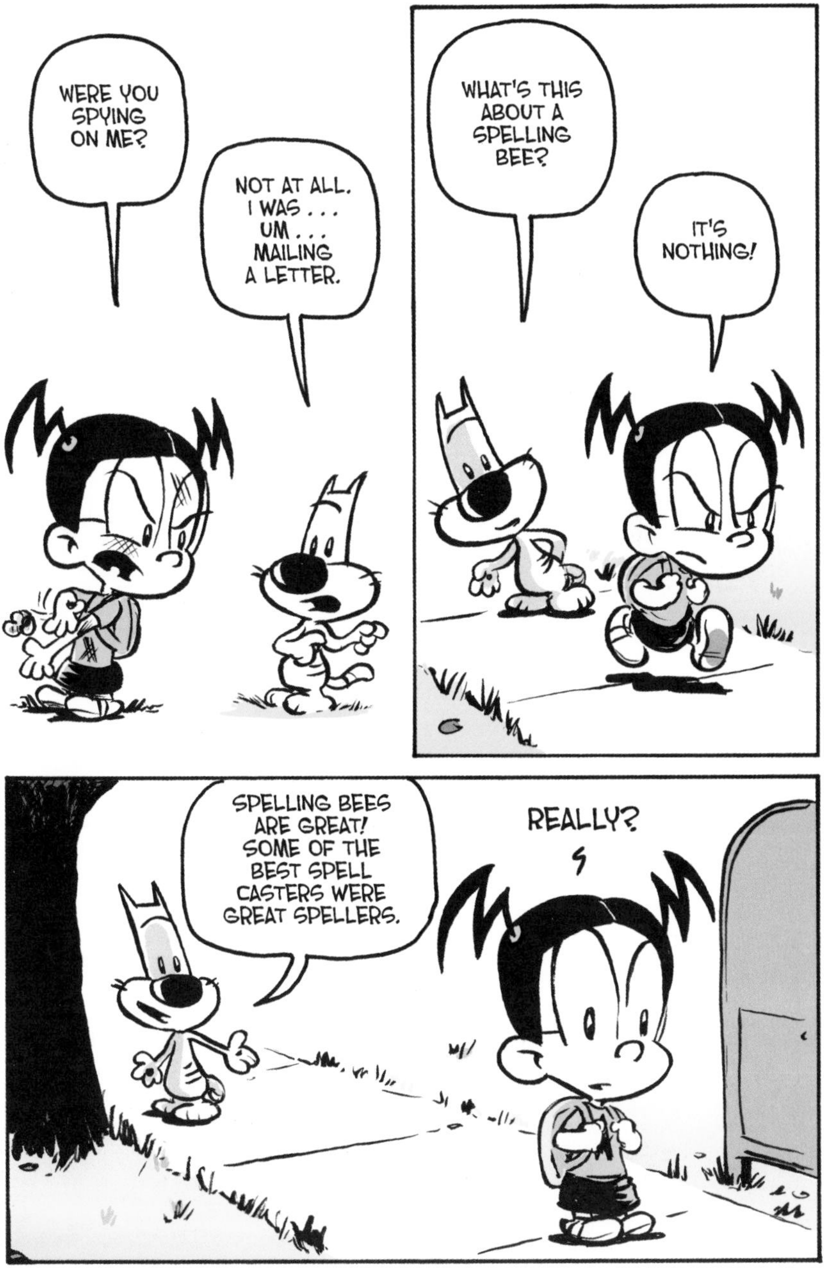
WERE YOU SPYING ON ME?
NOT AT ALL. I WAS . . . UM . . . MAILING A LETTER.
WHAT'S THIS ABOUT A SPELLING BEE?
IT'S NOTHING!
SPELLING BEES ARE GREAT! SOME OF THE BEST SPELL CASTERS WERE GREAT SPELLERS.
REALLY?

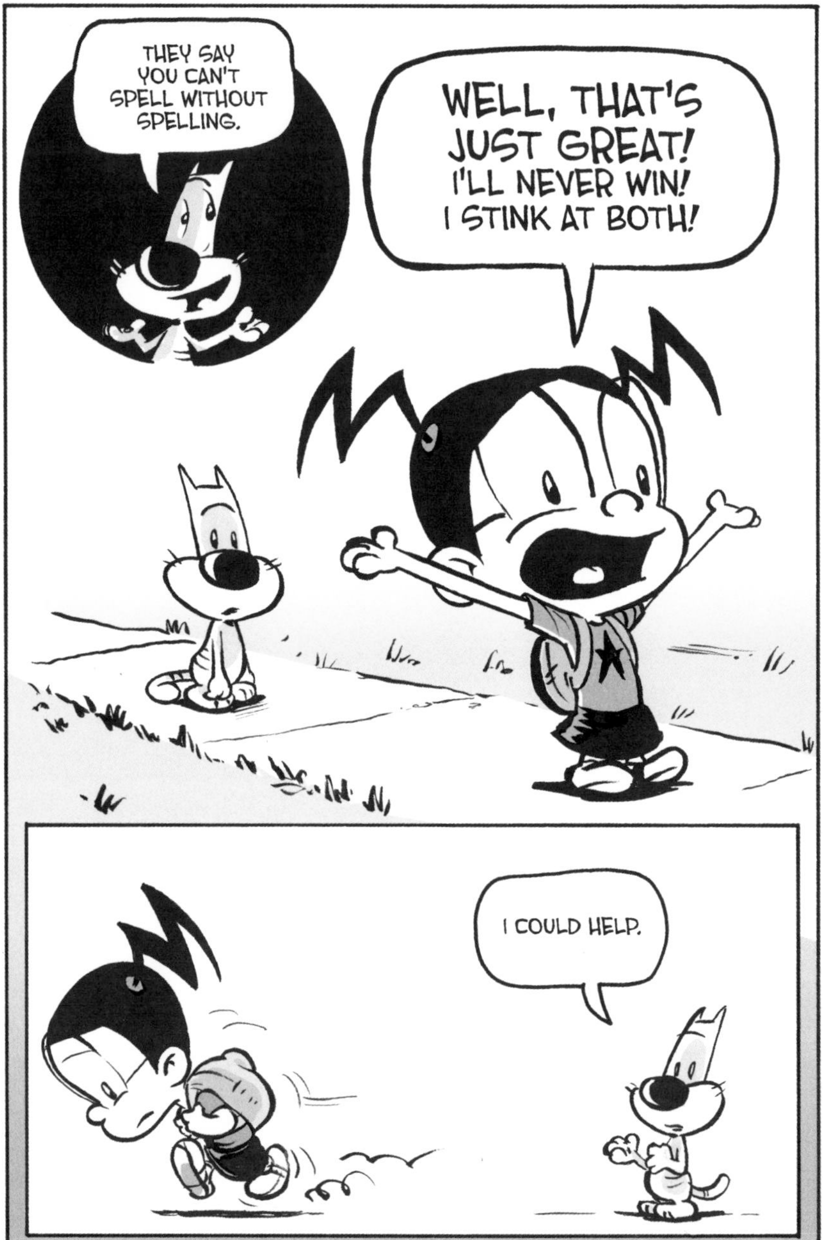
THEY SAY YOU CAN'T SPELL WITHOUT SPELLING.
WELL, THAT'S JUST GREAT! I'LL NEVER WIN! I STINK AT BOTH!
I COULD HELP.

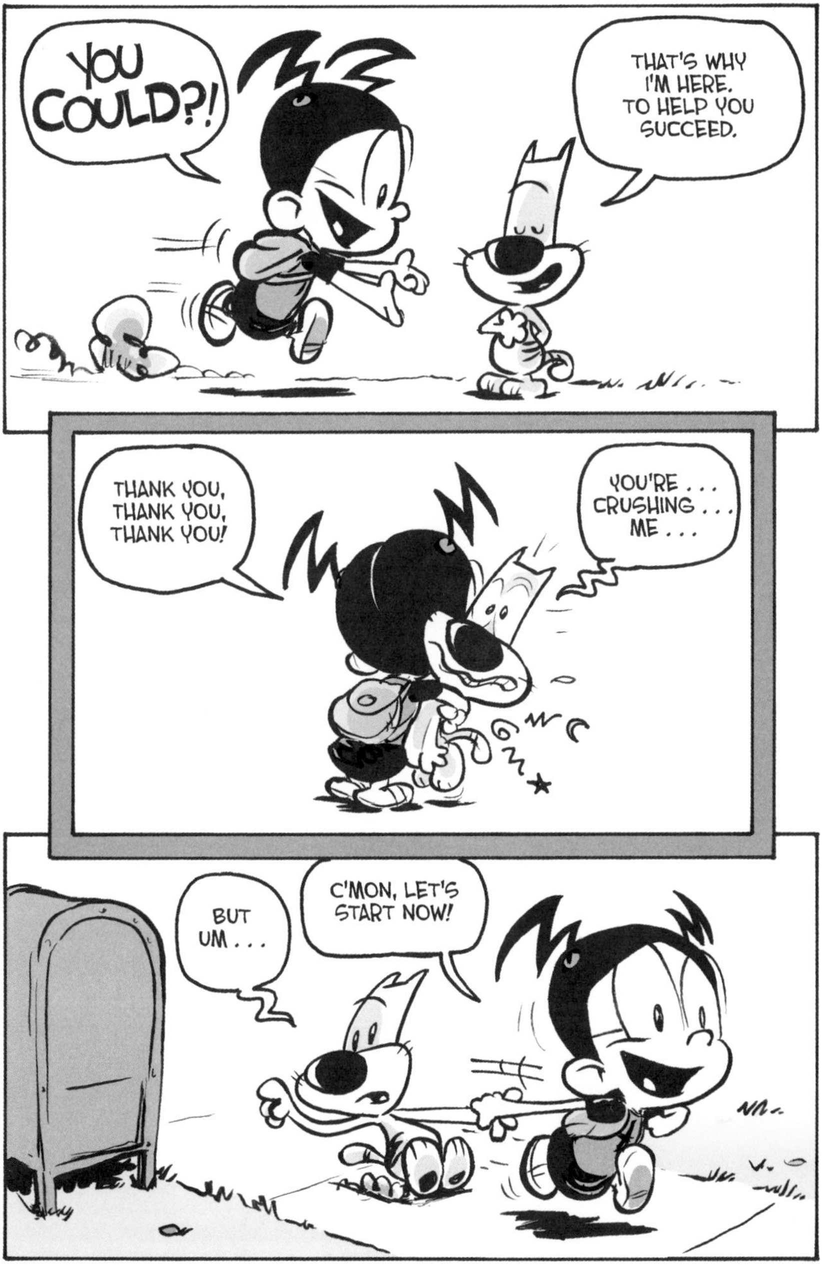
YOU COULD?!
THAT'S WHY I'M HERE. TO HELP YOU SUCCEED.
THANK YOU, THANK YOU, THANK YOU!
YOU'RE . . . CRUSHING . . . ME . . .
BUT UM . . .
C'MON, LET'S START NOW!

PART 3: SPELLING

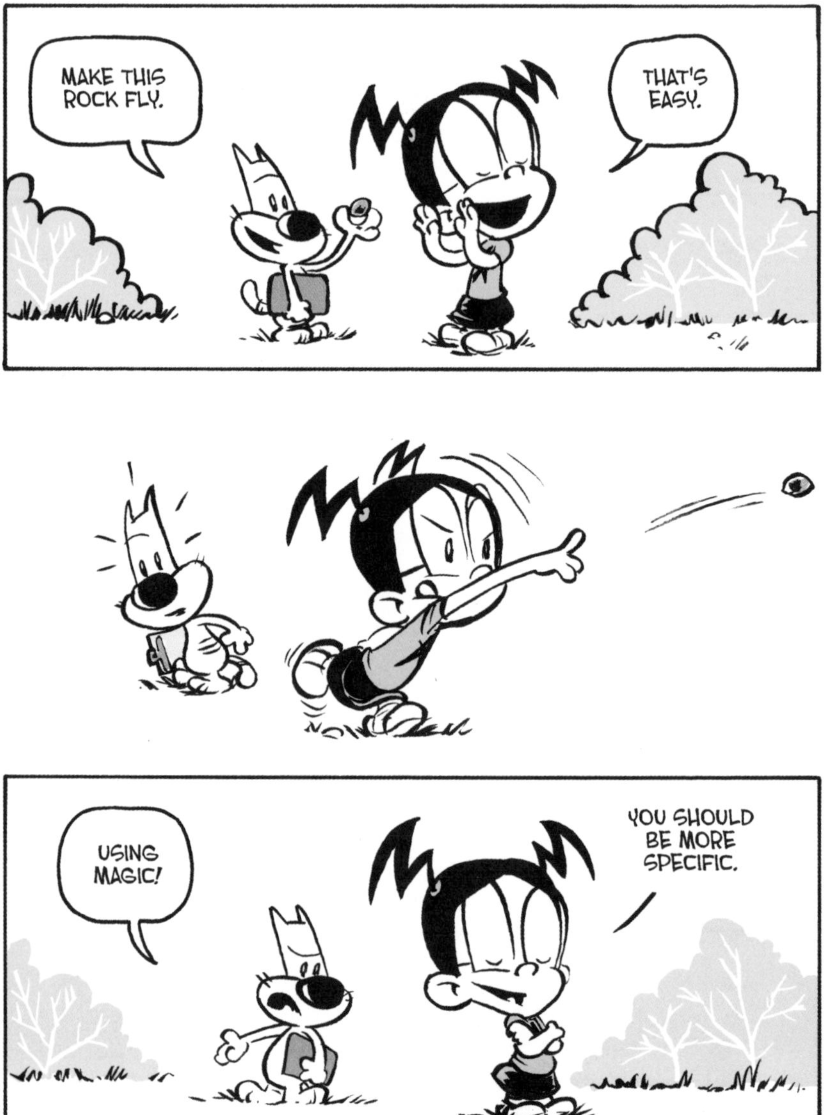
MAKE THIS ROCK FLY.
THAT'S EASY.
USING MAGIC!
YOU SHOULD BE MORE SPECIFIC.

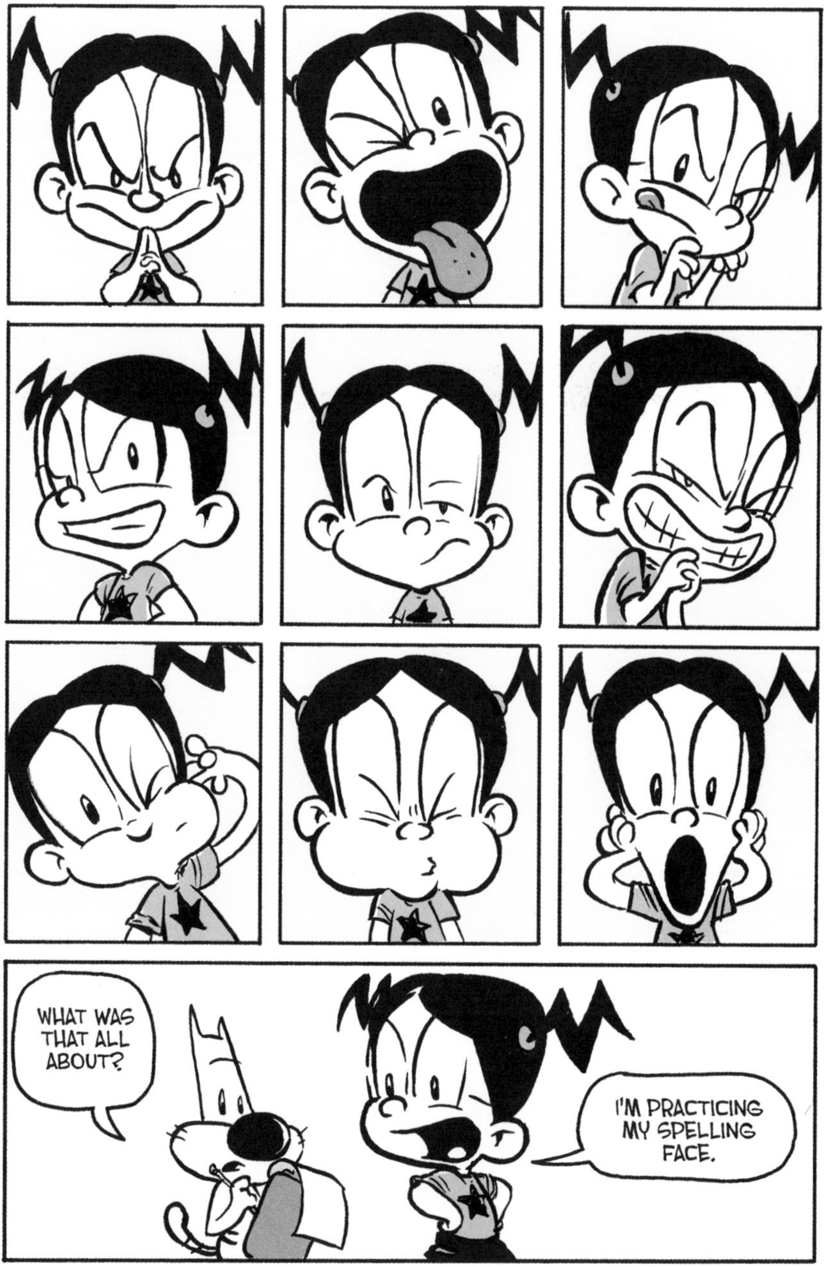
WHAT WAS THAT ALL ABOUT?
I'M PRACTICING MY SPELLING FACE.

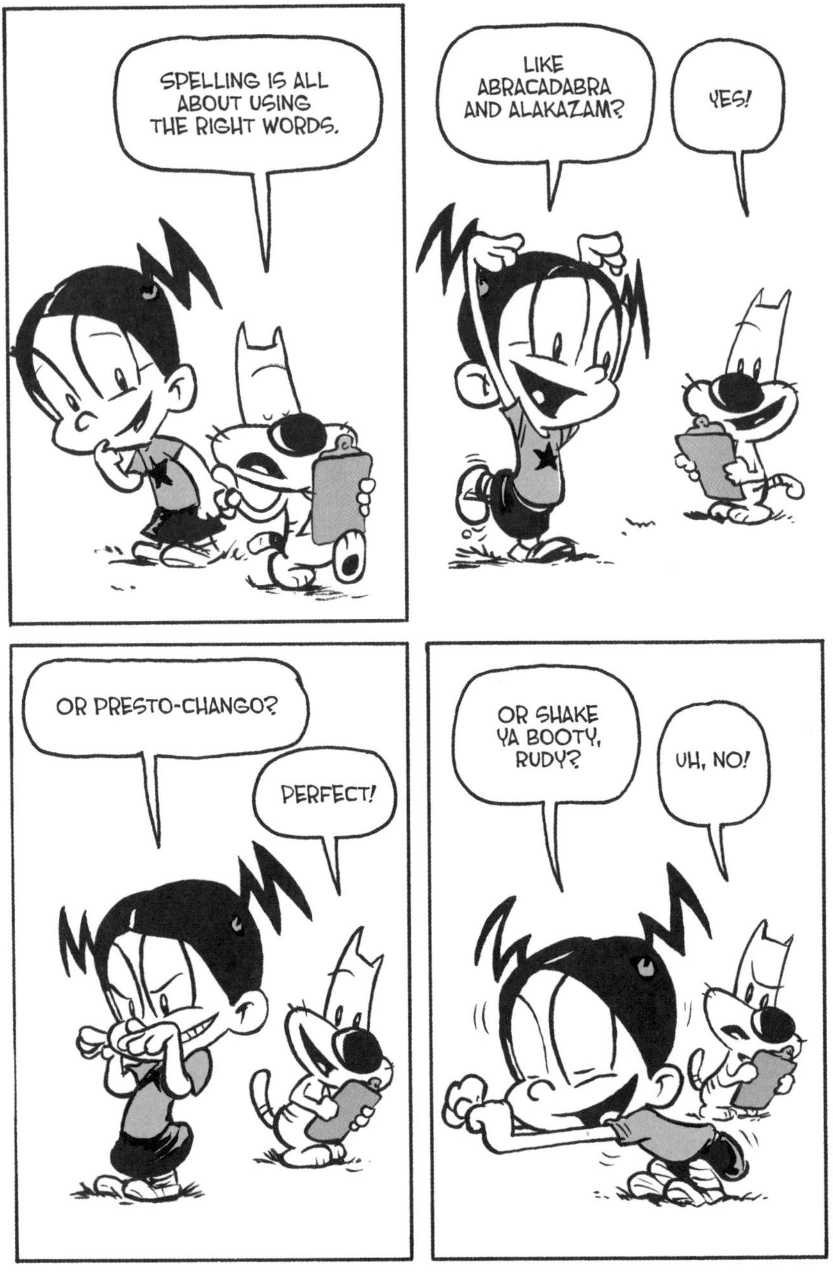
SPELLING IS ALL ABOUT USING THE RIGHT WORDS.
LIKE ABRACADABRA AND ALAKAZAM?
YES!
OR PRESTO-CHANGO?
PERFECT!
OR SHAKE YA BOOTY, RUDY?
UH, NO!

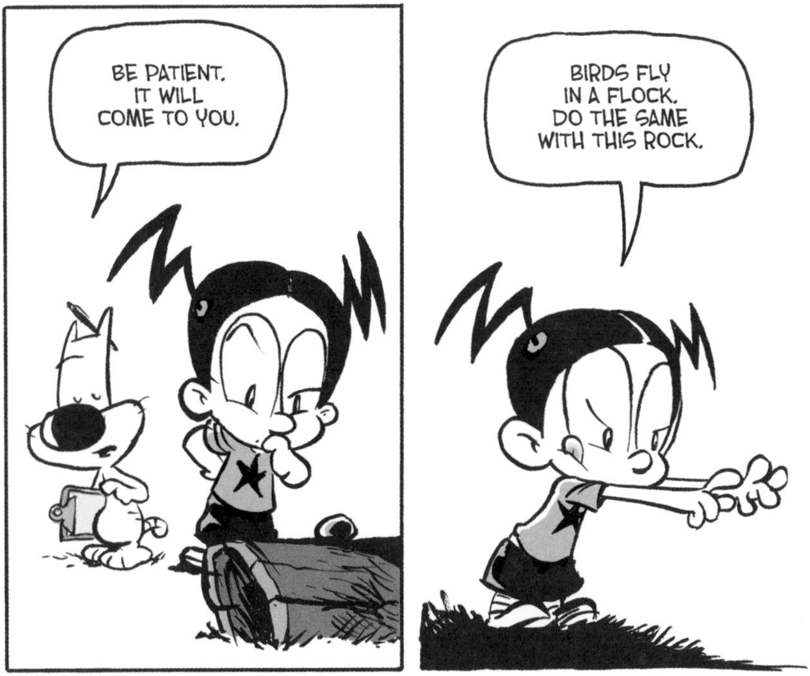
BE PATIENT. IT WILL COME TO YOU.
BIRDS FLY IN A FLOCK. DO THE SAME WITH THIS ROCK.

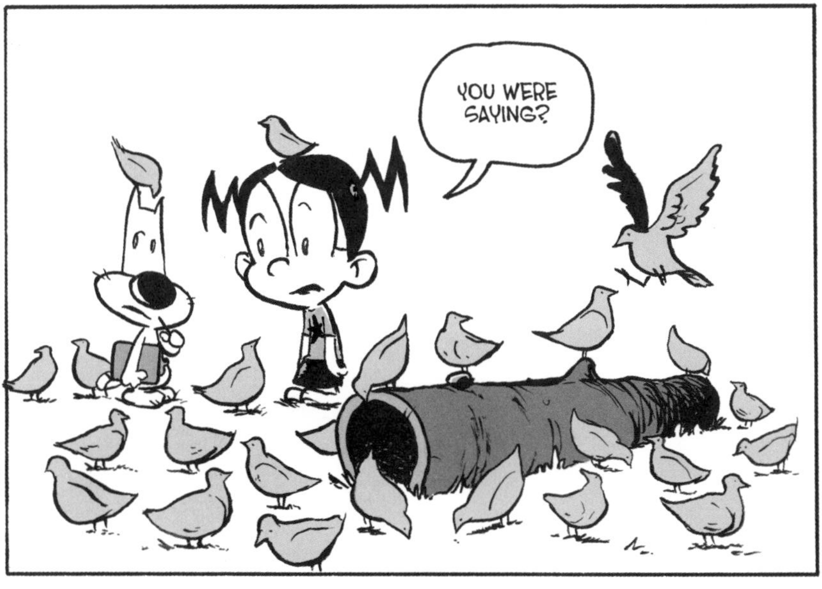
YOU WERE SAYING?

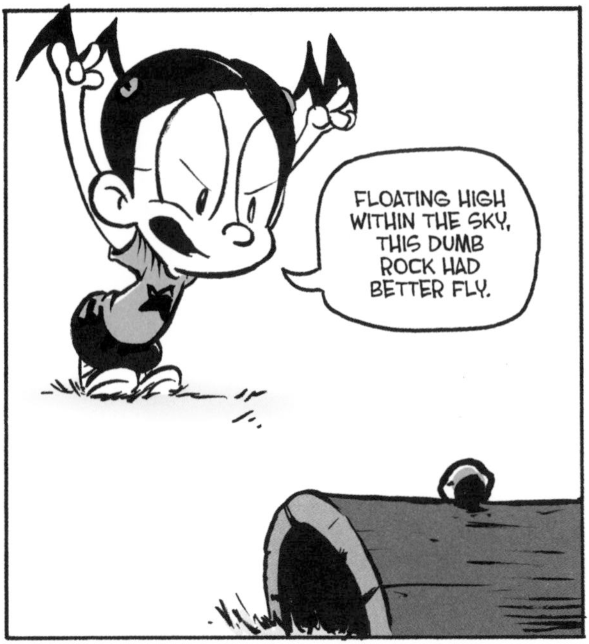
FLOATING HIGH WITHIN THE SKY, THIS DUMB ROCK HAD BETTER FLY.

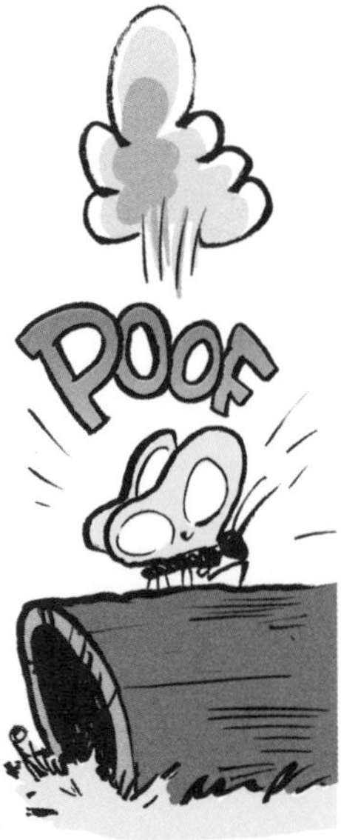
POOF

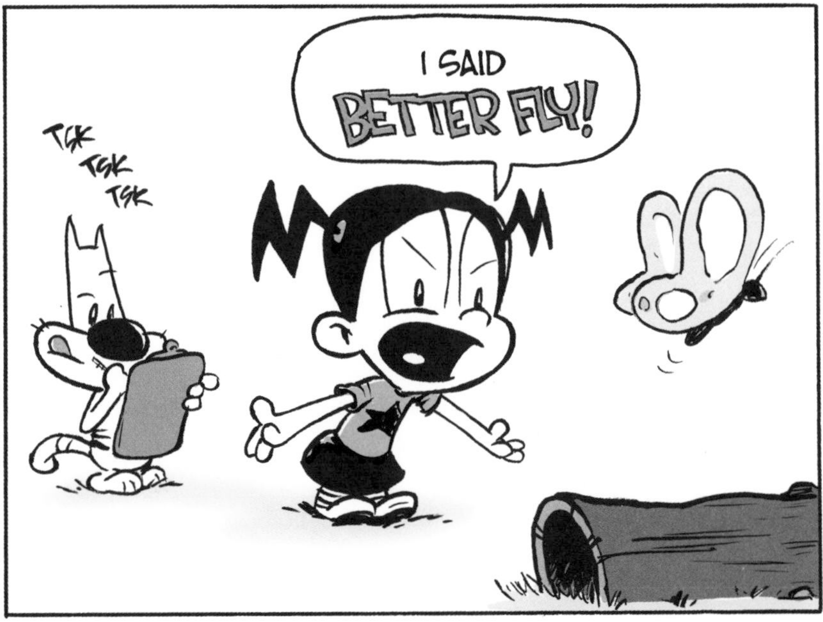
TSK
TSK
TSK
I SAID BETTER FLY!

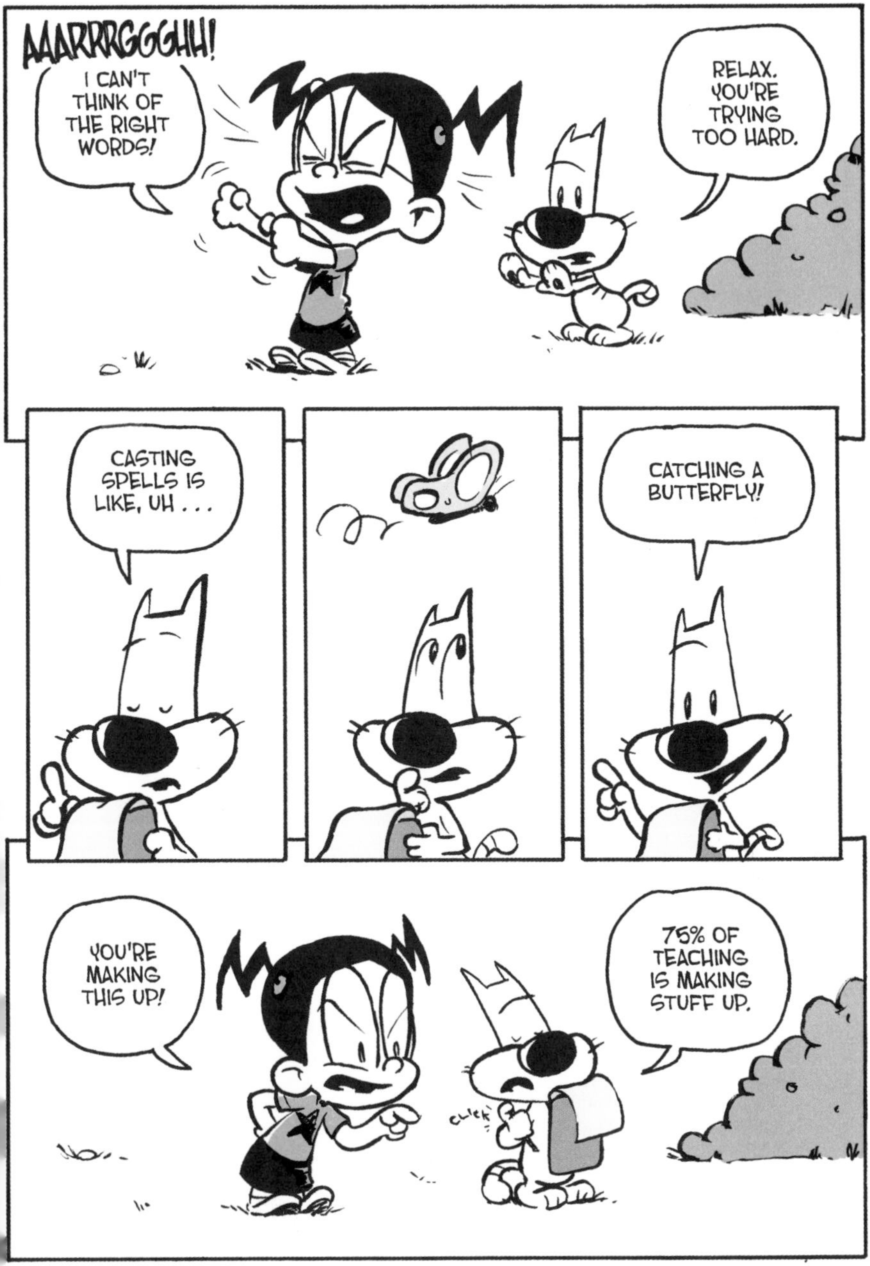
AAARRRGGGHH!
I CAN'T THINK OF THE RIGHT WORDS!
RELAX. YOU'RE TRYING TOO HARD.
CASTING SPELLS IS LIKE, UH . . .
CATCHING A BUTTERFLY!
YOU'RE MAKING THIS UP!
75% OF TEACHING IS MAKING STUFF UP.
CLICK

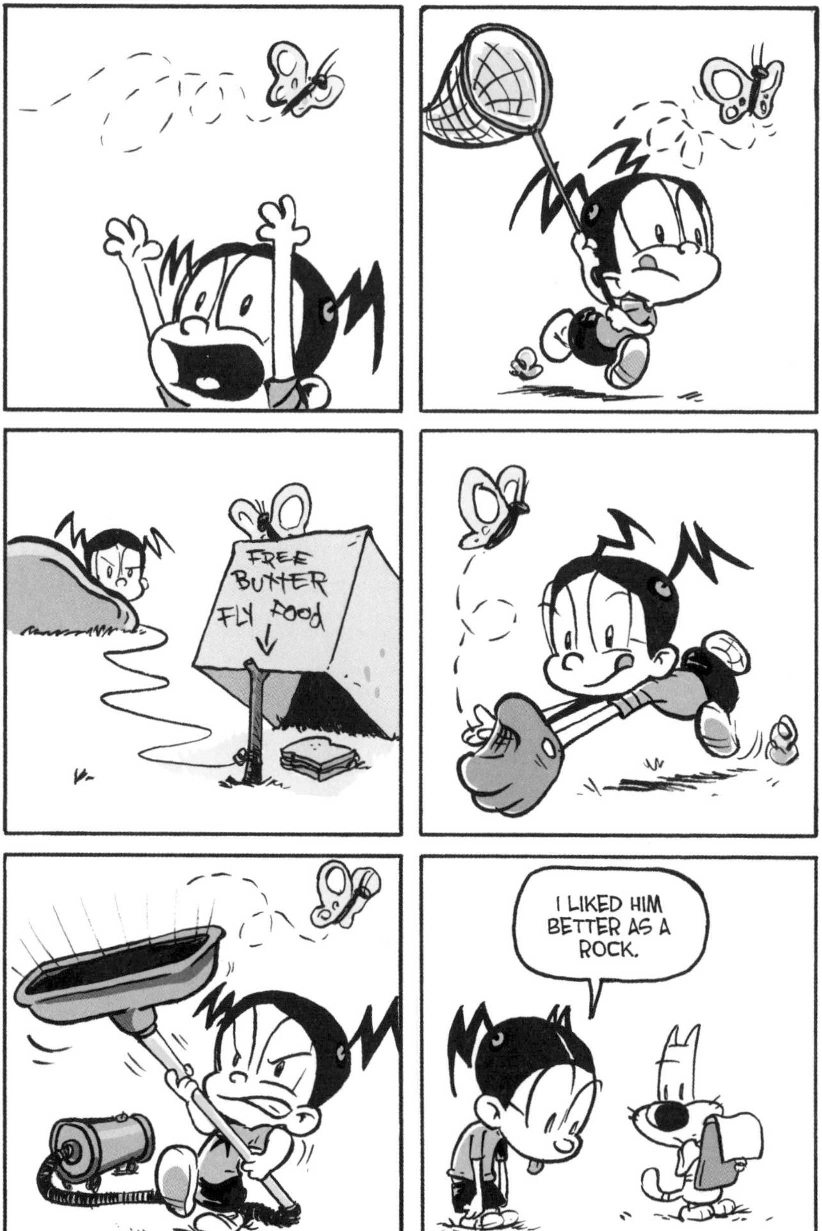
FREE BUTTER FLY FOOD
I LIKED HIM BETTER AS A ROCK.

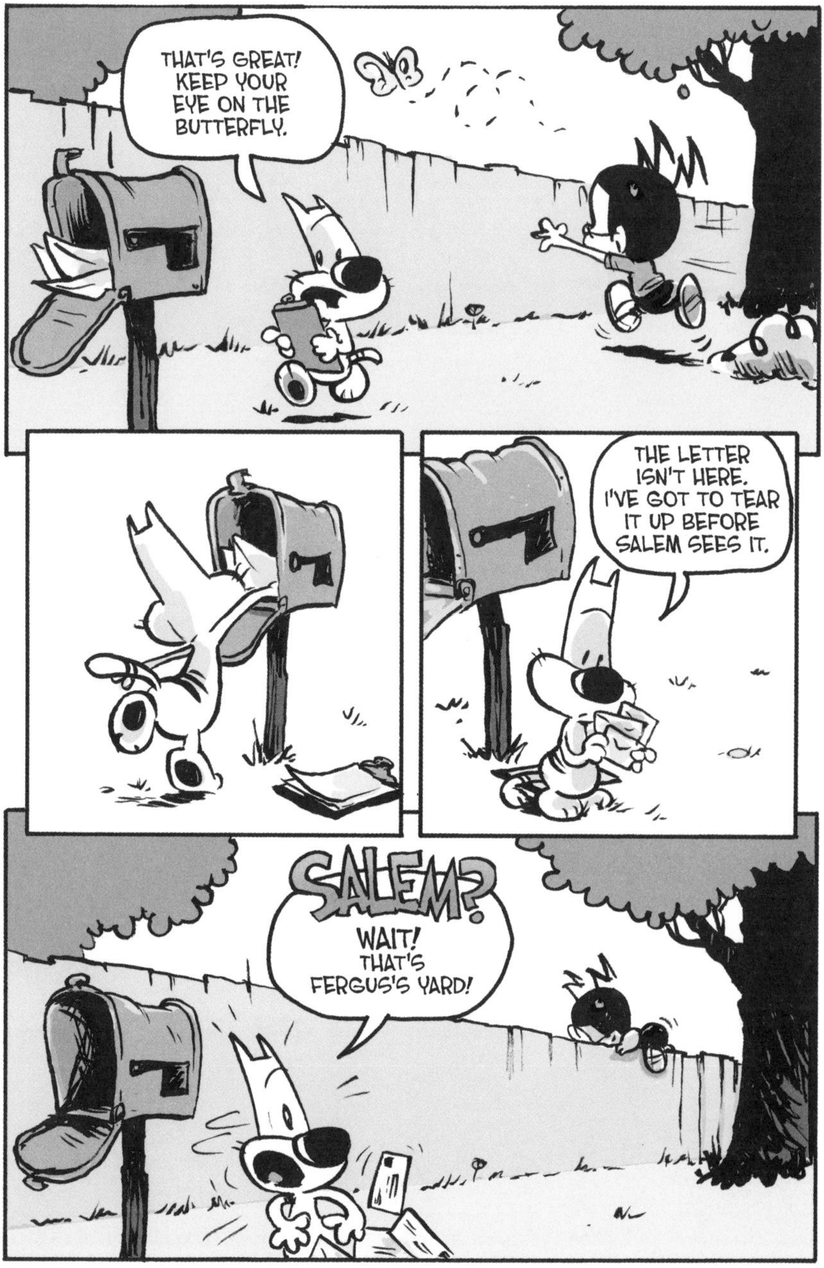
THAT'S GREAT! KEEP YOUR EYE ON THE BUTTERFLY.
THE LETTER ISN'T HERE. I'VE GOT TO TEAR IT UP BEFORE SALEM SEES IT.
SALEM?
WAIT! THAT'S FERGUS'S YARD!

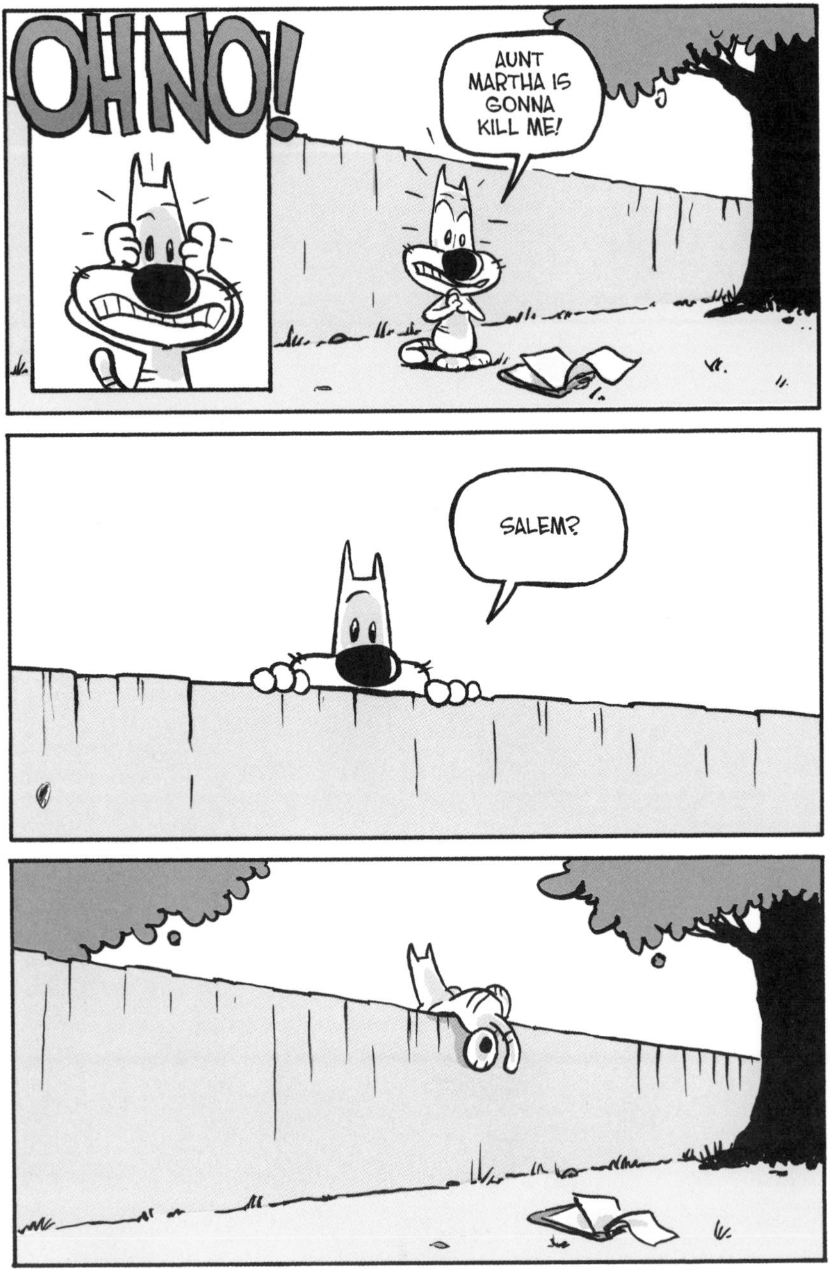
OH NO!
AUNT MARTHA IS GONNA KILL ME!
SALEM?

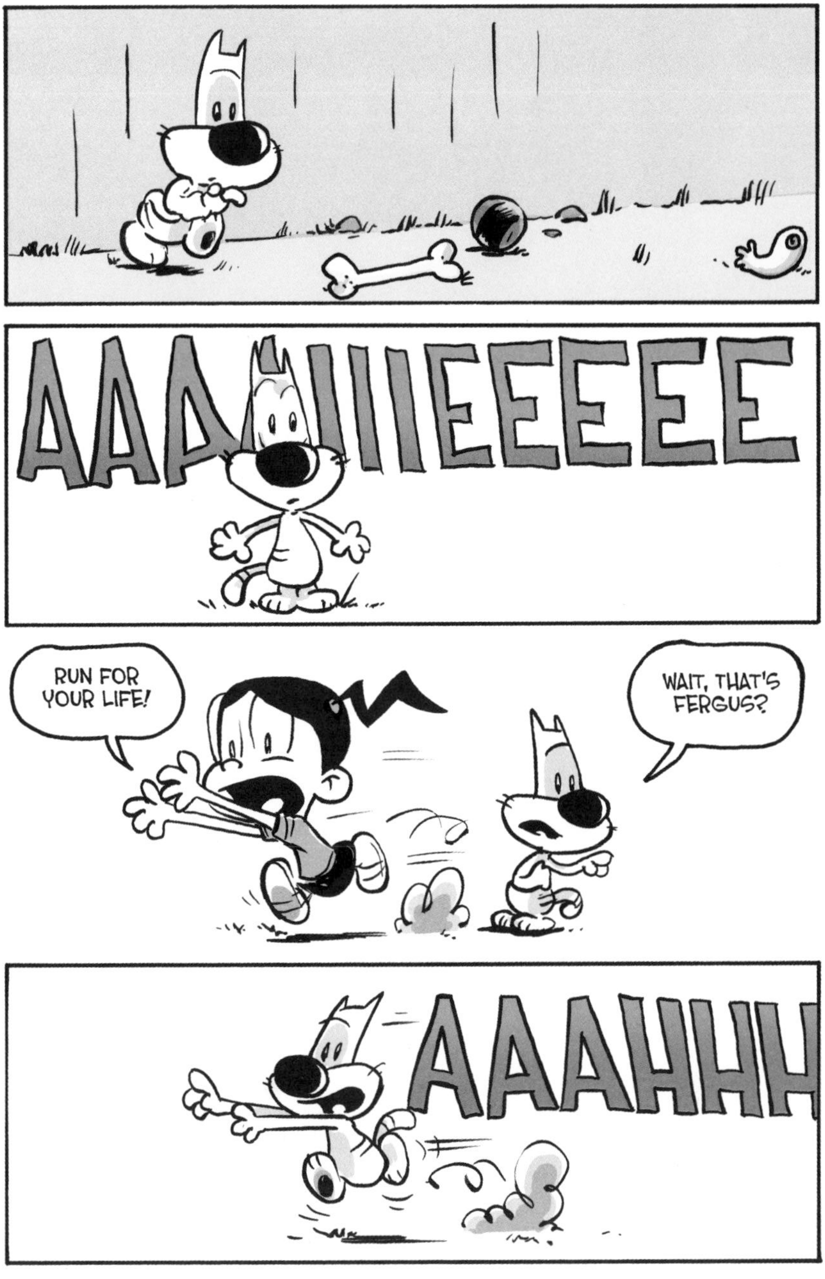

AAAIIIEEEEEE
RUN FOR YOUR LIFE!
WAIT, THAT'S FERGUS?
AAAHHH

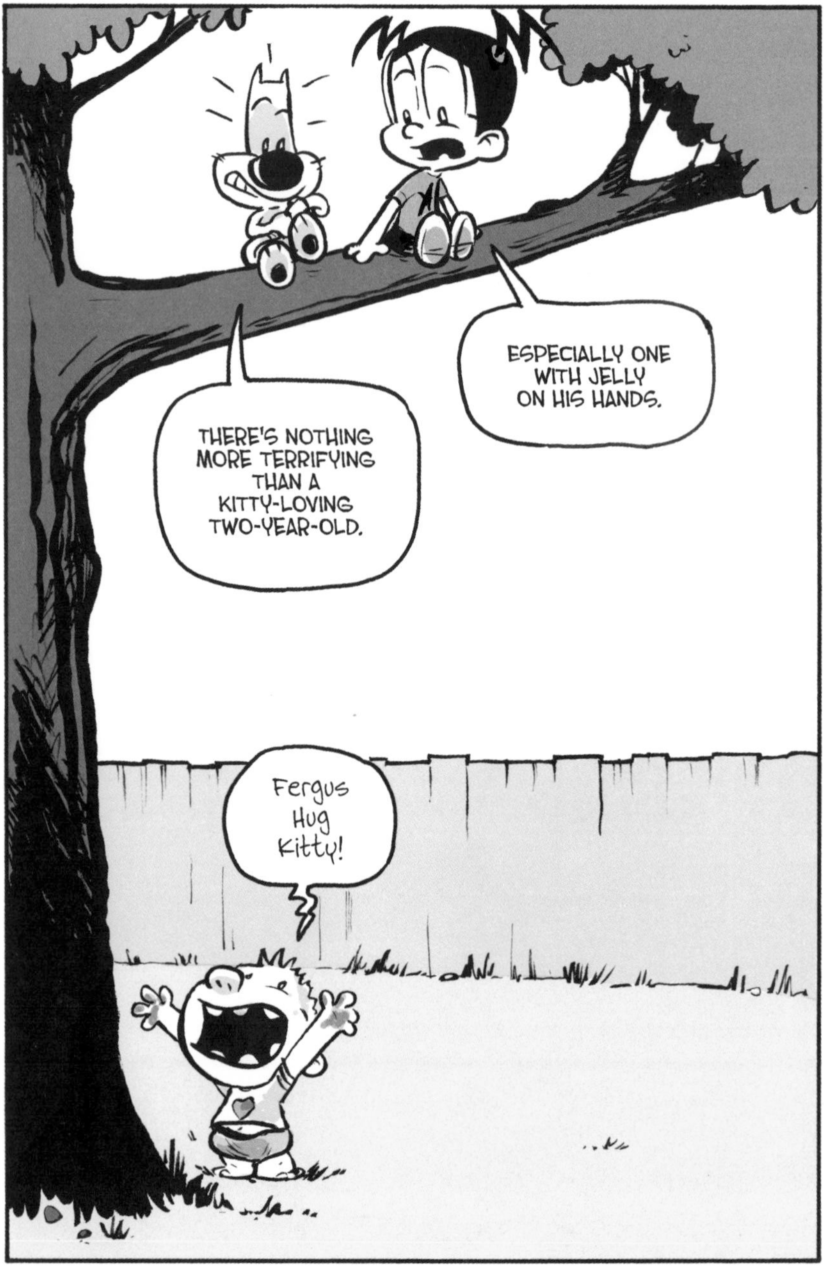
THERE'S NOTHING MORE TERRIFYING THAN A KITTY-LOVING TWO-YEAR-OLD.
ESPECIALLY ONE WITH JELLY ON HIS HANDS.
Fergus Hug Kitty!

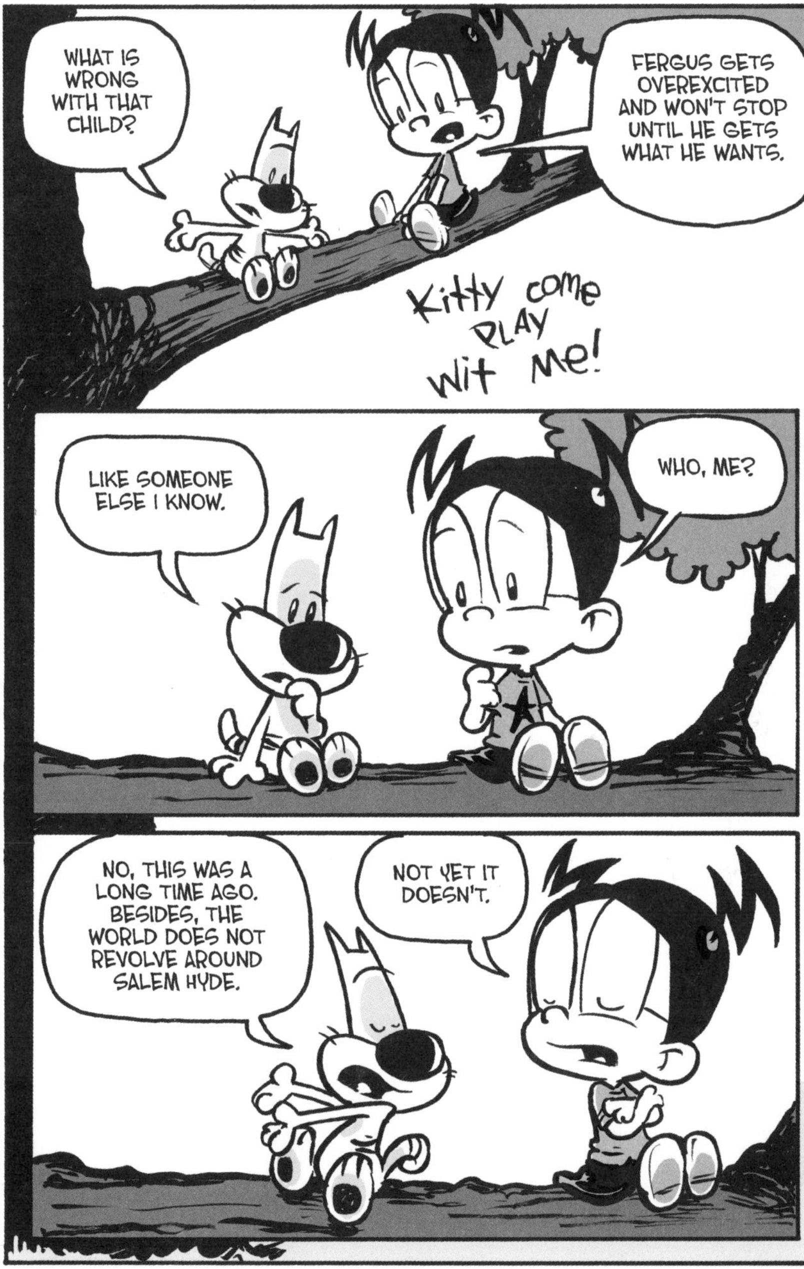
WHAT IS WRONG WITH THAT CHILD?
FERGUS GETS OVEREXCITED AND WON'T STOP UNTIL HE GETS WHAT HE WANTS.
Kitty come play wit me!
LIKE SOMEONE ELSE I KNOW.
WHO, ME?
NO, THIS WAS A LONG TIME AGO. BESIDES, THE WORLD DOES NOT REVOLVE AROUND SALEM HYDE.
NOT YET IT DOESN'T.

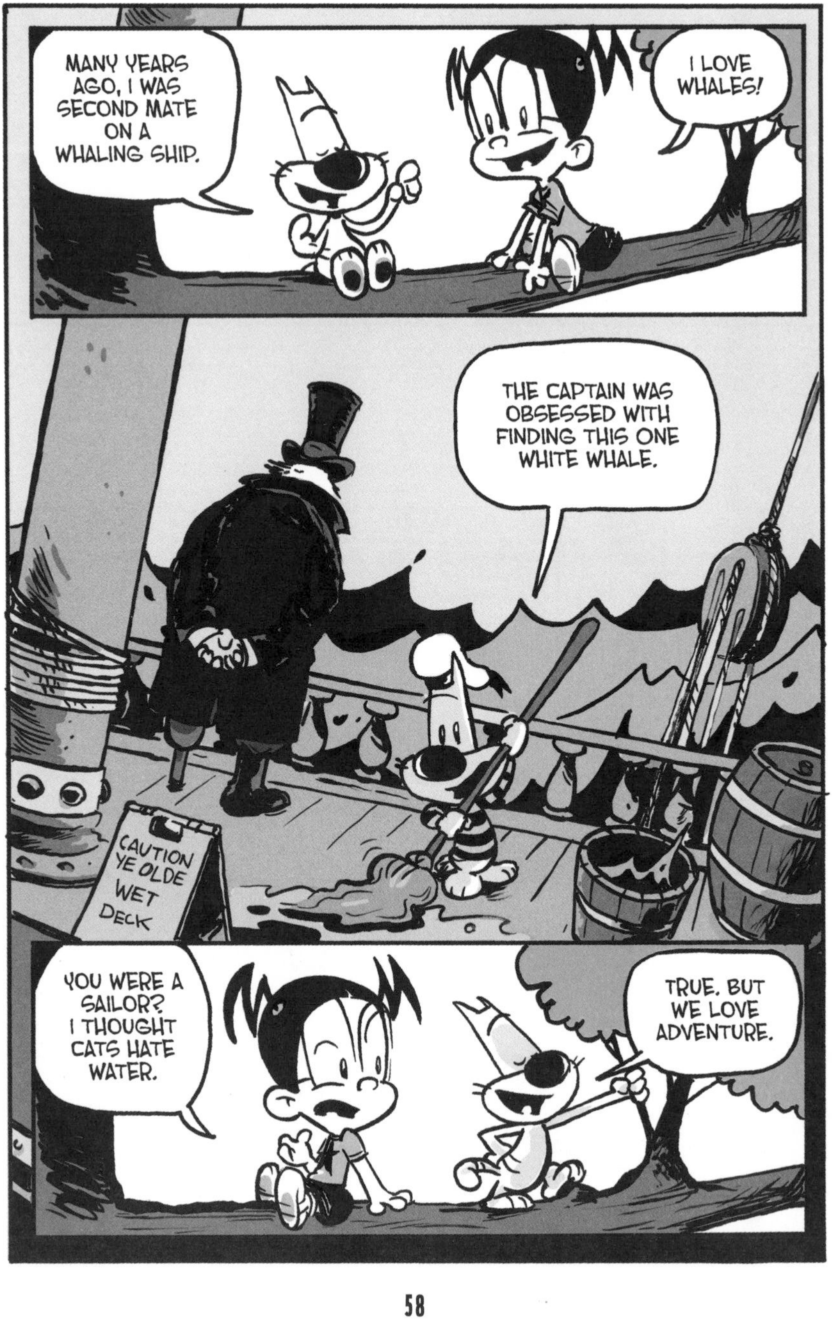
MANY YEARS AGO, I WAS SECOND MATE ON A WHALING SHIP.
I LOVE WHALES!
THE CAPTAIN WAS OBSESSED WITH FINDING THIS ONE WHITE WHALE.
CAUTION YE OLDE WET DECK
YOU WERE A SAILOR? I THOUGHT CATS HATE WATER.
TRUE. BUT WE LOVE ADVENTURE.

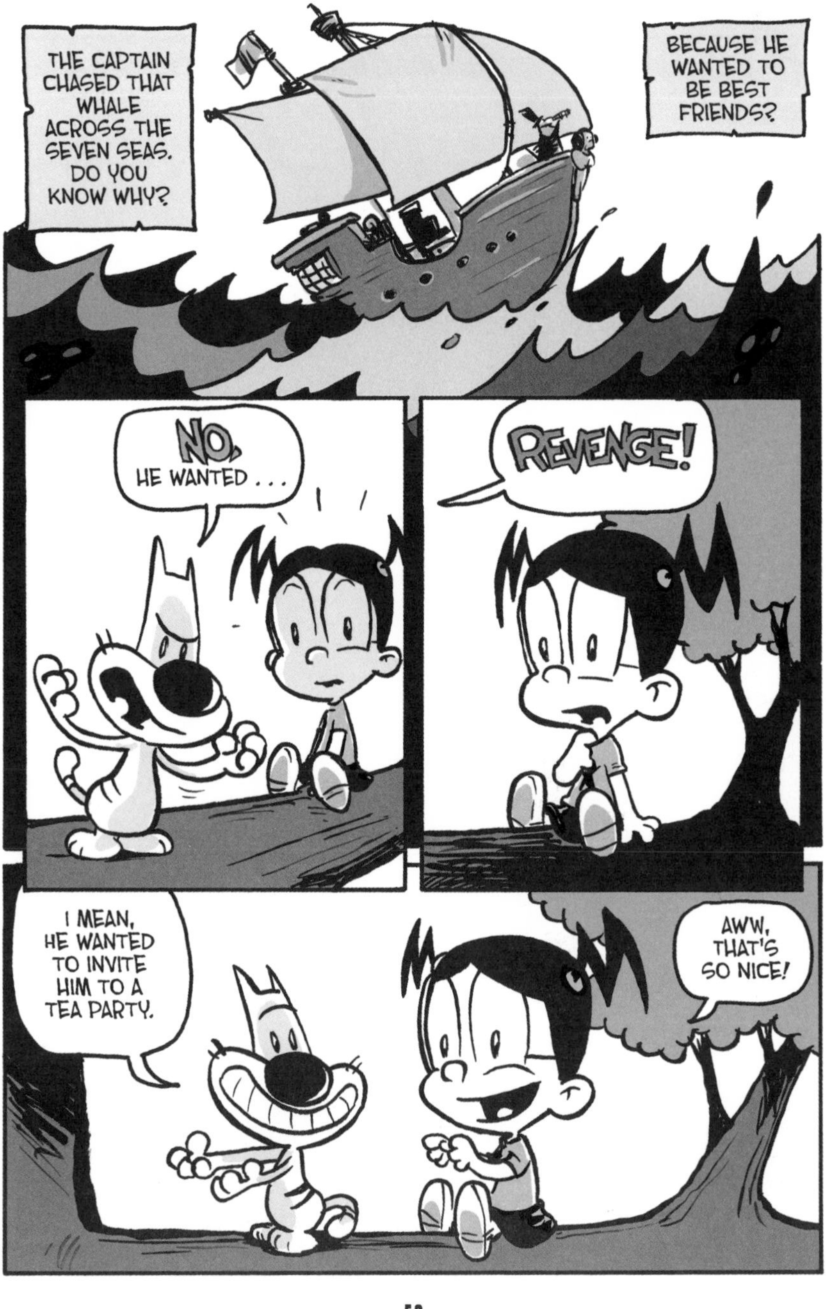
THE CAPTAIN CHASED THAT WHALE ACROSS THE SEVEN SEAS. DO YOU KNOW WHY?
BECAUSE HE WANTED TO BE BEST FRIENDS?
NO. HE WANTED . . .
REVENGE!
I MEAN, HE WANTED TO INVITE HIM TO A TEA PARTY.
AWW, THAT'S SO NICE!

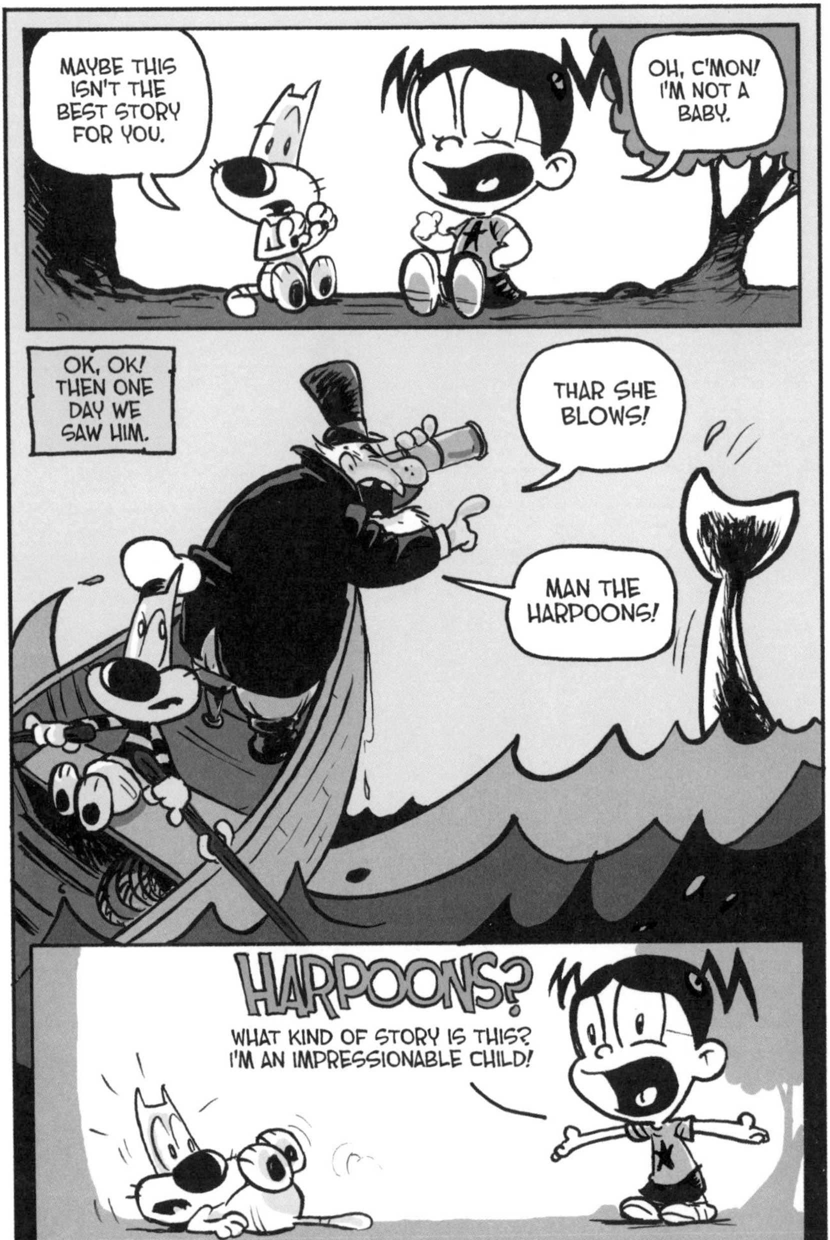
MAYBE THIS ISN'T THE BEST STORY FOR YOU.
OH, C'MON! I'M NOT A BABY.
OK, OK! THEN ONE DAY WE SAW HIM.
THAR SHE BLOWS!
MAN THE HARPOONS!
HARPOONS?
WHAT KIND OF STORY IS THIS? I'M AN IMPRESSIONABLE CHILD!

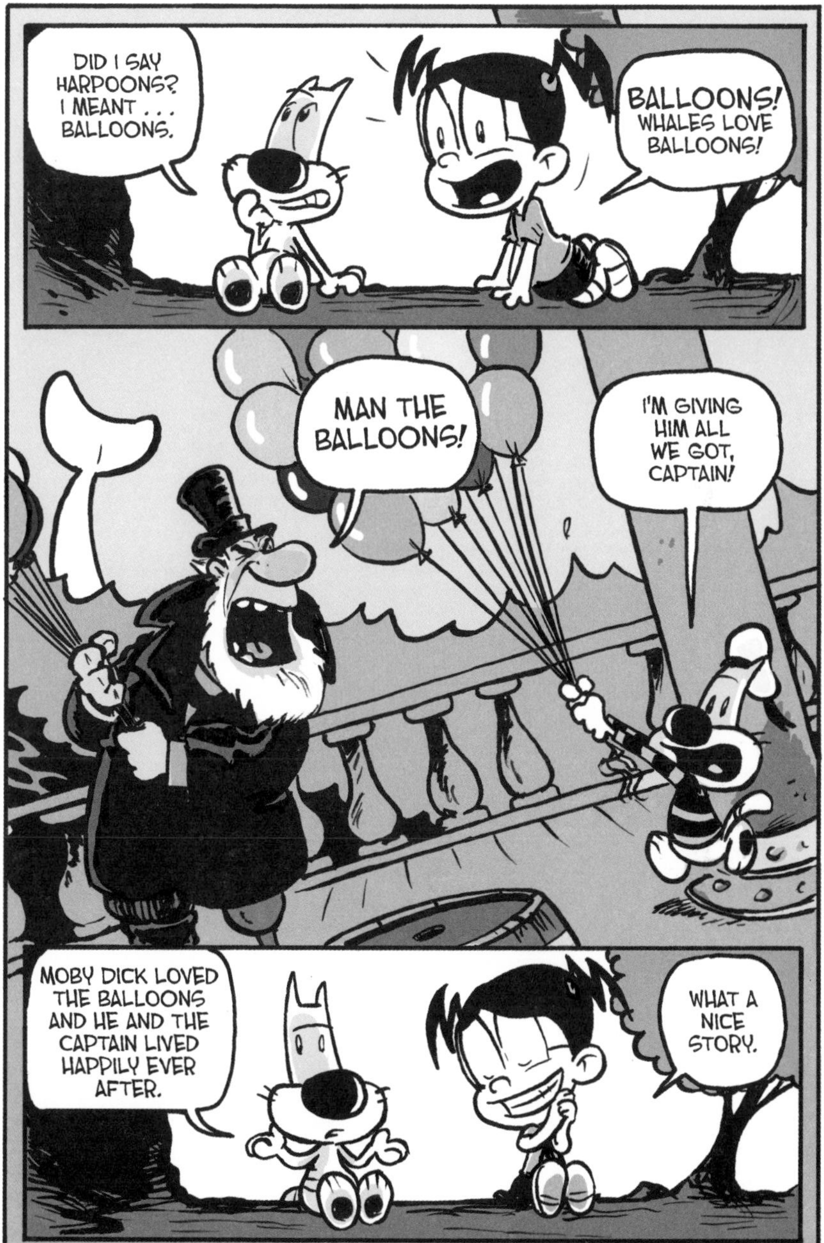

DID I SAY HARPOONS? I MEANT . . . BALLOONS.
BALLOONS! WHALES LOVE BALLOONS!
MAN THE BALLOONS!
I'M GIVING HIM ALL WE GOT, CAPTAIN!
MOBY DICK LOVED THE BALLOONS AND HE AND THE CAPTAIN LIVED HAPPILY EVER AFTER.
WHAT A NICE STORY.

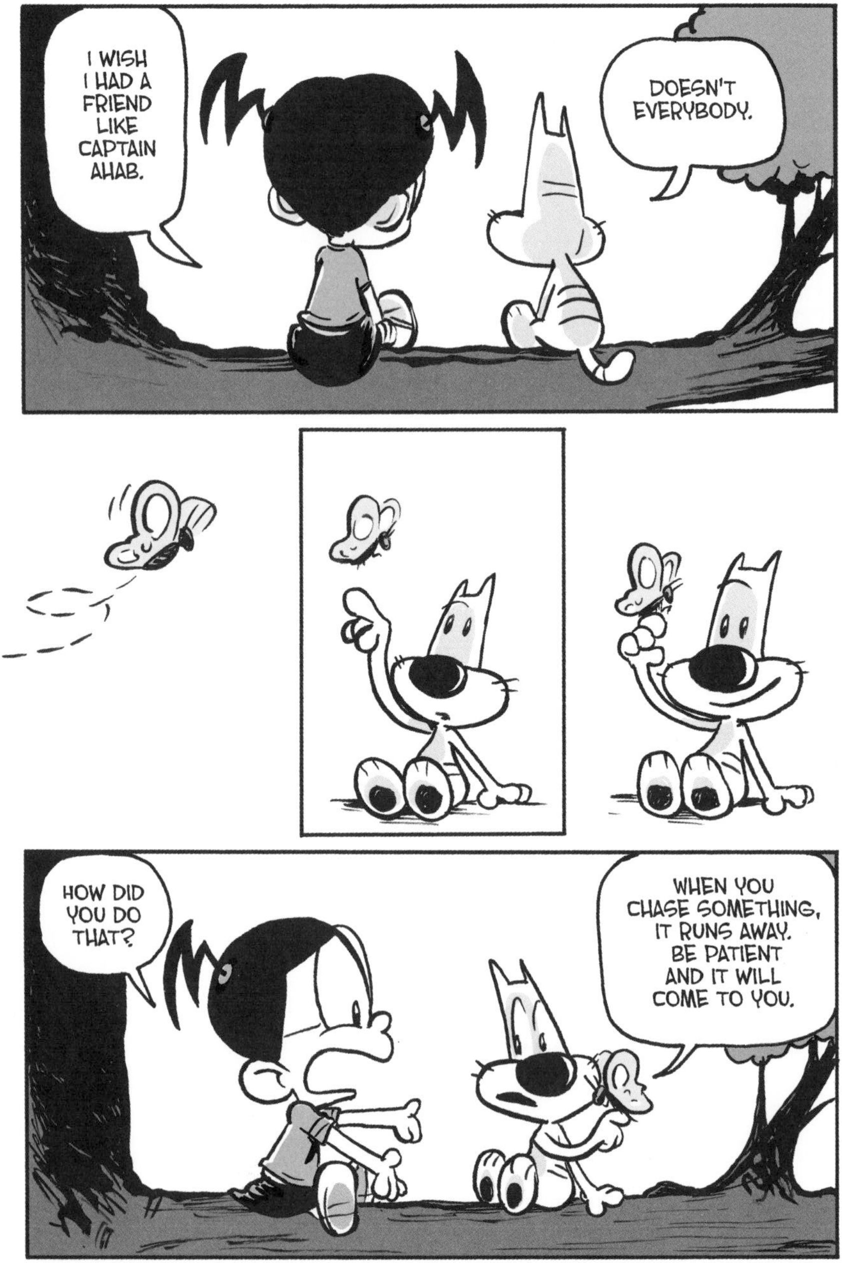
I WISH I HAD A FRIEND LIKE CAPTAIN AHAB.
DOESN'T EVERYBODY.
HOW DID YOU DO THAT?
WHEN YOU CHASE SOMETHING, IT RUNS AWAY. BE PATIENT AND IT WILL COME TO YOU.

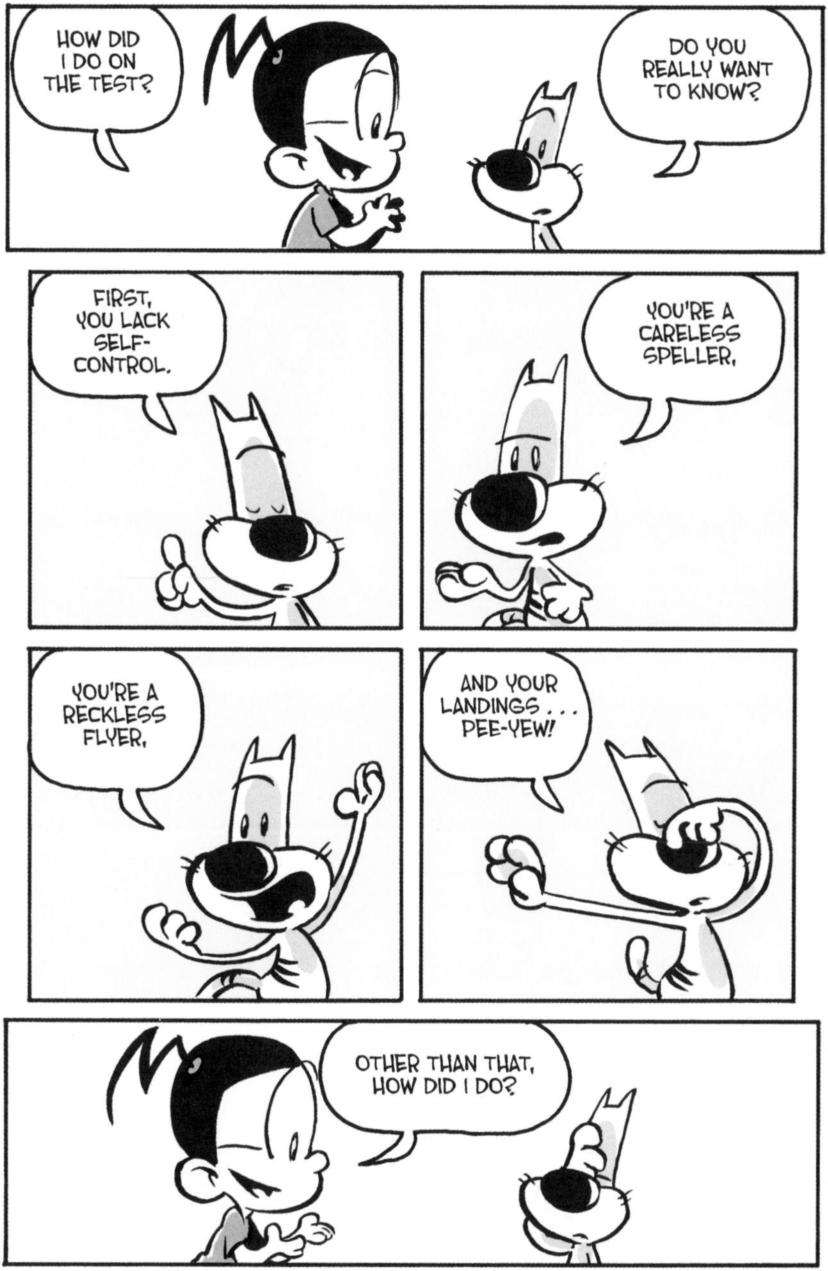
HOW DID I DO ON THE TEST?
DO YOU REALLY WANT TO KNOW?
FIRST, YOU LACK SELF-CONTROL.
YOU'RE A CARELESS SPELLER,
YOU'RE A RECKLESS FLYER,
AND YOUR LANDINGS . . . PEE-YEW!
OTHER THAN THAT, HOW DID I DO?

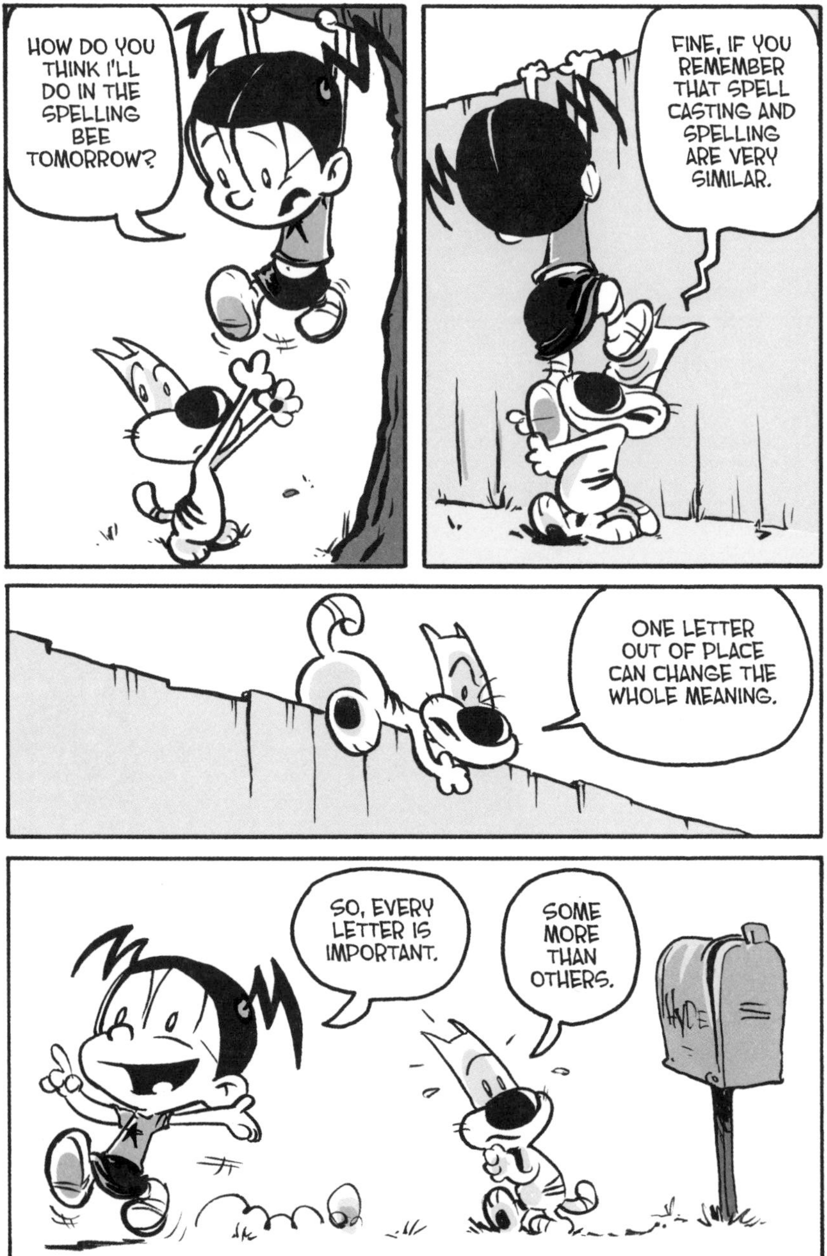
HOW DO YOU THINK I'LL DO IN THE SPELLING BEE TOMORROW?
FINE, IF YOU REMEMBER THAT SPELL CASTING AND SPELLING ARE VERY SIMILAR.
ONE LETTER OUT OF PLACE CAN CHANGE THE WHOLE MEANING.
SO, EVERY LETTER IS IMPORTANT.
SOME MORE THAN OTHERS.

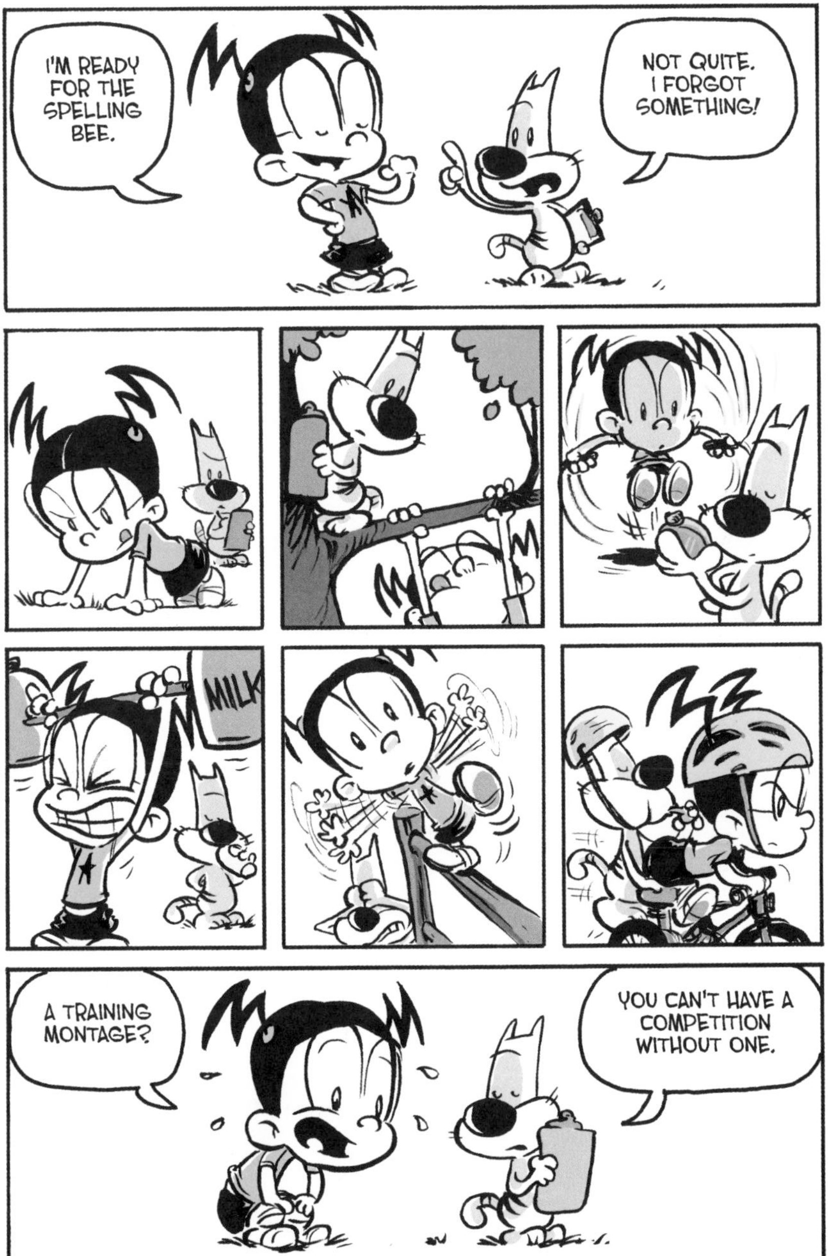
I'M READY FOR THE SPELLING BEE.
NOT QUITE. I FORGOT SOMETHING!
MILK
A TRAINING MONTAGE?
YOU CAN'T HAVE A COMPETITION WITHOUT ONE.

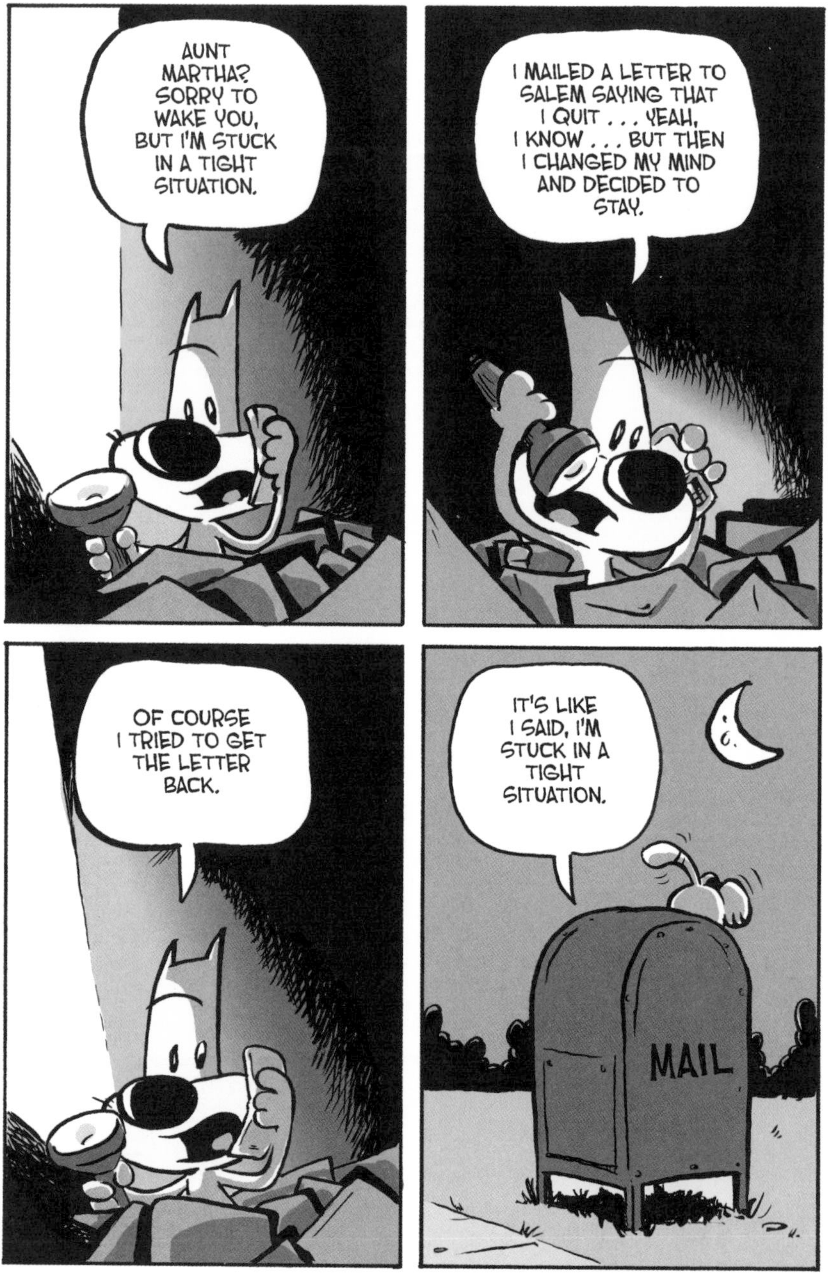
AUNT MARTHA? SORRY TO WAKE YOU, BUT I'M STUCK IN A TIGHT SITUATION.
I MAILED A LETTER TO SALEM SAYING THAT I QUIT . . . YEAH, I KNOW . . . BUT THEN I CHANGED MY MIND AND DECIDED TO STAY.
OF COURSE I TRIED TO GET THE LETTER BACK.
IT'S LIKE I SAID, I'M STUCK IN A TIGHT SITUATION.
MAIL

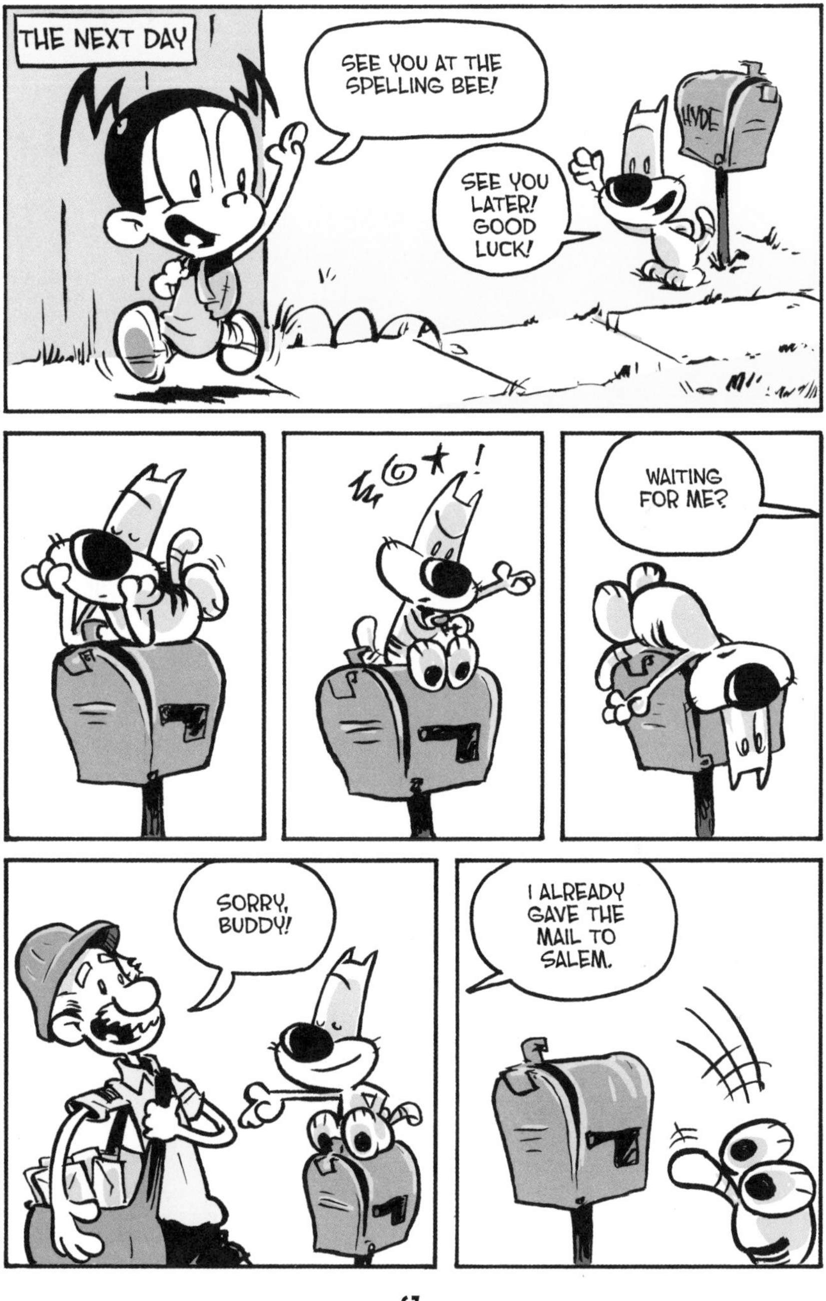
THE NEXT DAY
SEE YOU AT THE SPELLING BEE!
SEE YOU LATER! GOOD LUCK!
HYDE
WAITING FOR ME?
SORRY, BUDDY!
I ALREADY GAVE THE MAIL TO SALEM.

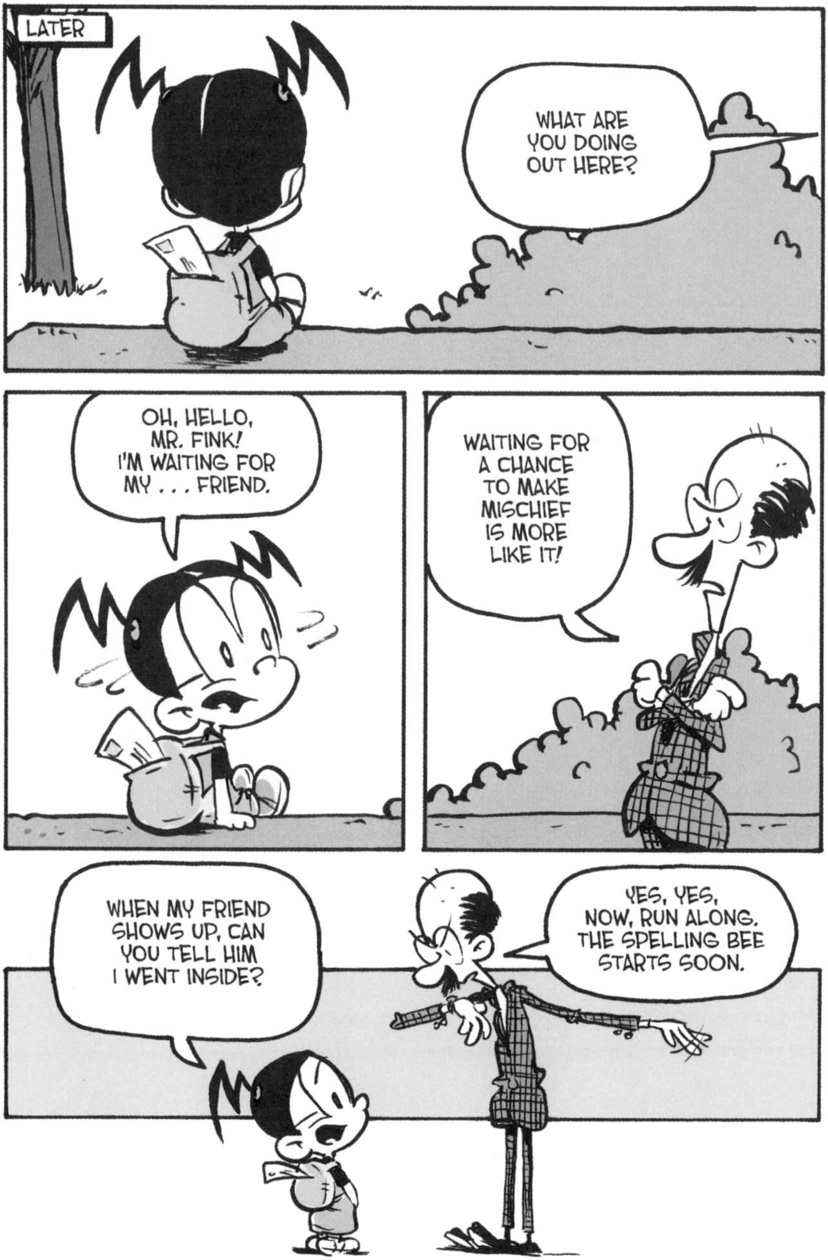
LATER
WHAT ARE YOU DOING OUT HERE?
OH, HELLO, MR. FINK! I'M WAITING FOR MY . . . FRIEND.
WAITING FOR A CHANCE TO MAKE MISCHIEF IS MORE LIKE IT!
WHEN MY FRIEND SHOWS UP, CAN YOU TELL HIM I WENT INSIDE?
YES, YES, NOW, RUN ALONG. THE SPELLING BEE STARTS SOON.

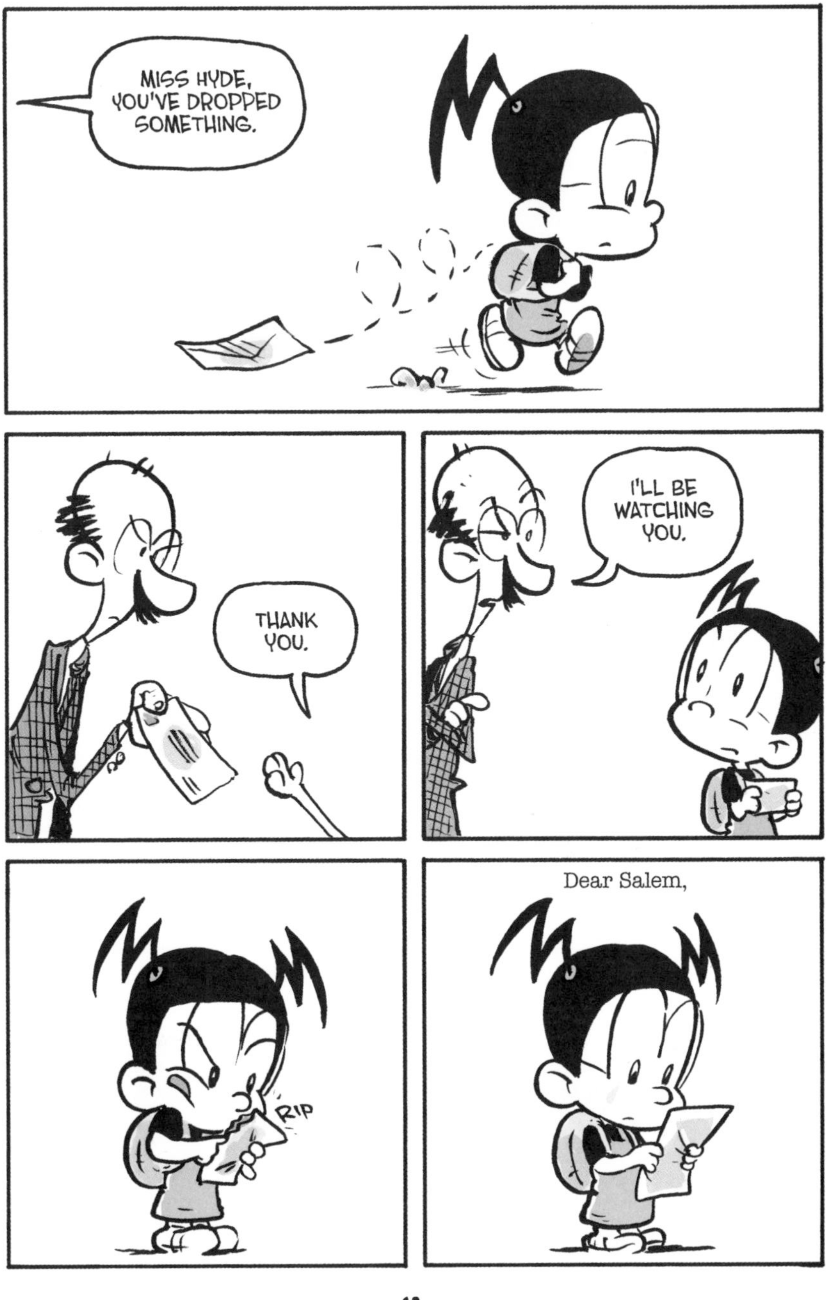
MISS HYDE, YOU'VE DROPPED SOMETHING.
THANK YOU.
I'LL BE WATCHING YOU.
RIP
Dear Salem,

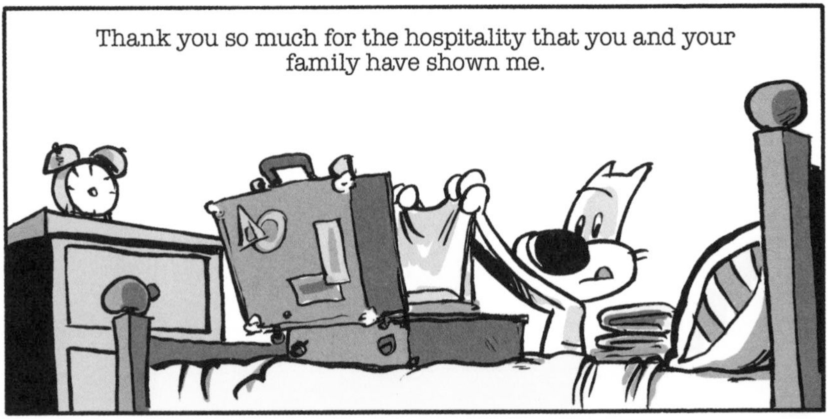
Thank you so much for the hospitality that you and your family have shown me.

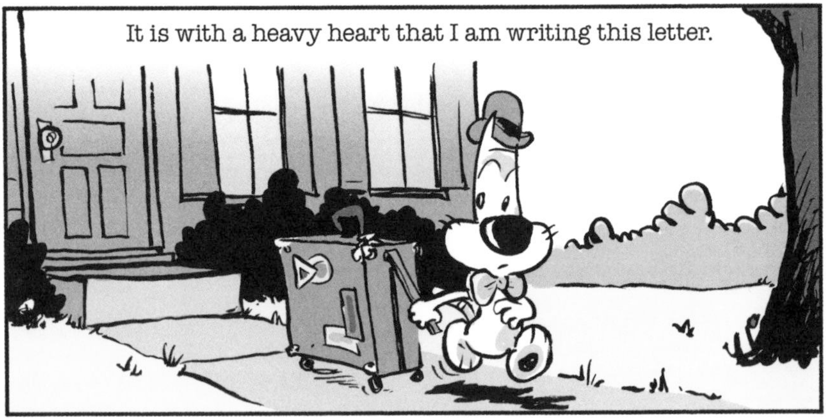
It is with a heavy heart that I am writing this letter.

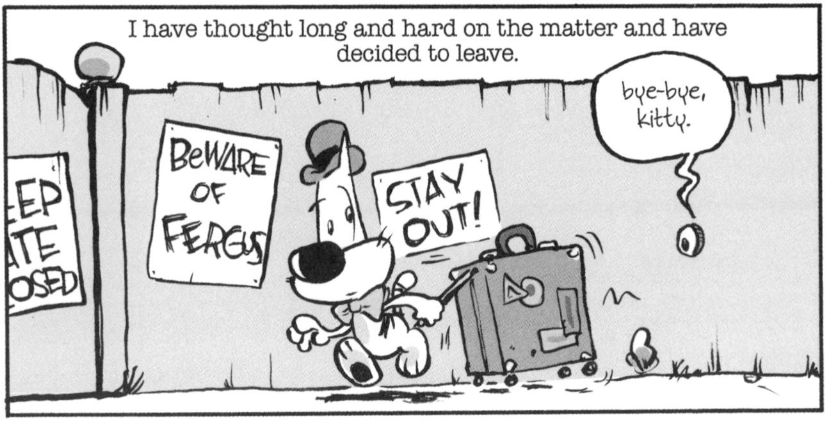
I have thought long and hard on the matter and have decided to leave.
BeWARE OF FERGUS
STAY OUT!
bye-bye, kitty.

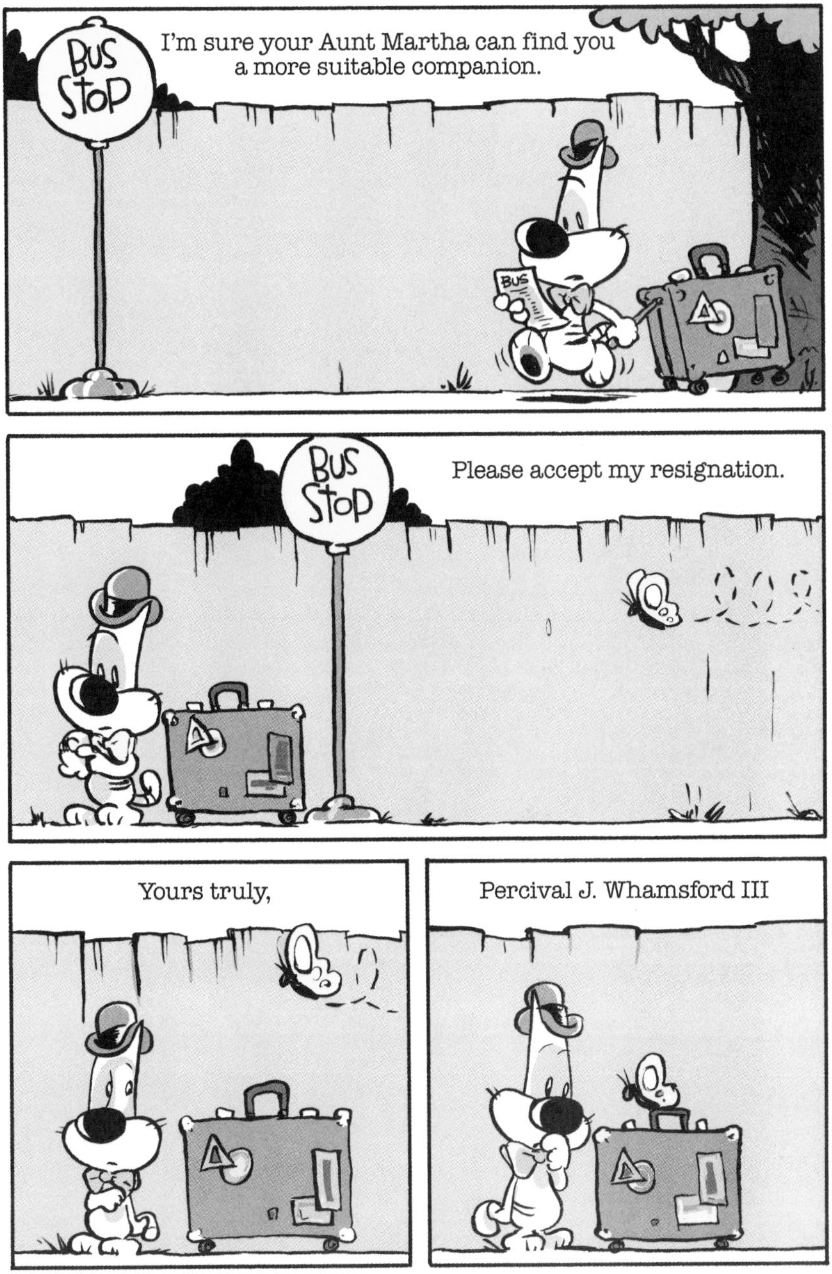
BUS STOP
I'm sure your Aunt Martha can find you a more suitable companion.
BUS
BUS STOP
Please accept my resignation.
Yours truly,
Percival J. Whamsford III

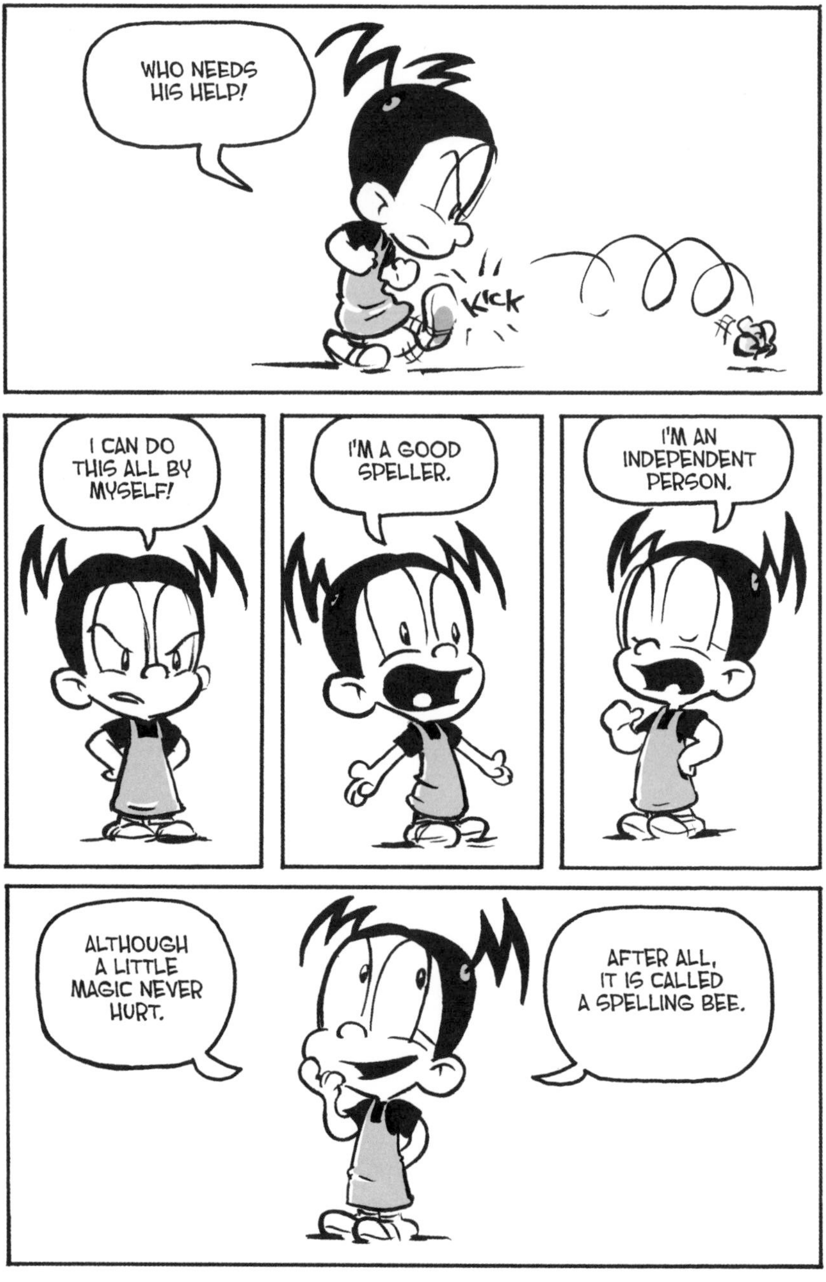
WHO NEEDS HIS HELP!
KICK
I CAN DO THIS ALL BY MYSELF!
I'M A GOOD SPELLER.
I'M AN INDEPENDENT PERSON.
ALTHOUGH A LITTLE MAGIC NEVER HURT.
AFTER ALL, IT IS CALLED A SPELLING BEE.

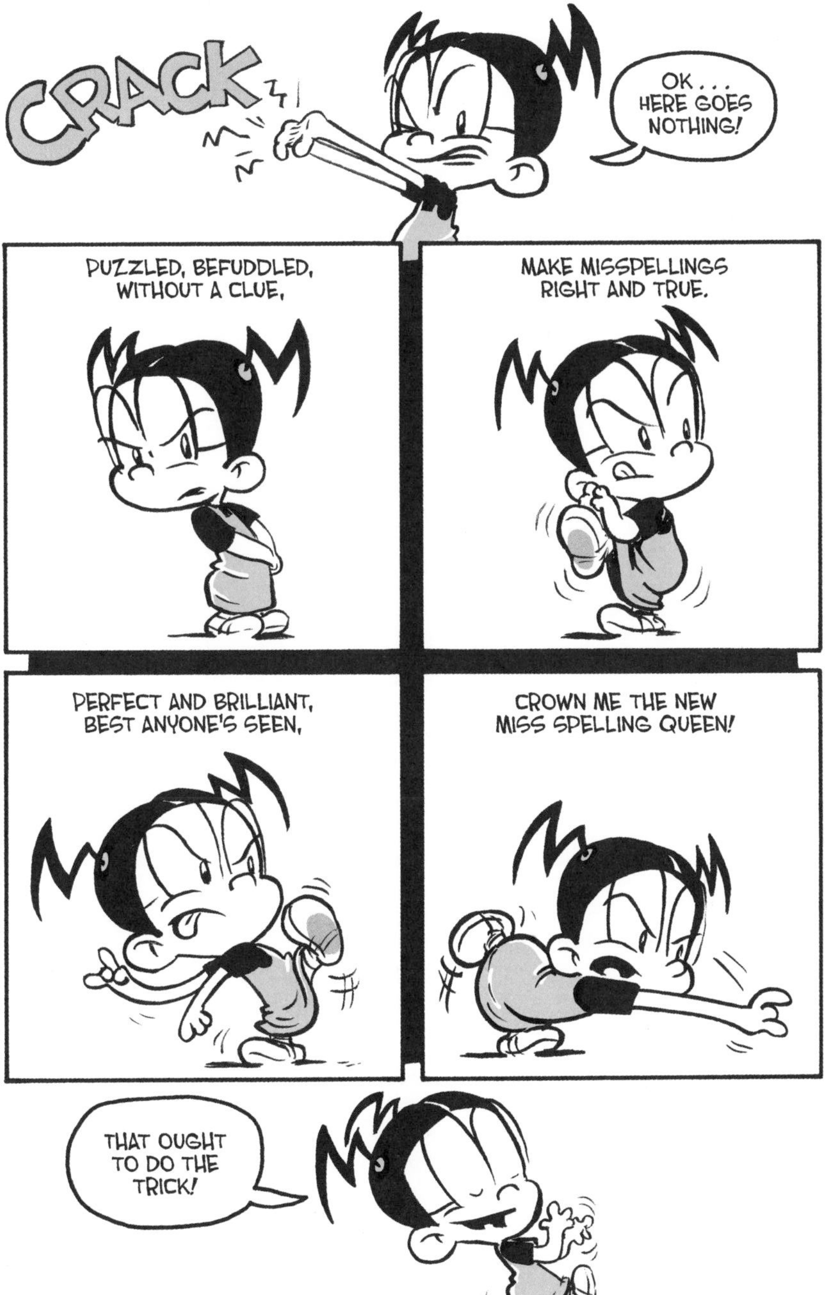
CRACK
OK . . . HERE GOES NOTHING!
PUZZLED, BEFUDDLED, WITHOUT A CLUE,
MAKE MISSPELLINGS RIGHT AND TRUE.
PERFECT AND BRILLIANT, BEST ANYONE'S SEEN,
CROWN ME THE NEW MISS SPELLING QUEEN!
THAT OUGHT TO DO THE TRICK!

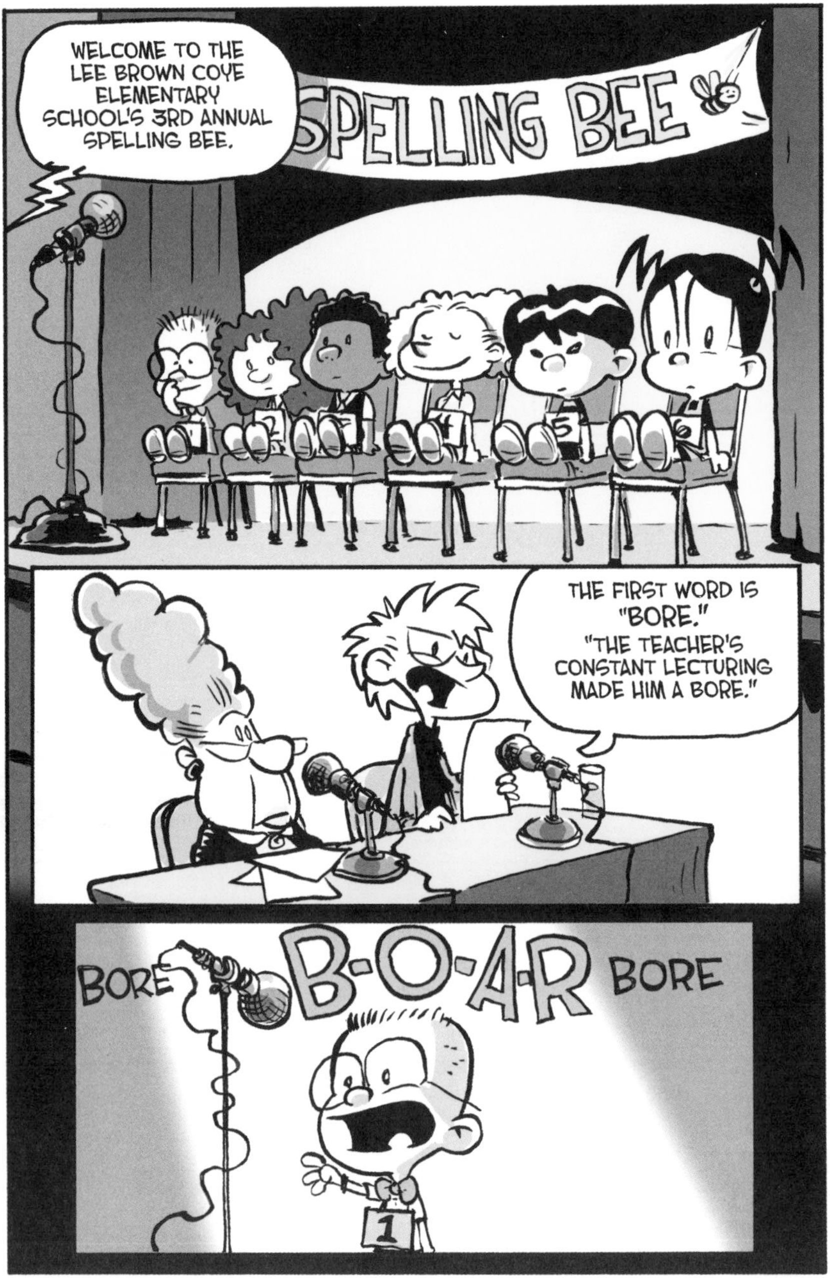
WELCOME TO THE LEE BROWN COYE ELEMENTARY SCHOOL'S 3RD ANNUAL SPELLING BEE.
SPELLING BEE
THE FIRST WORD IS "BORE." "THE TEACHER'S CONSTANT LECTURING MADE HIM A BORE."
BORE
B-O-A-R
BORE

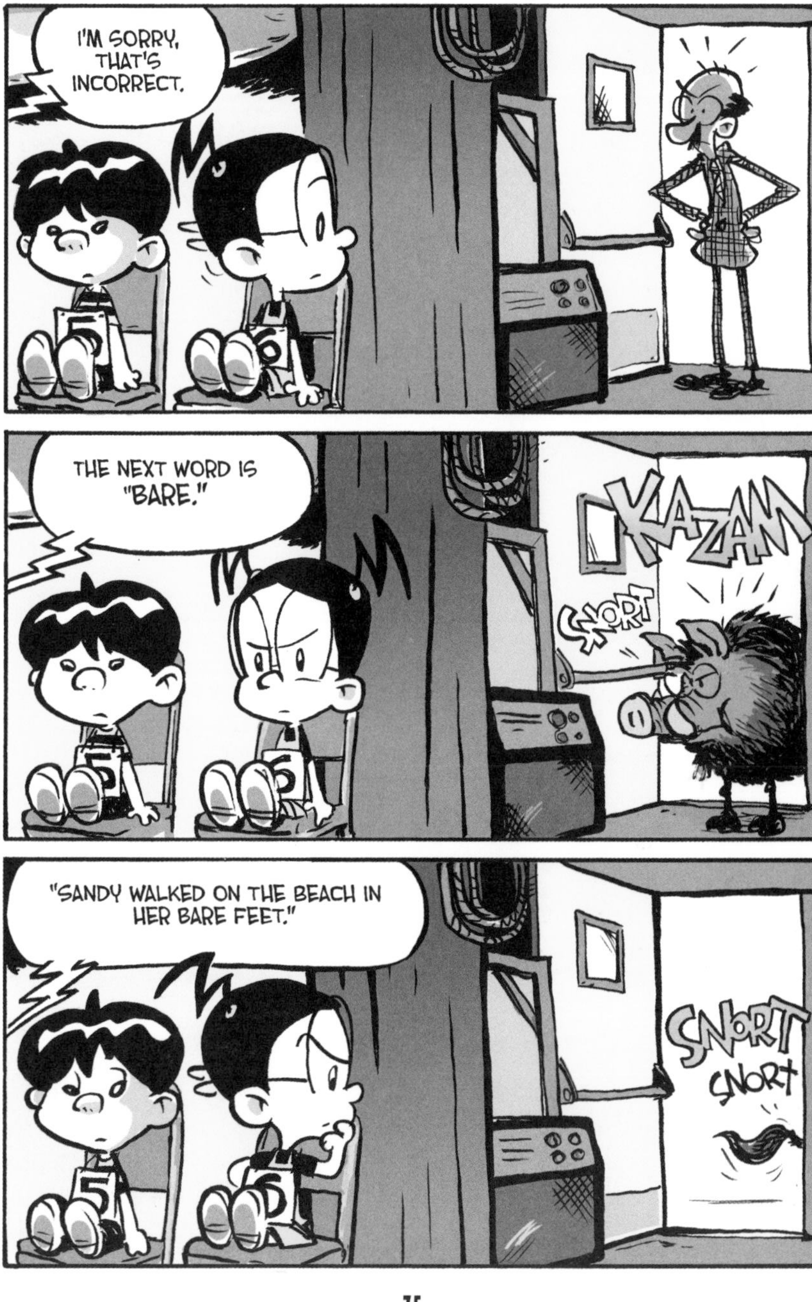
I'M SORRY, THAT'S INCORRECT.
THE NEXT WORD IS "BARE."
KAZAM
SNORT
"SANDY WALKED ON THE BEACH IN HER BARE FEET."
SNORT
SNORT

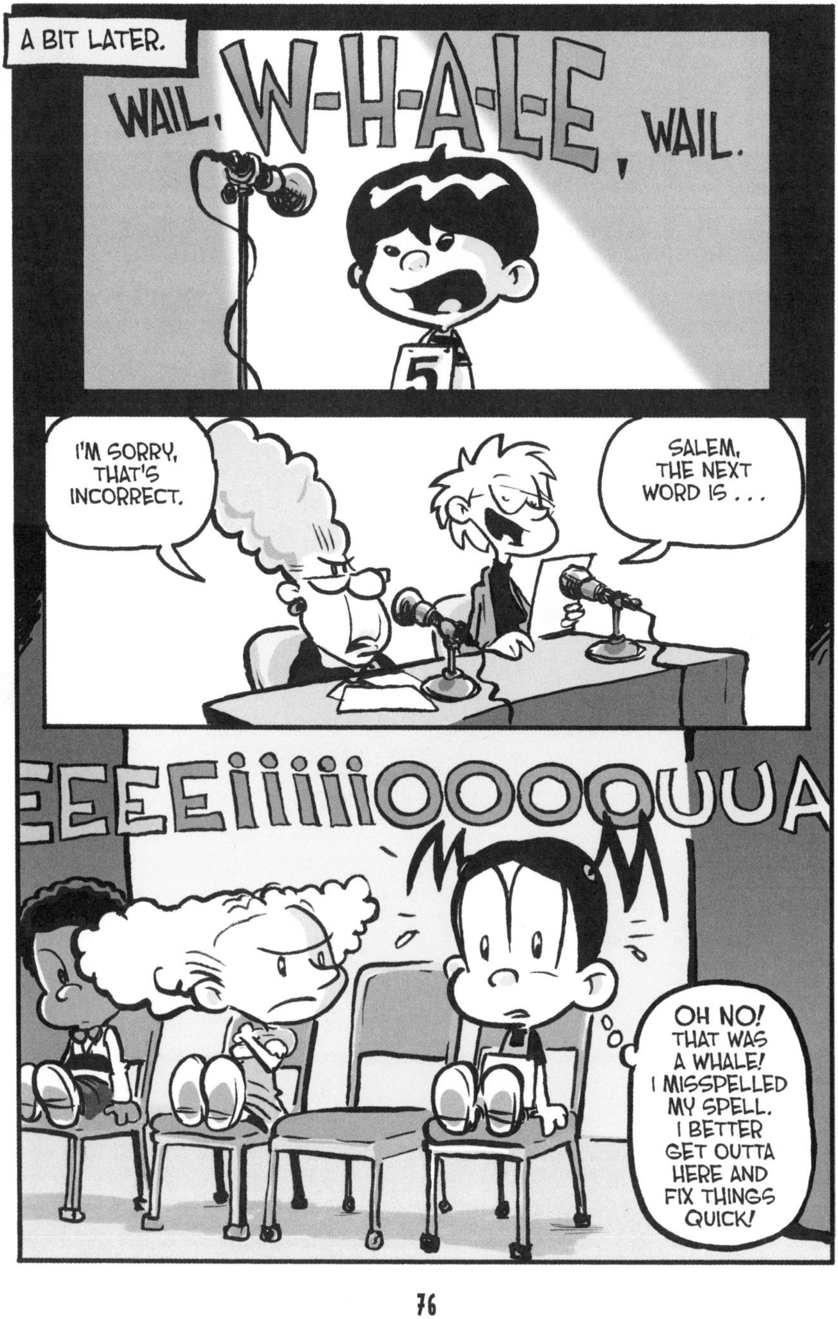

A BIT LATER.
WAIL, W-H-A-L-E, WAIL.
I'M SORRY, THAT'S INCORRECT.
SALEM, THE NEXT WORD IS . . .
EEEiiiiiOOOOUUA
OH NO! THAT WAS A WHALE! I MISSPELLED MY SPELL. I BETTER GET OUTTA HERE AND FIX THINGS QUICK!

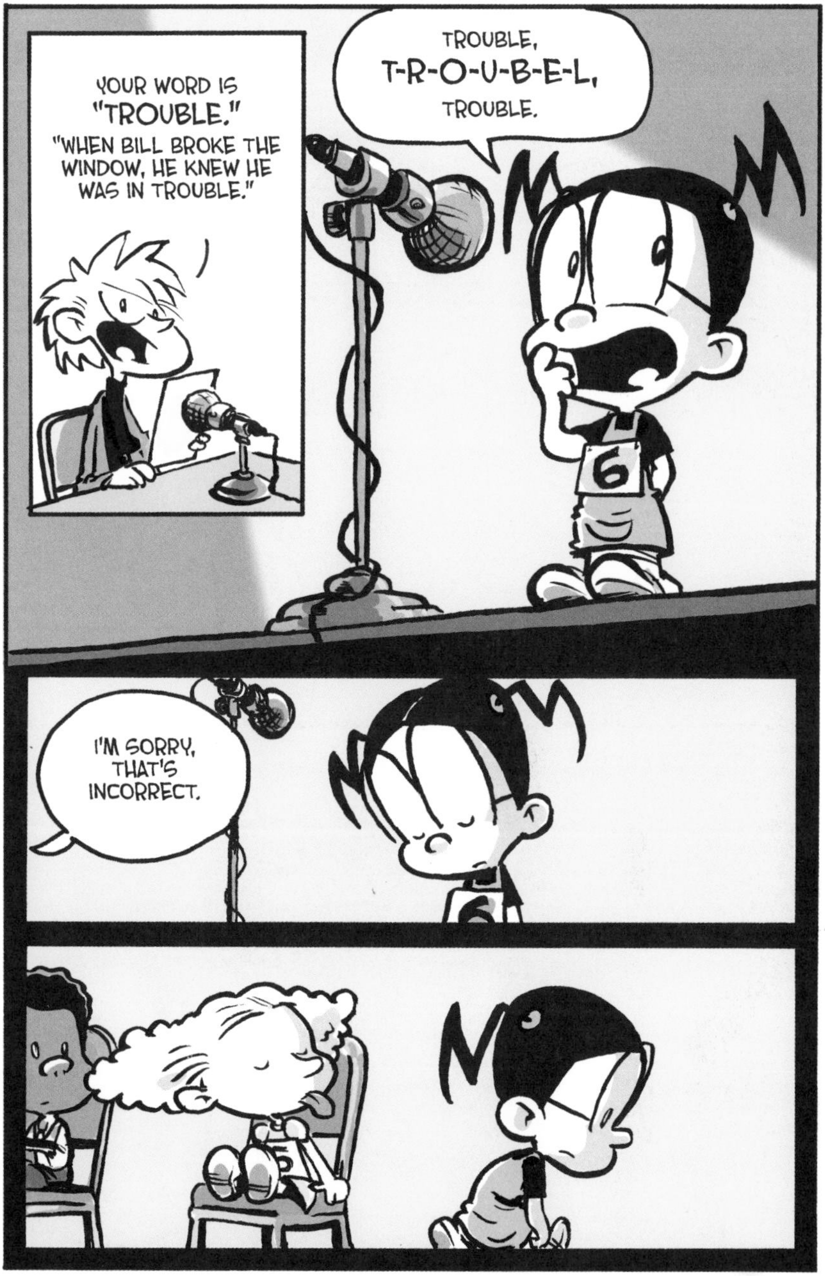
YOUR WORD IS "TROUBLE." "WHEN BILL BROKE THE WINDOW, HE KNEW HE WAS IN TROUBLE."
TROUBLE, T-R-O-U-B-E-L, TROUBLE.
I'M SORRY, THAT'S INCORRECT.

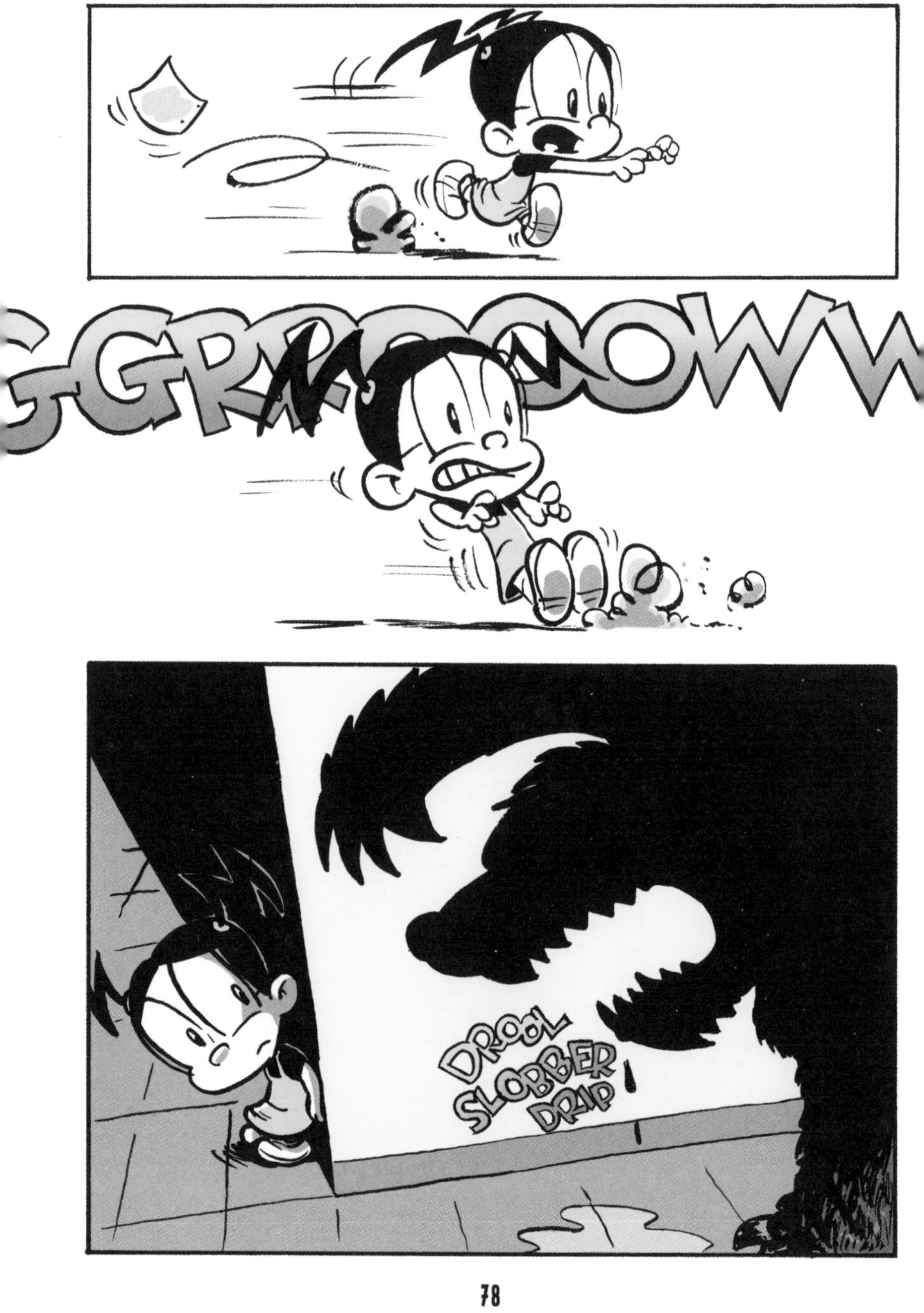
GGRROOOWW
DROOL
SLOBBER
DRIP

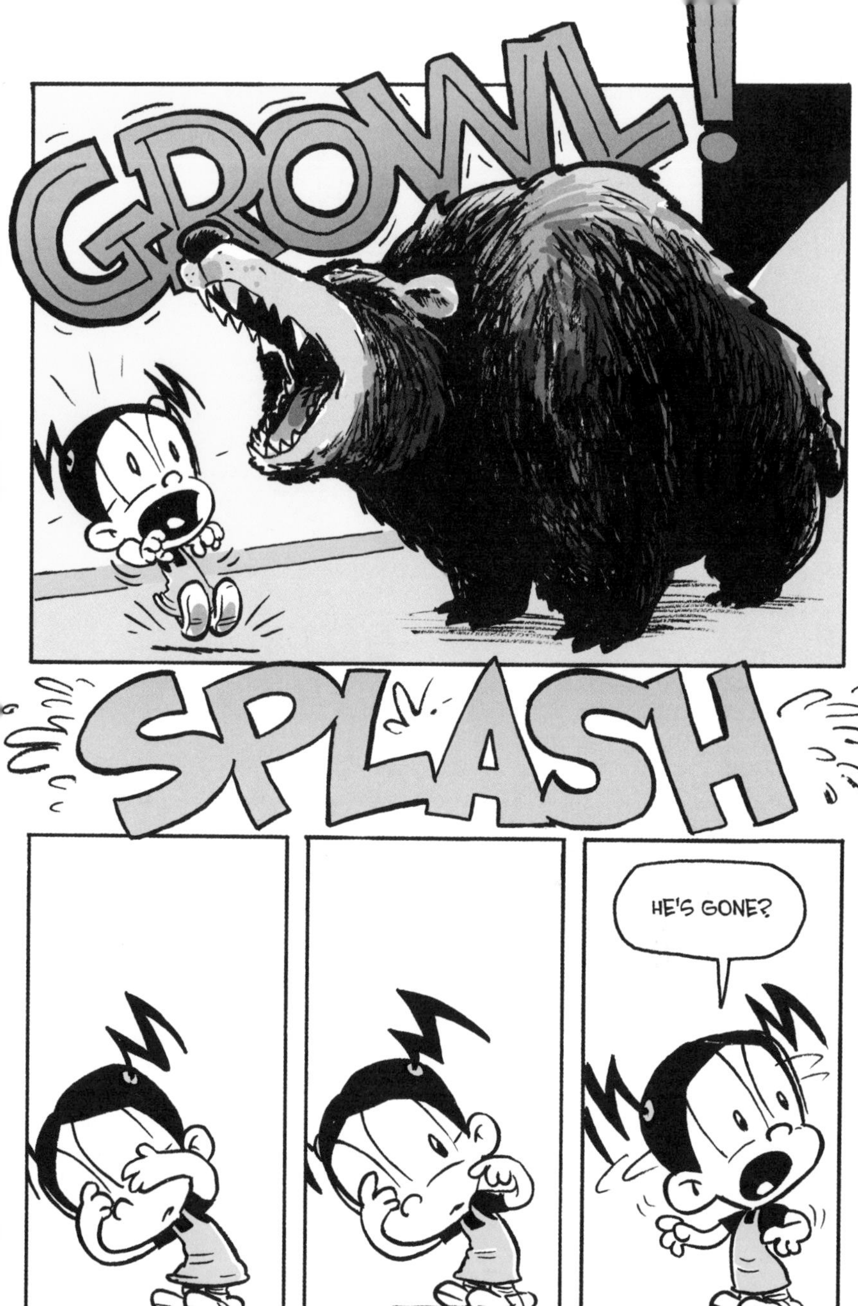
GROWL!
SPLASH
HE'S GONE?

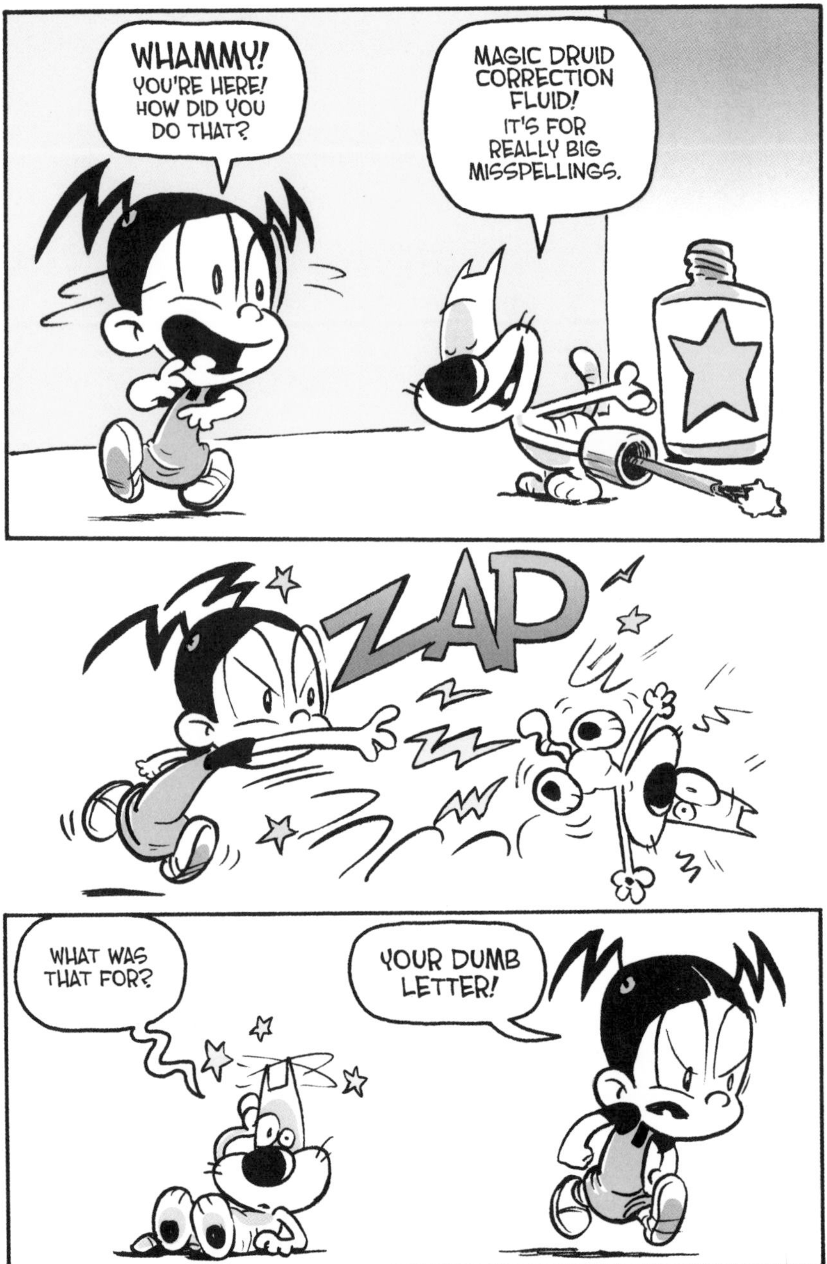
WHAMMY! YOU'RE HERE! HOW DID YOU DO THAT?
MAGIC DRUID CORRECTION FLUID! IT'S FOR REALLY BIG MISSPELLINGS.
ZAP
WHAT WAS THAT FOR?
YOUR DUMB LETTER!

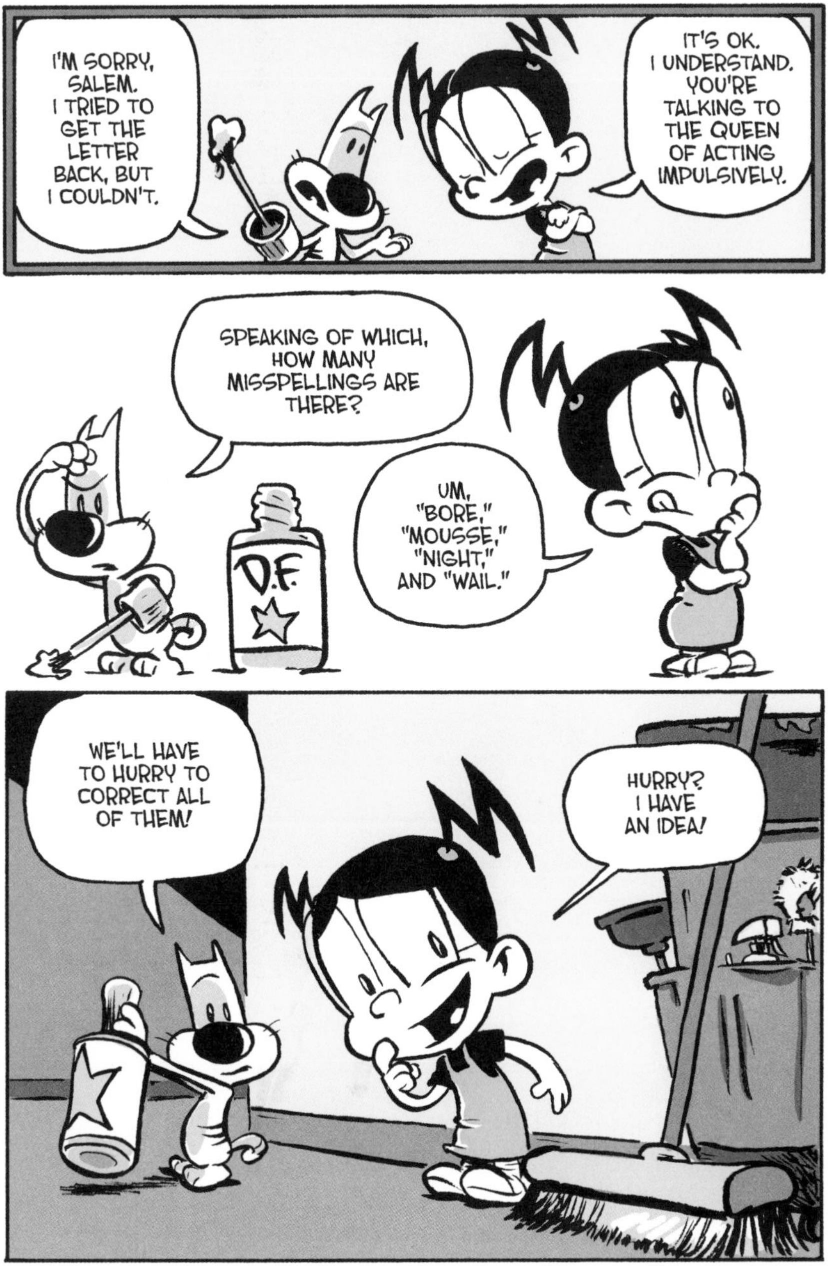

I'M SORRY, SALEM. I TRIED TO GET THE LETTER BACK, BUT I COULDN'T.
IT'S OK. I UNDERSTAND. YOU'RE TALKING TO THE QUEEN OF ACTING IMPULSIVELY.
SPEAKING OF WHICH, HOW MANY MISSPELLINGS ARE THERE?
D.F.
UM, "BORE," "MOUSSE," "NIGHT," AND "WAIL."
WE'LL HAVE TO HURRY TO CORRECT ALL OF THEM!
HURRY? I HAVE AN IDEA!

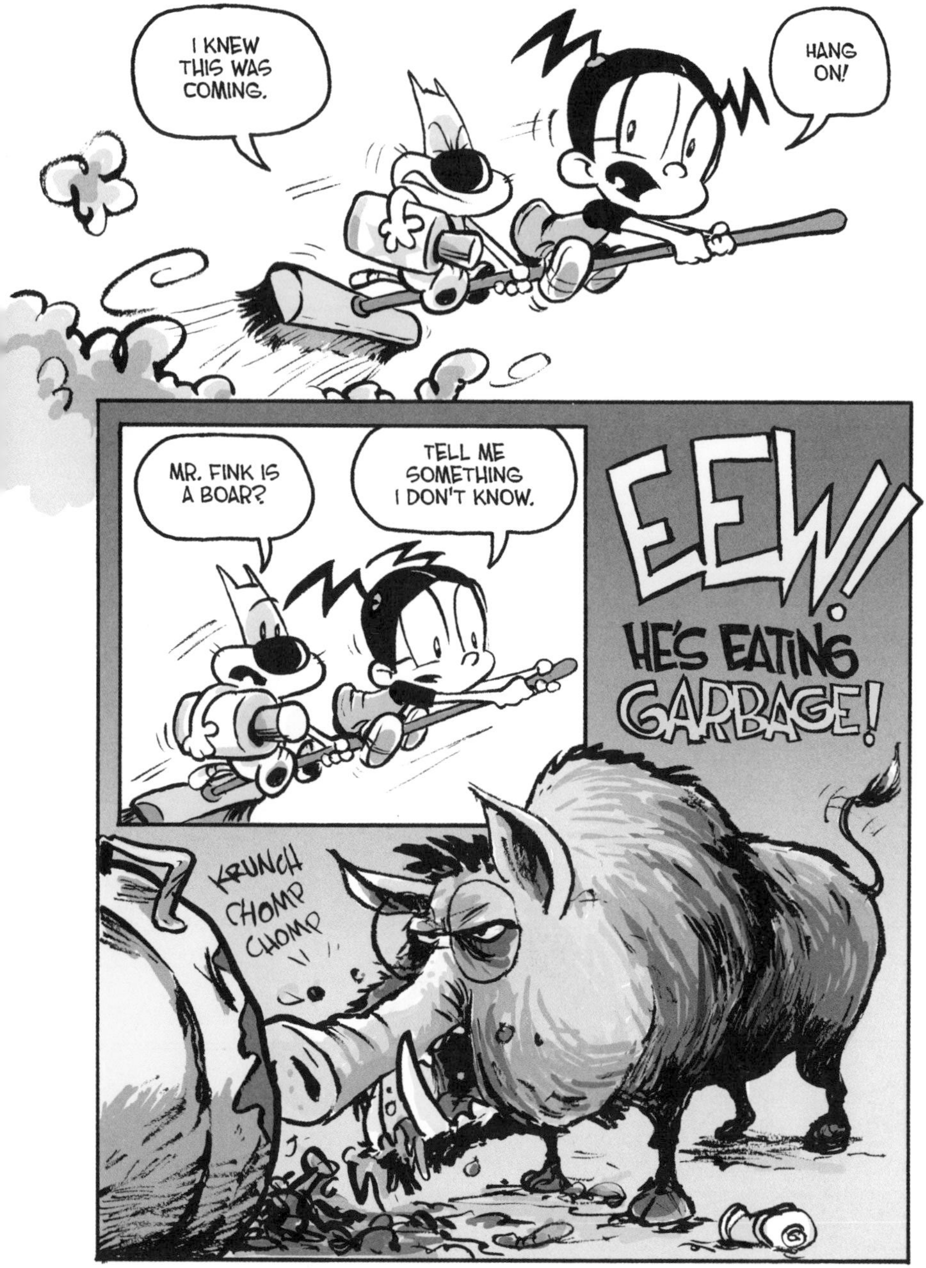

I KNEW THIS WAS COMING.
HANG ON!
MR. FINK IS A BOAR?
TELL ME SOMETHING I DON'T KNOW.
EEW!!
HE'S EATING GARBAGE!
KRUNCH CHOMP CHOMP

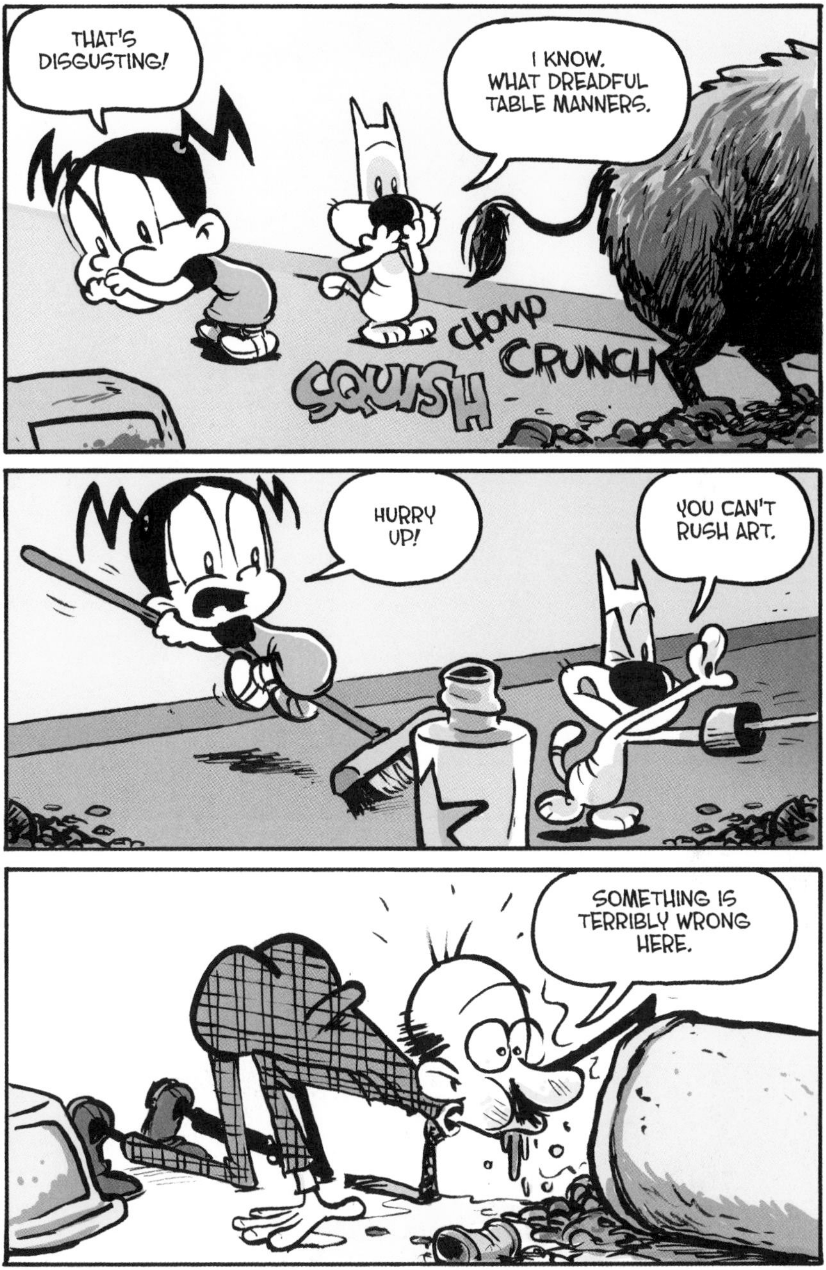
THAT'S DISGUSTING!
I KNOW. WHAT DREADFUL TABLE MANNERS.
CHOMP
SQUISH
CRUNCH
HURRY UP!
YOU CAN'T RUSH ART.
SOMETHING IS TERRIBLY WRONG HERE.

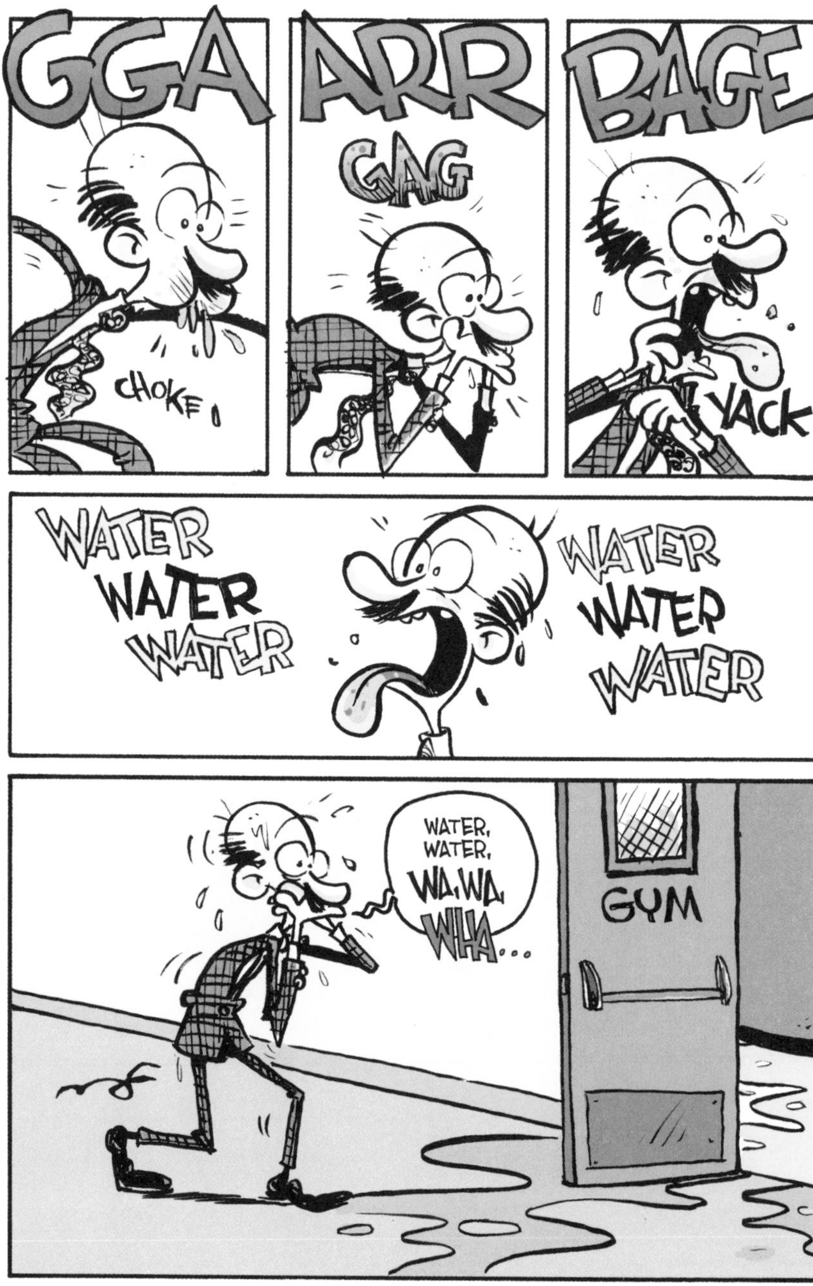
GGA
ARR
BAGE
CHOKE
GAG
YACK
WATER
WATER
WATER
WATER
WATER
WATER
WATER,
WATER,
WA, WA,
WHA...
GYM

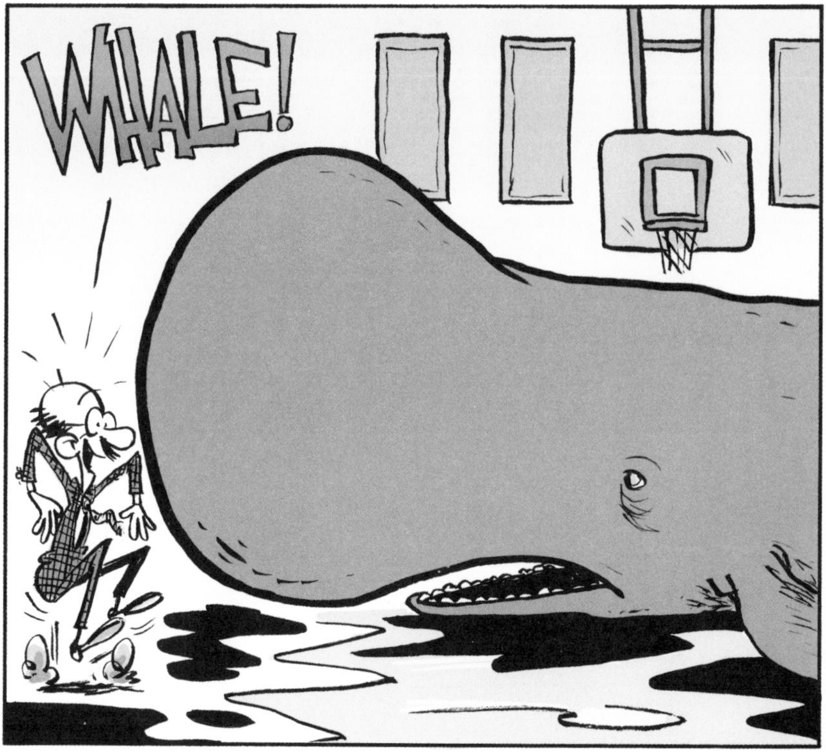
WHALE!

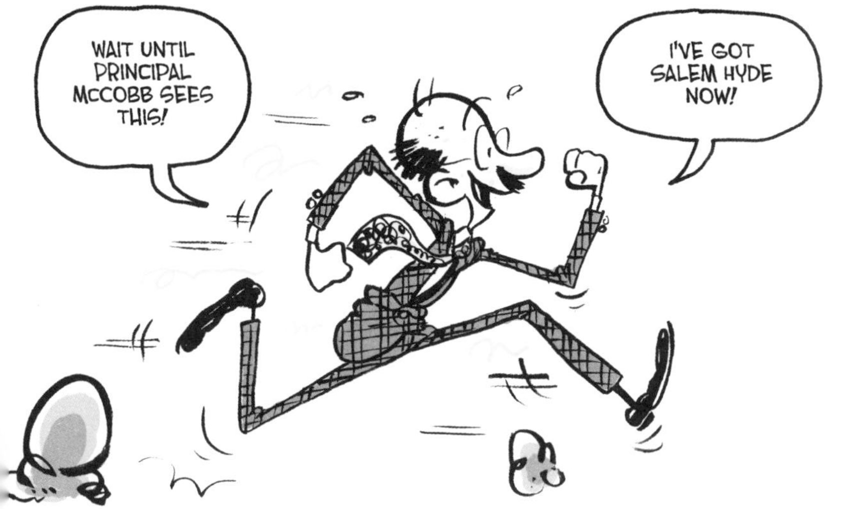
WAIT UNTIL PRINCIPAL MCCOBB SEES THIS!
I'VE GOT SALEM HYDE NOW!

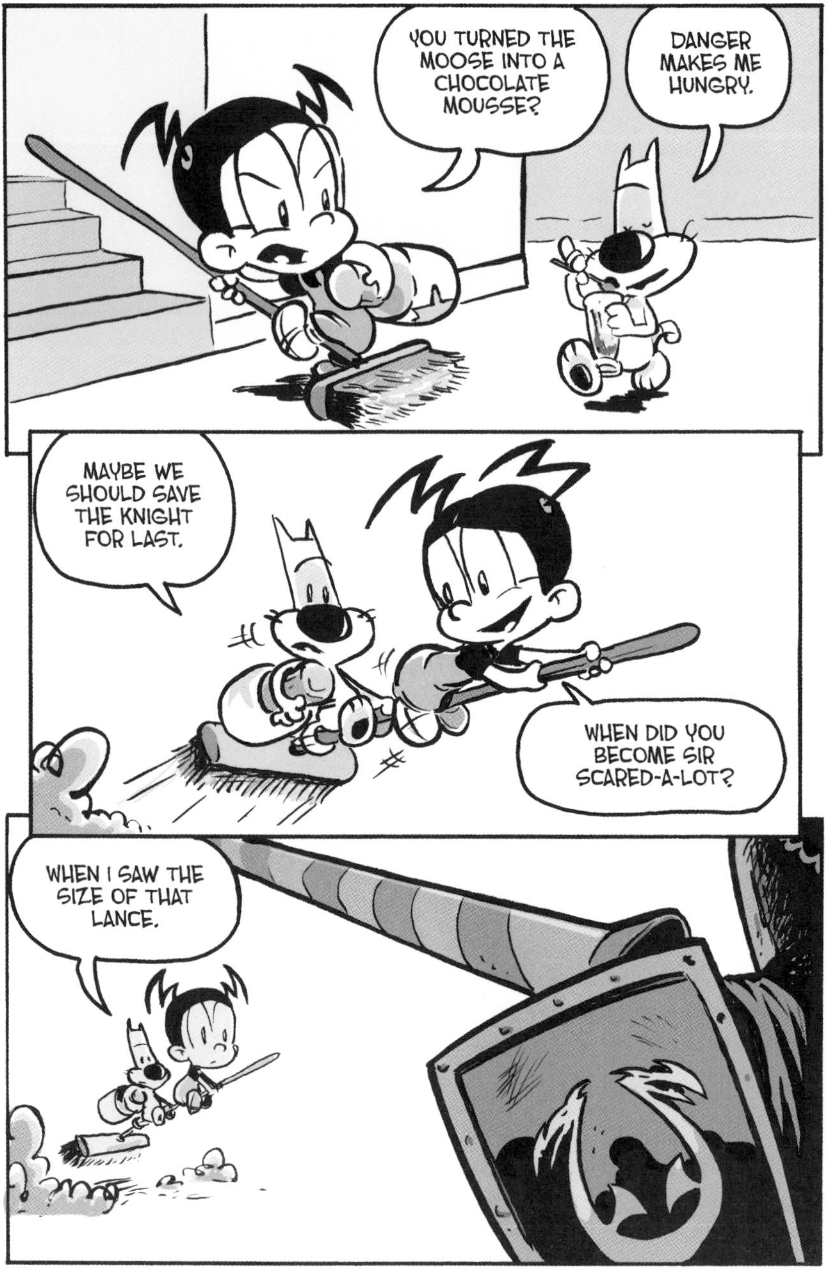
YOU TURNED THE MOOSE INTO A CHOCOLATE MOUSSE?
DANGER MAKES ME HUNGRY.
MAYBE WE SHOULD SAVE THE KNIGHT FOR LAST.
WHEN DID YOU BECOME SIR SCARED-A-LOT?
WHEN I SAW THE SIZE OF THAT LANCE.

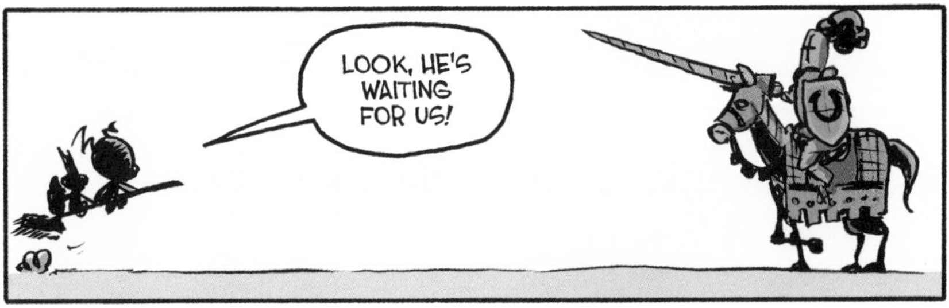
LOOK, HE'S WAITING FOR US!

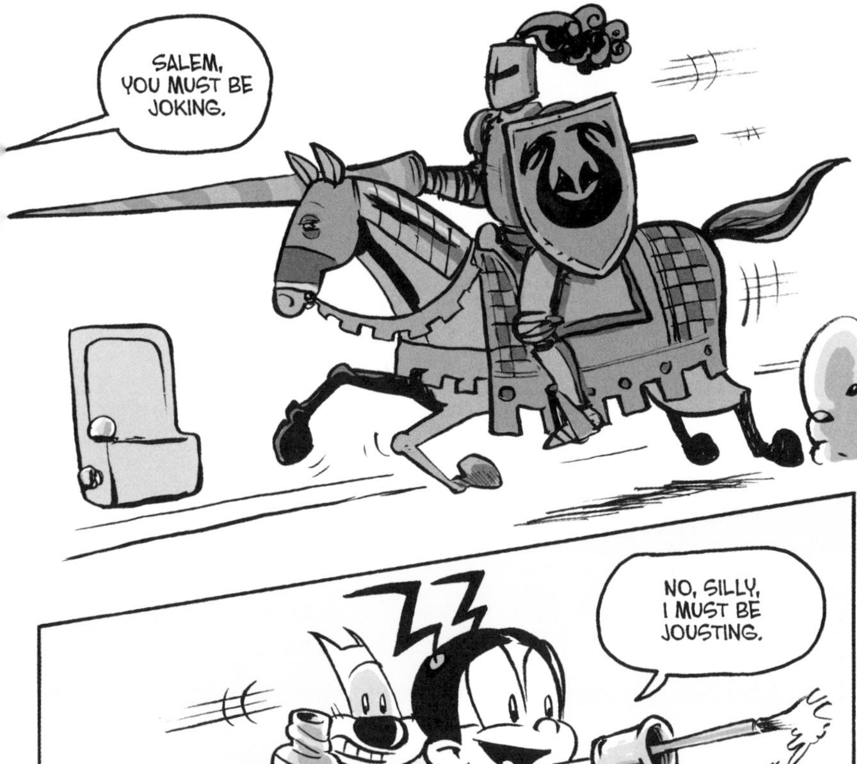
SALEM, YOU MUST BE JOKING.

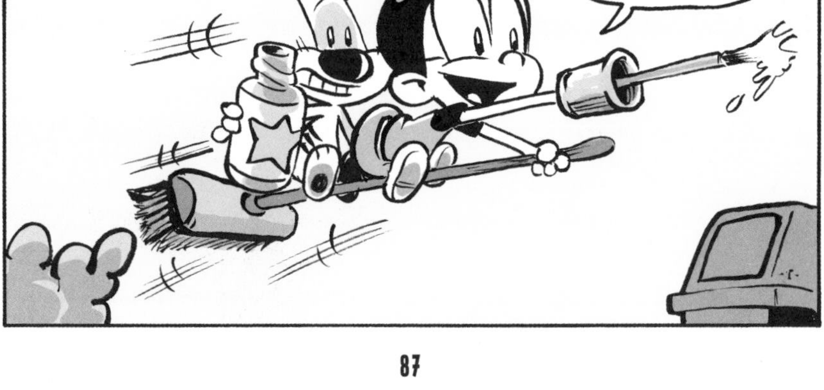
NO, SILLY, I MUST BE JOUSTING.

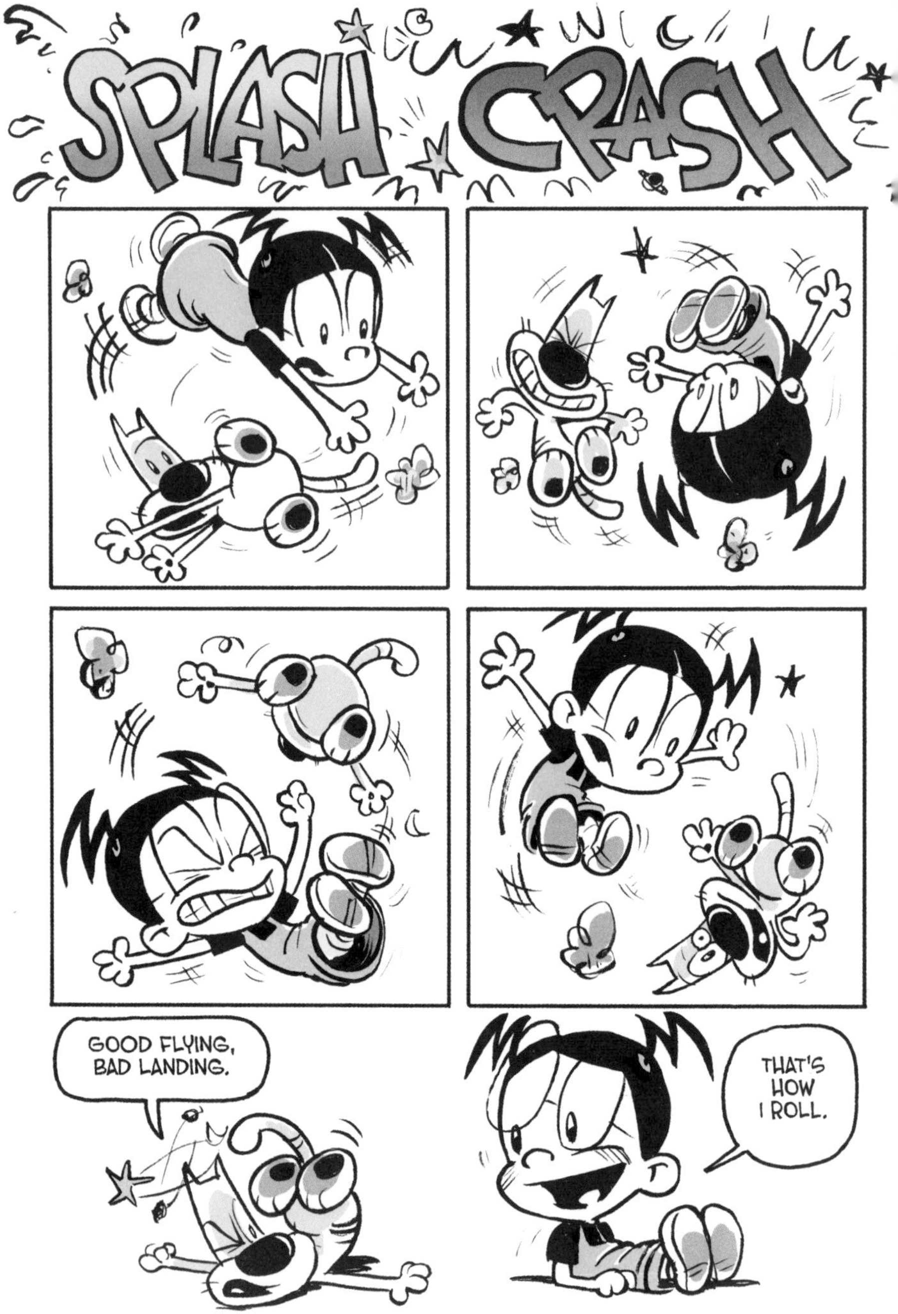
SPLASH CRASH
GOOD FLYING, BAD LANDING.
THAT'S HOW I ROLL.

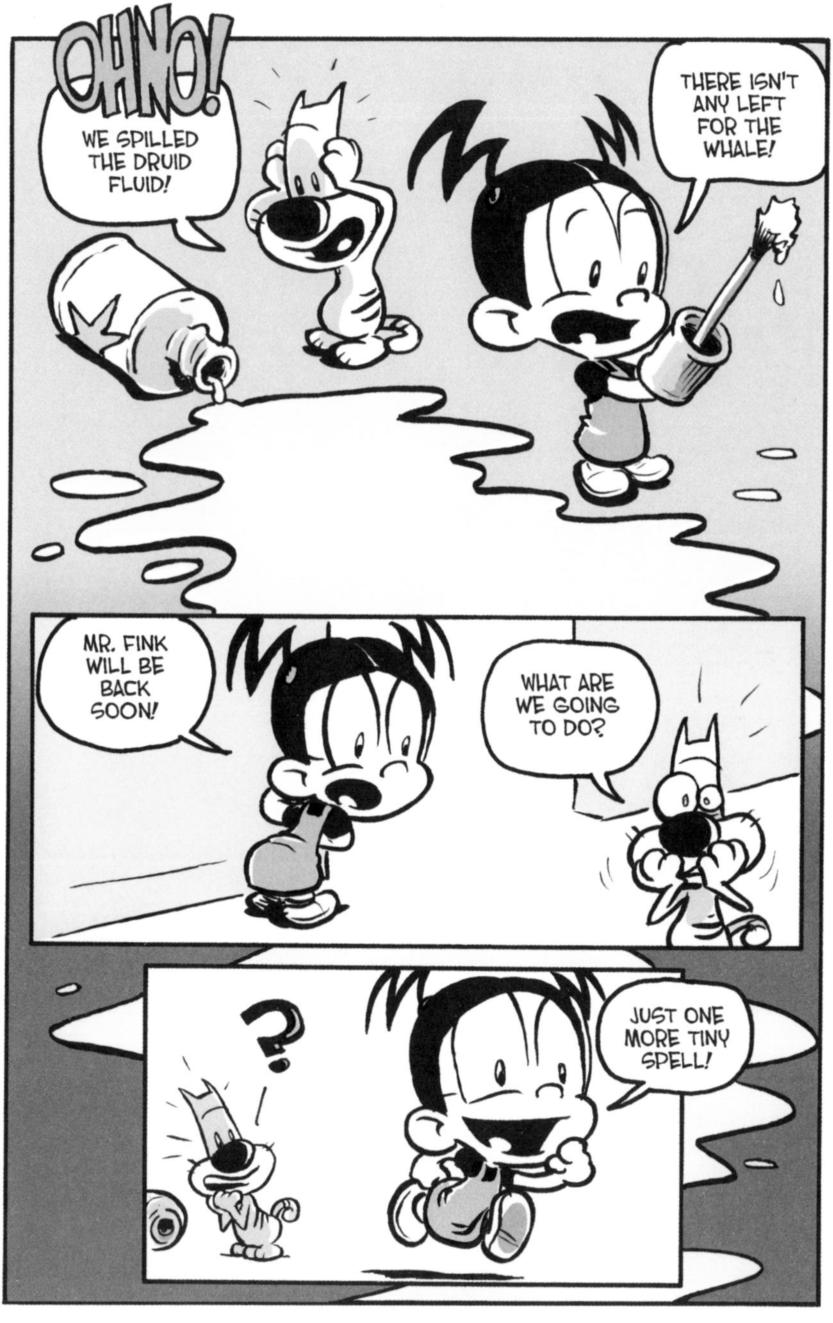
OHNO!
WE SPILLED THE DRUID FLUID!
THERE ISN'T ANY LEFT FOR THE WHALE!
MR. FINK WILL BE BACK SOON!
WHAT ARE WE GOING TO DO?
?
JUST ONE MORE TINY SPELL!

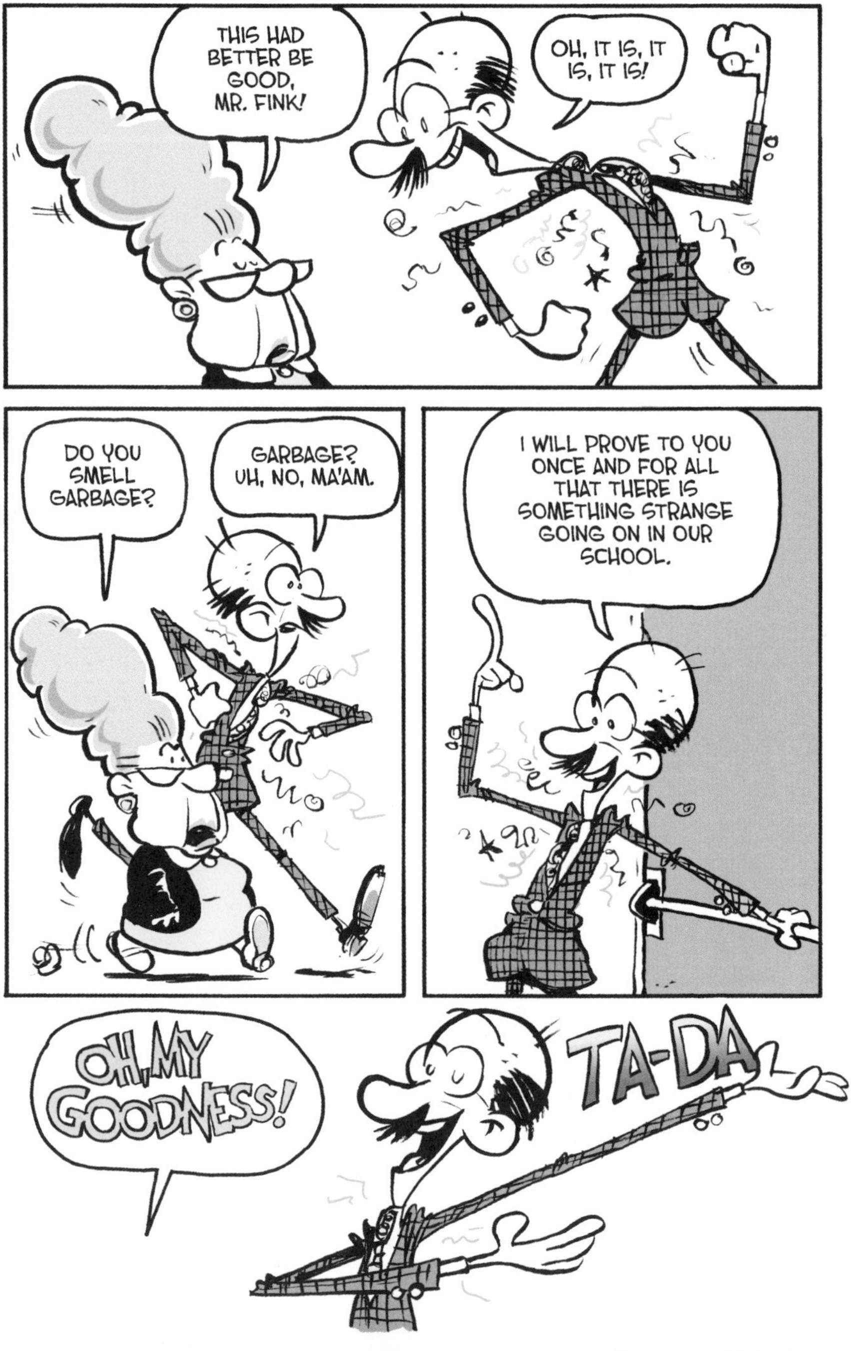
THIS HAD BETTER BE GOOD, MR. FINK!
OH, IT IS, IT IS, IT IS!
DO YOU SMELL GARBAGE?
GARBAGE? UH, NO, MA'AM.
I WILL PROVE TO YOU ONCE AND FOR ALL THAT THERE IS SOMETHING STRANGE GOING ON IN OUR SCHOOL.
OH, MY GOODNESS!
TA-DA

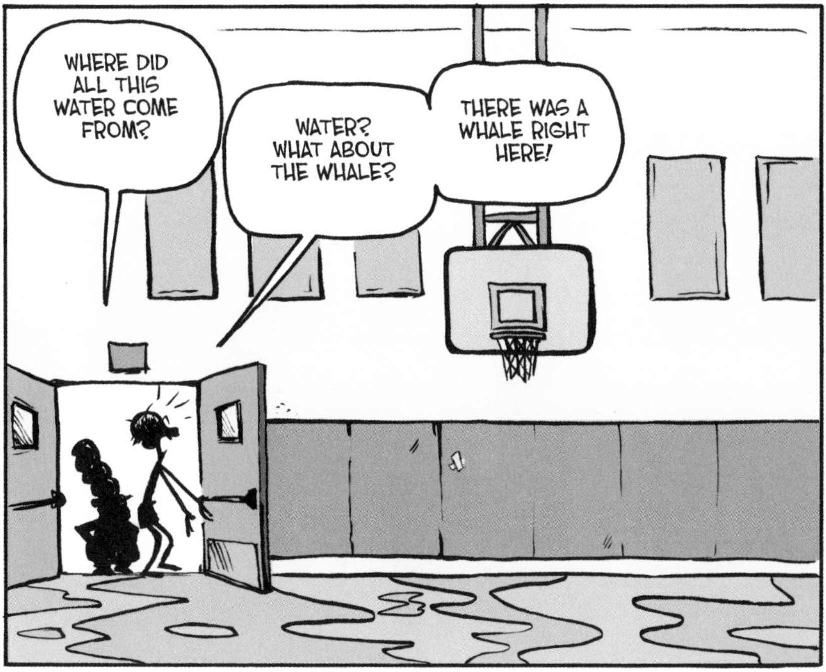
WHERE DID ALL THIS WATER COME FROM?
WATER? WHAT ABOUT THE WHALE?
THERE WAS A WHALE RIGHT HERE!

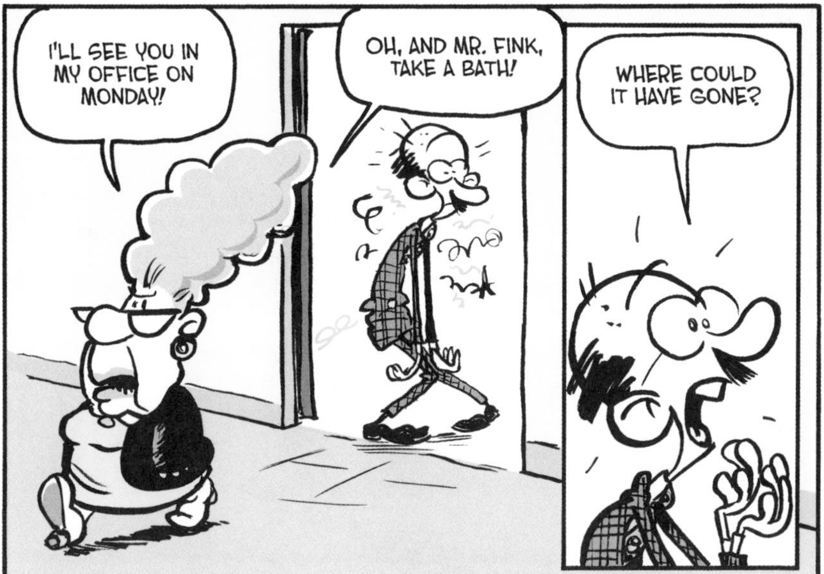
I'LL SEE YOU IN MY OFFICE ON MONDAY!
OH, AND MR. FINK, TAKE A BATH!
WHERE COULD IT HAVE GONE?

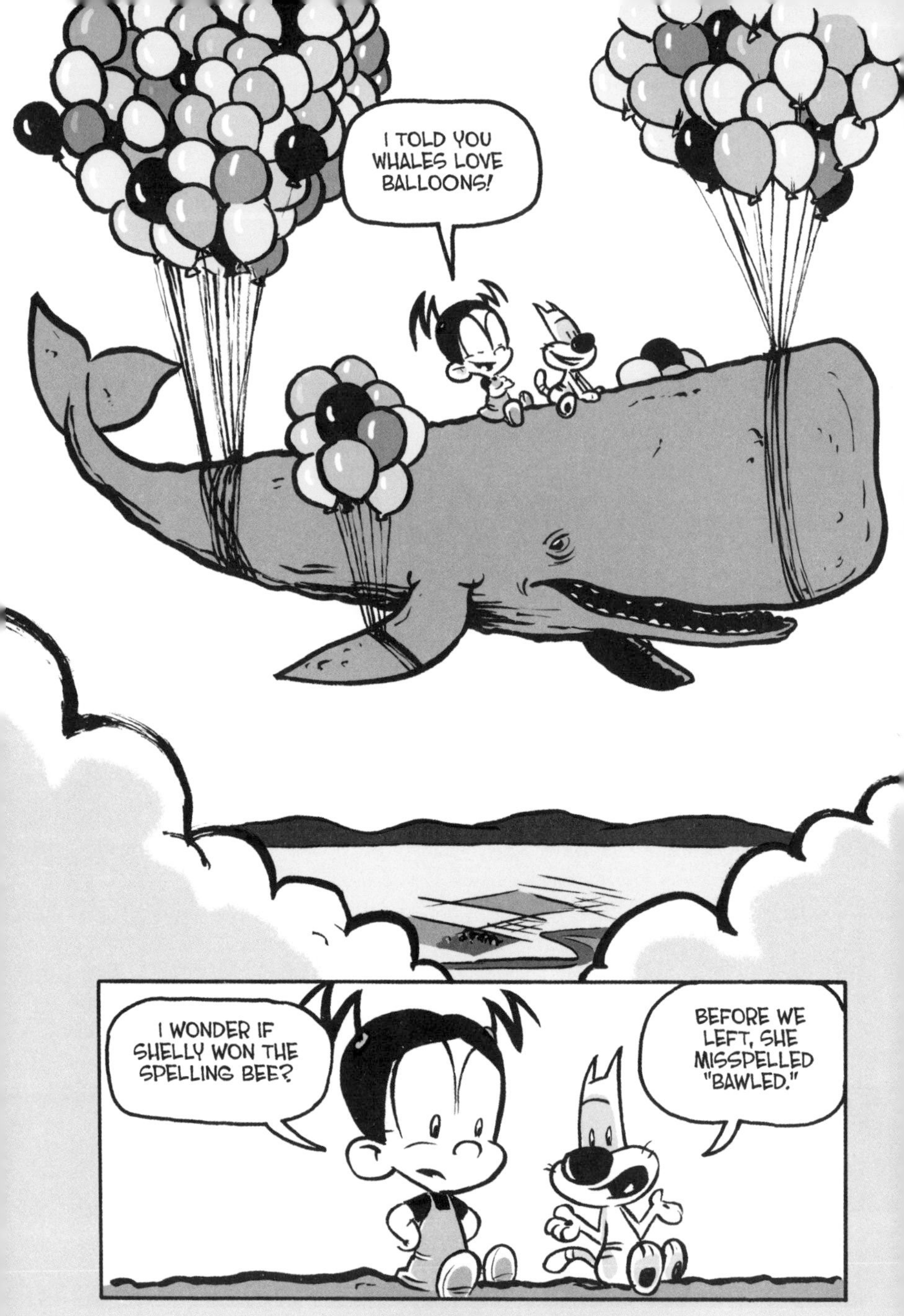
I TOLD YOU WHALES LOVE BALLOONS!
I WONDER IF SHELLY WON THE SPELLING BEE?
BEFORE WE LEFT, SHE MISSPELLED "BAWLED."

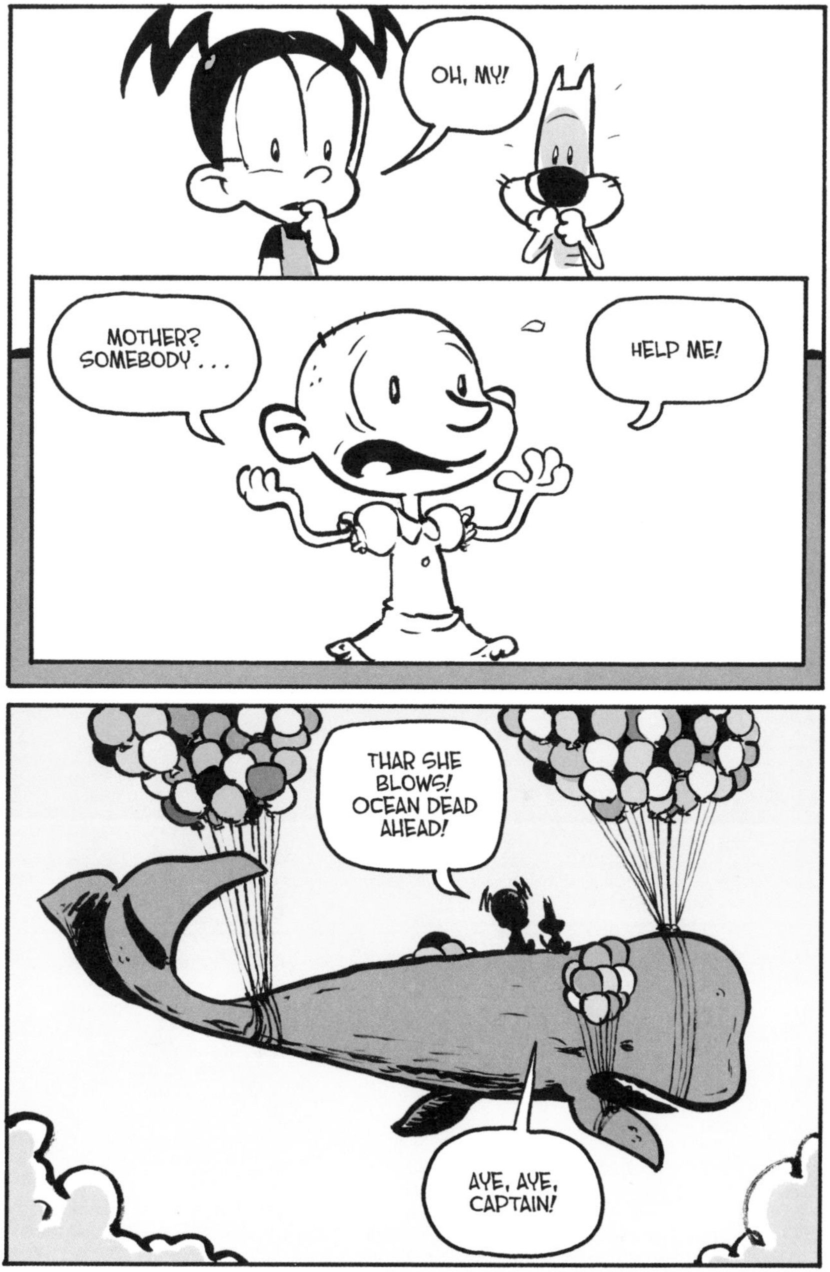
OH, MY!
MOTHER? SOMEBODY . . .
HELP ME!
THAR SHE BLOWS! OCEAN DEAD AHEAD!
AYE, AYE, CAPTAIN!

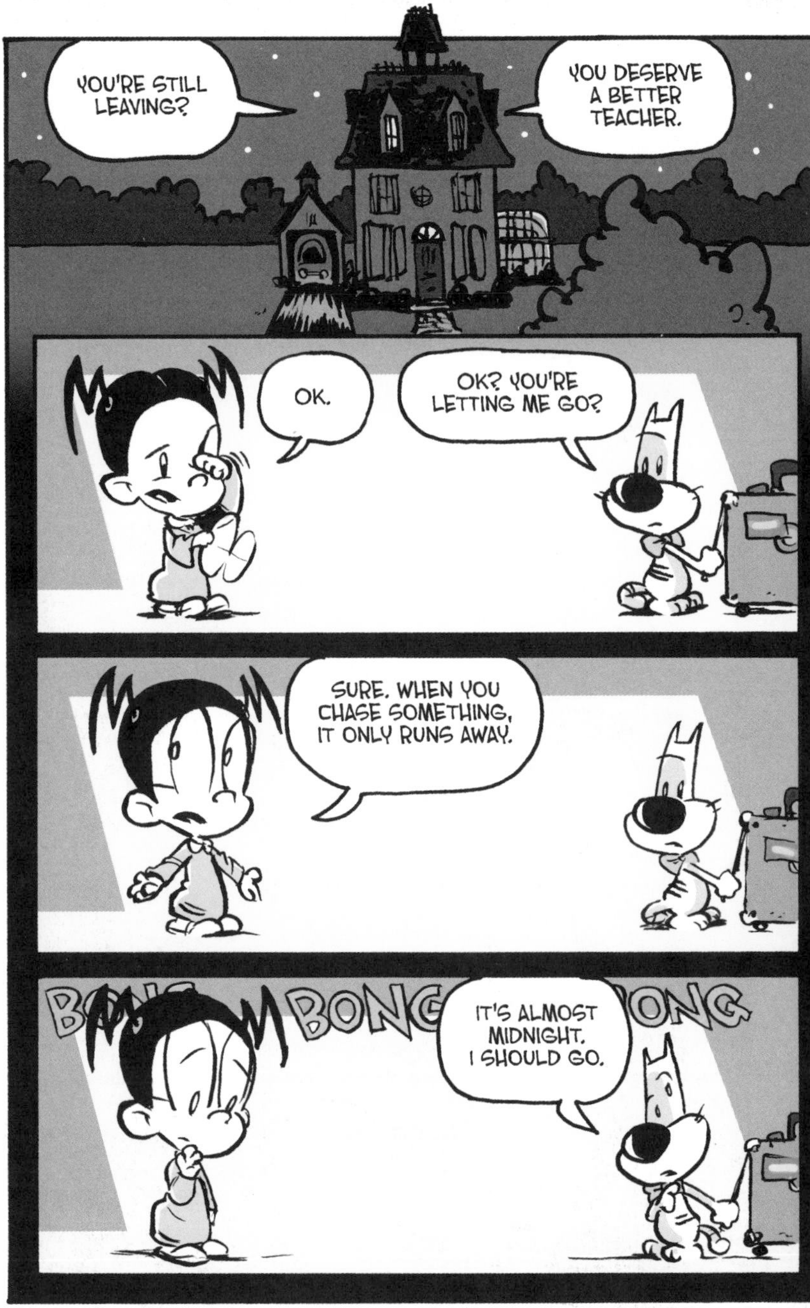
YOU'RE STILL LEAVING?
YOU DESERVE A BETTER TEACHER.
OK.
OK? YOU'RE LETTING ME GO?
SURE. WHEN YOU CHASE SOMETHING, IT ONLY RUNS AWAY.
BONG
IT'S ALMOST MIDNIGHT. I SHOULD GO.

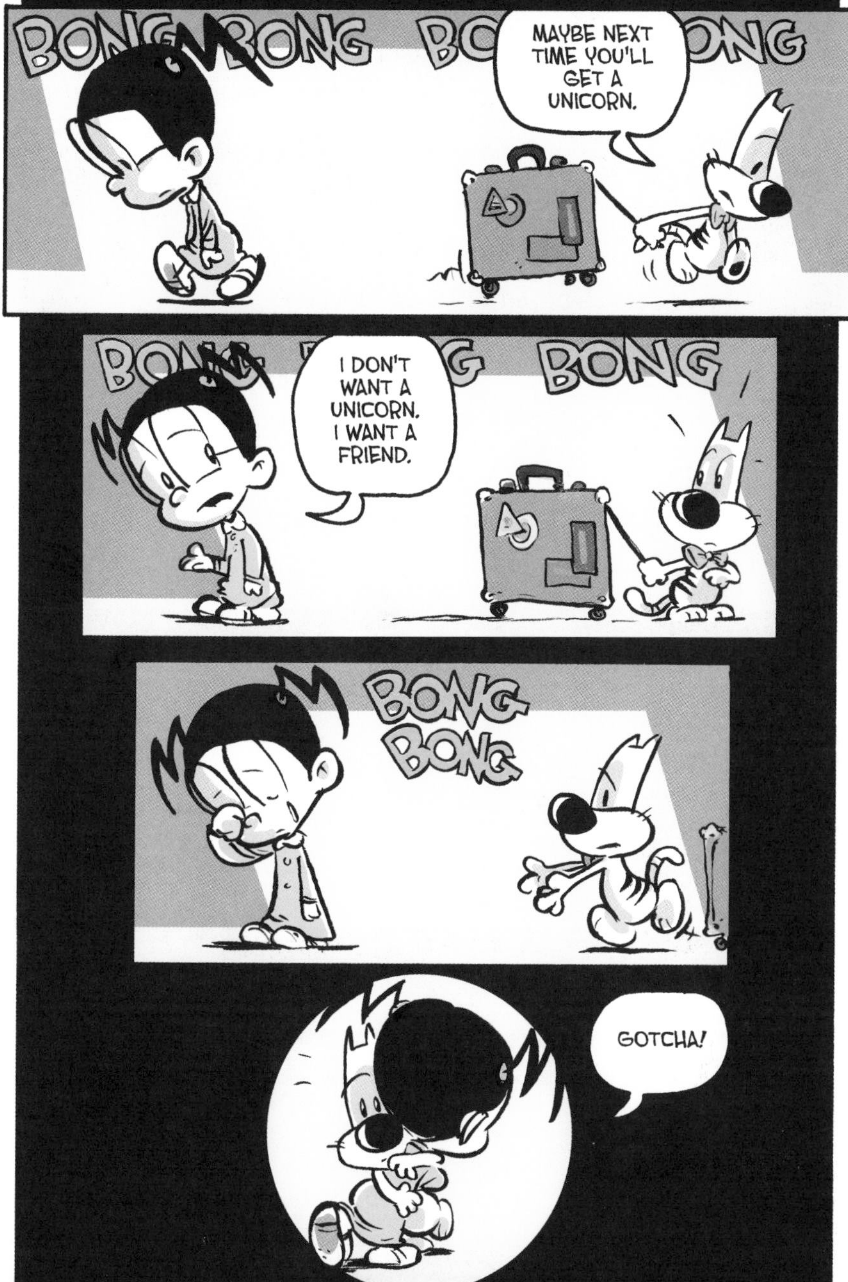
BONG BONG BONG BONG
MAYBE NEXT TIME YOU'LL GET A UNICORN.
BONG BONG
I DON'T WANT A UNICORN. I WANT A FRIEND.
BONG
BONG BONG
GOTCHA!

Getting to KNOW FRANK CAMMUSO

FRANK LIKES
1. SPENDING TIME WITH HIS FAMILY
2. PIZZA (ALL KINDS)
3. MAKING COMICS
4. READING COMICS

FRANK DISLIKES
1. TUNA FISH
2. MAYONNAISE (ALL KINDS)
3. MOWING THE LAWN
4. BULLIES

FUN FACT: DID YOU KNOW THAT FRANK CAMMUSO WROTE AND DREW THIS BOOK IN HIS PAJAMAS?

SPECIAL THANKS TO . . .

Sheila Keenan, Kathy Leonardo, Nancy Iacovelli, Hart Seely, Judy Hansen, Tom Peyer, Charlie Kochman, Nathan Hale, Maggie Lehrman, Sara Corbett, Chad Beckerman, and finally to my wife and son for allowing me to abandon them.

For more fun stuff about Salem, Whammy, and me, check out my website at . . .
www.cammuso.com